Let's Face the Music and Dance

MERRY FARMER

MIDLOTHIAN COUNCIL LIBRARY
WITHDRAWN

W0006289

LET'S FACE THE MUSIC AND DANCE

Copyright ©2022 by Merry Farmer

This ebook is licensed for your personal enjoyment only. This ebook may not be re-sold or given away to other people. If you would like to share this book with another person, please purchase an additional copy for each recipient. If you're reading this book and did not purchase it, or it was not purchased for your use only, then please return to your digital retailer and purchase your own copy. Thank you for respecting the hard work of this author.

This book is a work of fiction. Names, characters, places, and incidents are products of the author's imagination or are used fictitiously. Any resemblance to actual events or locales or persons, living or dead, is entirely coincidental.

Cover design by Erin Dameron-Hill (who is completely fabulous)

ASIN: B09KQT3XWV

Paperback: 9798427462884

Click here for a complete list of other works by Merry Farmer.

If you'd like to be the first to learn about when the next books in the series come out and more, please sign up for my newsletter here: http://eepurl.com/RQ-KX

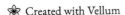 Created with Vellum

Chapter One

Backstage at the Concord Theater in the middle of the morning on a Tuesday was not precisely the place one would expect to find the son of a marquess on the brink of losing his fortune and his reputation, but it was the only place that Mr. Dean Rathborne-Paxton had any interest in being.

"Watch yourself," one of the stagehands—a young person who dressed like a boy but called herself Lily—called out, ducking, as Dean swung around with a load of boards over one shoulder. He nearly knocked Lily's cap clean off her head.

"Sorry," Dean apologized, face heating with embarrassment. He stole a quick look toward the center of the stage, where rehearsal for Niall Cristofori's new play, *The Marshall*, was taking place. "I didn't mean any harm," he went on, speaking to Lily while staring at the heavenly sight that was Mademoiselle Nanette D'Argent.

"No worries. I've been dodging your clumsiness for

months," Lily said with a laugh, taking some of the boards from Dean's shoulder and nudging him to walk with her to the space near the very back of the stage, where construction of the sets for *The Marshall* was underway. "I've learned to be nimble on my feet when you're in Mlle. D'Argent's presence."

Part of Dean heard what Lily had said, but too much of him was busy gazing at the thing of beauty that was Nanette.

Nanette D'Argent was beauty and grace and perfection. She had arrived in London less than five years ago, a tender ingenue in the limelight for the first time, and took that season by storm. She'd trained in the ballet in Paris and could dance as magnificently as any of the ballerinas on the stage of the Royal Ballet Theater, but her truest talents lay in the dulcet tones of her singing voice and in her incomparable acting skills. She was the female lead that every playwright and director of the West End theaters wanted for their productions, and that every theater-going man in London simply wanted.

Her face now graced advertisements for soaps and facial creams as the ideal of feminine beauty—not to mention appearing on the wrappings of chocolate bars and other sweets as the epitome of something a gent might like to eat. Dean had even spent a small fortune purchasing packets of biscuits that bore the images of celebrities so that he could own the collectable card with her face as a keepsake, even though he detested the biscuits themselves. His father—and even his oldest brother, Francis—had scorned those cards as a tasteless bit of modern frippery that heralded the destruction of all good morals and manners, but Dean hardly cared. He slept with Nanette's card propped against the lamp on his bedside table all the same, dreaming of the day when he might have the real Nanette D'Argent in his bed.

A burst of laughter shook him out of his admittedly foolish thoughts. He turned swiftly to see who was laughing at him now, and in the process, he slapped the end of his boards against the tall bundles of rolled-up canvas that Martin Piper —one of the Concord Theater's comic actors, who also helped with the sets and props—carried. The canvas rolls spilled to the floor, but that only made Martin laugh harder.

"I've got them, I've got them!" Martin continued to chuckle as he bent to pick up the rolls.

On the stage, Nanette spoke one of her lines in a louder voice, and Dean twisted back to her. Which meant he swung the boards on his shoulder around just as Martin was straightening. The end of one of the boards thumped the back of Martin's head, and the man dropped the canvas rolls all over again. One of them escaped the string that tied it shut and began to roll across the stage toward the rehearsing actors.

Dean leapt into action, dropping his boards—one of which fell on Martin's toe, causing him to yelp and Lily to burst into raucous laughter—and rushed to fetch the runaway roll before it could even think of doing Nanette any harm. Of course, he kicked it just as he was about to snatch it up, sending it spinning even closer to Nanette and her scene partner, Everett Jewel.

"Hold, hold!" the irritated director, Mr. Abrams, shouted from his place in the first few rows of seats in the house.

Everything came to a complete stop. Even the stage crew stopped their work to see what had upset Mr. Abrams this time. Dean caught the canvas and yanked the unspooling roll into his arms, then stood. He found himself faced with not only a furious Mr. Abrams, but an amused Mr. Jewel. And much to his horror, Nanette was now staring at him as well. Only, instead of gazing fondly at Dean, as though he were the hero she had always waited for, Nanette grinned at him, as though he were a poodle that had been trained to wear a tutu and dance at a circus.

"Is zere a problem, Mr. Rathborne-Paxton?" Nanette asked in her delicious, French accent, one of her dark eyebrows arched fetchingly.

"No! No, not at all, *mademoiselle*," Dean said, smiling broadly at her. "I was just helping with the sets."

"I see." Nanette's smile widened and her eyes sparkled. "Zen perhaps you might return to your endeavors and allow us to return to ours, *non*?"

Dean gulped. She was smiling at him. She found him amusing. He was certain that she liked him, even though she barely paid him any mind whenever they were working in the same space. Acting was Nanette's profession and her means of supporting herself—which she did spectacularly well, if rumors could be believed—whereas helping out with the sets was simply Dean's way to fill his days with something other than the idleness of his class.

"*Monsieur* Rathborne-Paxton?" Nanette asked. Her use of the French word snapped Dean out of his reverie.

"Oh. Right. Sorry," Dean said, bowing to her and backing up, pulling all of the canvas that had unrolled around him as he did. "Terribly sorry. Didn't mean to interrupt. Carry on."

Nanette laughed at him. The sound was like golden sunshine. Dean sighed like a schoolboy, then felt as though the sun had gone behind a cloud when Nanette turned back to Mr. Jewel and resumed the rehearsal.

Just like that, it was as though he meant nothing to her again. He let his shoulders drop and walked to the back of the stage, where Lily and Martin were standing with their heads together, clearly laughing at him.

"Don't worry, mate," Martin said, thumping Dean's shoulder as he handed the bunched-up canvas and roll back to him. "We all find true love eventually."

"Speak for yourself," Lily said with a voice of mock offense, as though love was the last thing she wanted.

"I do speak for myself," Martin said, beaming ridiculously. "Edward and I are very happy."

Dean barely flinched at the reminder of the sort of people he delighted in surrounding himself with as he volunteered at the Concord Theater. Martin was happily involved with a Member of Parliament, one Edward Archibald. Everett Jewel was together with his bobby-turned-bodyguard, Mr. Patrick Wrexham. The stage manager, Ted York, lived with two of the chorus girls, Nancy and Eloise, and went around telling everyone the three of them were married. And even Niall Cristofori was famously in a love partnership with recently-divorced duke and father of three, Blake Williamson. And that was all without counting Lily, who lived as though she were a boy without caring what anyone else thought. Theater people were a wicked and scandalous lot.

Dean loved it. He loved every naughty, immoral, poten-tially illegal relationship and individual around him. Not only that, the circles in which he chose to move—when he was not obligated to spend time with his own class—were what had inspired him to pursue something a bit wicked and unconven-tional himself. He'd always expected that, eventually, he'd be forced to find a respectable wife and make a good match—though the idea of courting someone like Nanette as a mistress had also appealed to him—but now that his family's world had been turned upside down, other ideas had whispered to him, courtesy of his theatrical friends.

As if entering the stage perfectly on cue as he returned to the boards he'd abandoned earlier, Dean spotted his brother, Francis, walking anxiously through the clutter and activity of the backstage area toward him. It was Dean's turn to laugh. In his exquisitely tailored suit, perfectly groomed, back straight, Francis appeared as out of place in the wild world of the theater as an ostrich would have been at Eton.

"Dean, thank God," Francis said, picking up his pace and

stepping around a cluster of open paint cans as he made his way toward Dean. "I've been searching everywhere for you. I should have listened to Joseph, who'd said you would be here."

"Who's Joseph?" Martin asked, staying to listen to the conversation instead of carrying the canvas to the other side of the stage, as he'd looked like he would do.

"My youngest brother," Dean explained with a smirk that told Martin not to get his hopes up. He then turned to Francis. "What is the matter, *frater*?" he asked, his concern apparent by his use of Latin, which his brothers only did when they were feeling particularly fraternal. "You wouldn't dare set foot in a place like this unless London was burning."

"Quiet backstage!" Mr. Abrams shouted from the house.

Dean hunched slightly, sending the director an apologetic look. His gaze drifted straight to Nanette, but she was busy perusing her rehearsal script.

Francis looked surprisingly cowed as well. He nodded to Mr. Abrams and Mr. Jewel—who winked salaciously at him, despite the fact that his darling Mr. Wrexham was a mere twenty feet away, painting one of the flats for the set. Mr. Wrexham merely shook his head and grinned at Mr. Jewel, who then blew him a kiss. That entire exchange made Francis visibly uncomfortable.

"I have no idea whatsoever how you can choose to spend your time in a place like this," Francis muttered.

"Because it is fun," Dean answered, dropping everything to go stand in front of his brother, arms crossed. "Did you come here to insult my friends?"

"I did not," Francis answered. At least he had the decency to bow respectfully to Martin and Lily—who were now watching as though Dean and Francis were the show. "I have no objections to how anyone chooses to conduct their lives. Now more than ever." Francis sent Dean a telling look. The two of them along with their brothers, Sam and Joseph, had

had piety shoved down their throats from birth, but those lessons had failed to take hold with any of them. Except, perhaps, Joseph. In fact, the more their father had harangued them with virtue, the more the brothers had rebelled when left to their own devices. And when it had come to light recently that their father was a horrific hypocrite who had gambled away nearly all of the family's money and involved himself in such nefarious activities that, should the truth be made public, the entire family would be instant social pariahs, the sons had rebelled even more.

Francis cleared his throat once more. "I need to speak to you about arrangements for Mother."

Dean's mood shifted again. "Oh?" He softened toward his brother, taking a supportive step toward him. "What do you need me to do? I'll do anything for Mother."

"Is this Lady Vegas we're talking about?" Lily asked, inching forward herself.

Francis looked astounded at Lily's audacity in involving herself in a conversation between aristocratic brothers, but Dean answered, "Yes. Muriel Rathborne-Paxton, Marchioness of Vegas, and one of the loveliest, most wronged women to ever grace this earth with her presence."

Lily made a sound as though she were impressed. "Go on," she said.

Francis looked more annoyed than ever, but he did go on. "I think I've found a suitable flat for her here in London so that she can be near us again, but the landlord requires some sort of collateral before he will let it to her."

"What? A landlord requiring collateral for a *marchioness* to rent a flat from him?" Martin asked, incredulous, stepping forward as well.

Francis's scowl darkened, and he pressed his lips together for a moment before saying, "Our family is experiencing a bit of trouble with ready funds at the moment."

"Montrose," Lily whispered to Martin.

"Good God." Martin held a hand to his throat.

Dean winced. So it seemed that all of London knew about the vicious and merciless Mr. Montrose and his quest to ruin and impoverish any and all families from the aristocracy that he felt had done him some sort of wrong. Montrose had bankrupted earls, publicly disgraced viscounts, and caused a baron to take his own life, all within the last year. He was in the process of attempting to destroy the Rathborne-Paxton family—thanks to the sins of their father, Lord Vegas—and had nearly ruined the life and reputation of Dean and Francis's brother Sam's wife, Alice, just the month before.

Sam and Alice had moved to Francis's estate in Hampshire a fortnight ago, but before they'd left, they'd uncovered information that could be vital to defeating Montrose. The man was in a precarious financial position himself. His machinery of destruction needed to be oiled with money, and Montrose's money was swiftly running out. It was valuable to know, but neither Dean nor Francis nor anyone else in their family had yet discovered what to do with the information.

"Yes, well." Francis drew Dean's attention back to the moment at hand. "This is not about Montrose. We need to secure a London flat for Mother. To do that, we need money. And you know what that means."

Dean smiled. "Yes, I do." He sent a longing glance across the stage to Nanette. He hadn't quite found the nerve to begin his conquest yet, but he already had his eyes set on his prize. Forget making Nanette his mistress. Everything had changed, and now he was dead-set on making the magnificent woman his wife.

"*I* don't know what that means," Lily said, glancing between Dean and Francis. "What does it mean?"

Francis frowned at Lily, then turned to Dean. "Perhaps I

was wrong to address this matter with you now. It can wait until supper tonight."

"But you came all the way to the theater," Martin argued, looking as though he were trying not to grin.

Francis's scowl deepened. "I found myself in the area," he said. "I did not realize my brother and I would have an audience for such a private conversation."

"You are at a theater, my lord," Lily said with a cheeky sort of pretend respect. "You will always an audience here."

Dean was shocked that his brother would allow an adolescent girl in boy's clothes to get away with such insolent behavior, but Lily stood confidently where she was, and Francis was clearly out of his depth. So much so that he cleared his throat yet again, tugged at his jacket, and said, "I will continue my errands, then. We will discuss the matter in more detail over supper tonight."

"As you wish, Francis," Dean said, laughing and thumping his brother's shoulder. "Thank you for at least attempting to meet me on my own ground."

After Francis nodded and turned to leave the theater, Lily glanced to Dean and asked, "Is this your own ground? I'm not certain you can claim it as your own when you aren't paid to be here, like the rest of us."

"Nonsense," Martin blurted—so loudly that he earned their group another censorious glare from Mr. Abrams. "Nonsense," he repeated in a whisper. "Dean is one of us." He paused. "Though perhaps he should pay his dues by informing us of the meaning of 'he knows what that means', as Lord Cathraiche implies."

Both Martin and Lily grinned like a cat who had caught a canary and turned to Dean. They even crossed their arms in tandem and stared at him in a way that implied they would not ease up until they knew everything.

Oddly, even though it was a private family matter, Dean

found that he had no qualms at all about sharing the truth. "Our family needs money," he said with a shrug. "Francis has suggested that we obtain that money the way noblemen have been filling their coffers for centuries. He has proposed that we all marry wealthy women."

"But your brother was married last month, and as far as I understand it, Mrs. Alice Rathborne-Paxton was penniless," Martin said with a confused frown.

"She was his mistress, was she not?" Lily asked.

"She was," Dean said. "And that is the other part of Francis's plan for all of us." He stepped in closer to Lily and Martin and lowered his voice even beyond what Mr. Abrams would have required of him. "You see, Montrose is still after us. And the only way to thwart the man's intent to destroy the family utterly is if we destroy ourselves first."

Martin and Lily exchanged looks as though that were the most ridiculous thing they'd ever heard.

"Go on," Lily said, her eyes alight with excitement.

Dean shifted, leaning even closer. "When Sam announced his intent to marry Alice, believing her to have money, it occurred to Francis that if the four of us marry women with means and wealth, but who are social pariahs with reputations that are already ruined, then Montrose will have no weapons to wield against us. His intentions for our ruination will be thwarted, and he will be forced to leave us alone."

"That," Martin began slowly, "is either the stupidest...or the most brilliant plan I've ever heard of."

"No, it's brilliant!" Lily said. "Imagine the freedom that gives them."

Martin made a noise as though he didn't believe her.

"Truly," Lily went on. "If everything I've heard and the things I've read in the gossip columns are correct, Mr. Samuel Rathborne-Paxton got to marry the woman he loved, a woman he'd never be able to marry otherwise."

"Precisely," Dean said, pleased that someone understood the situation.

Lily's smile broadened even more. "That means our Dean here will be able to marry the woman he loves as well."

Dean's face flushed hot. "Yes, well, I have yet to address the matter at all." He peeked over his shoulder to where Nanette and Mr. Jewel were running through the new script.

"Fantastic!" Martin exclaimed, apparently piecing the puzzle together. "Oh, I like this. I like this very much."

"As do I," Lily laughed. She schooled her face to solemnity and took a step toward Dean, clapping a hand on his shoulder. "Mr. Rathborne-Paxton, I hereby humbly grant you my blessing to pursue Mlle. Nanette D'Argent, a woman we all know you adore, and to make her your own."

"Oh, I say," Dean stammered, flushing hotter. It was absurd for him to feel so pleased—or so sheepish—over a theater girl granting him her approval to pursue the object of his fantasy.

"Alright," Mr. Abrams called out at that moment. "We'll end there for now. Half hour break, and then we'll have the chorus work with the choreographer for that Act One finale."

The sound of shuffling and footsteps as actors and stagehands left what they were doing to begin their break rose up like the rumble before a storm. Lily grasped Dean's shoulders, then turned him toward Nanette. Nanette continued to stand closer to the apron of the stage, writing something in her script with a stubby pencil. Dean's heart lifted at the sight of her, then thumped wildly against his ribs as Lily pushed him forward.

This was it. This was the moment he had dreamed of and dreaded ever since Francis had concocted the idea of them all marrying unsuitable brides. The son of a marquess marrying a famous actress and dancer would tear through the scandal sheets like a hot knife through butter, which was precisely what they wanted. To Dean, though, it was more than that. His heart was on the line.

As he took a step forward, just as Nanette glanced up at him with a banal smile, he wondered if he was mad or if this was the beginning of a life that would be happier than he could ever have imagined.

Chapter Two

Nan bit the end of her pencil, then sketched a few more notes about blocking into her script as the rest of the cast and crew began their break. She'd given as much of her attention to running through the scene with Everett and Mr. Abrams as she could, but her mind was scattered in a thousand directions. Not only was the stage itself a hive of activity that continuously pulled her focus away from her work, the cares and concerns that she took home with her when she left the theater seemed to loom larger than usual as well.

As if to underscore that point, a flash of movement caught the corner of her eye, and when she turned to see what it was, she spotted Lily Logan pushing Mr. Dean Rathborne-Paxton toward her. Mr. Rathborne-Paxton's face was a charming shade of red, and along with the adoration that the man was never able to hide, there was a great deal of apprehension.

Of course, Nan knew precisely what that was about. Stage Door Johnnies were as common in her profession as needles were in a seamstress's shop. Not a day had gone by for years now when she wasn't greeted at the stage door by a dozen men with flowers or chocolates and worshipful looks every time she left. She received at least two proposals of marriage a week as well. She'd taken to having Everett's Patrick walk her home a time or two when some of the men had looked as though they wanted more than autographed pictures of her. For the most part, those men were entirely harmless.

Mr. Rathborne-Paxton was harmless as well. She supposed it was a mark of his class that he'd been able to make his way inside the theater instead of lingering around the stage door, like the others. He was useful when it came to helping construct and paint sets—although she hadn't been blind to the comedy show that he and Martin had inadvertently put on earlier—and if she were honest with herself, he wasn't bad to look at either. He had expressive eyes, a fit physique, a sensual mouth, and a thick head of hair that she daydreamed about running her fingers through in moments of particular desperation.

But Mr. Rathborne-Paxton was just another admirer who would lose interest over time. And if—heaven forbid—he discovered who she really was, he would likely be the first to turn against her and to throw her to the wolves for her deception.

She closed her script and sent the man another polite smile before starting off for her dressing room. Instead of just grinning at her, like he usually did, Mr. Rathborne-Paxton hurried forward, intercepting her with that adoring look in his eyes.

"Mlle. D'Argent, would you do me the honor of escorting you to lunch?" he blurted, nearly tripping over his words and his feet as he did.

A small flutter filled Nan's stomach. It wasn't that his offer was unique. She might never have to purchase her own food again if she took up every offer for a meal from an admirer. But she was well aware of the true cost of those meals and what the gentlemen who paid for them expected in return.

"You are too kind, Mr. Rathborne-Paxton," she said with what she hoped was a smile kind enough to soothe the sting of her refusal. "But I am afraid zat I must learn my lines, and zerefore, I cannot go with you."

"Oh, but the play doesn't open for another three weeks, right?" Mr. Rathborne-Paxton protested. "Surely, you could take some time to have a quick bite with me."

Nan smiled. The man was sweet, really. But so were the three dozen others who had made her the same offer in the last fortnight.

"Truly, I cannot, *monsieur*. But I am ever so grateful for your offer."

She tried to move on, but froze when Mr. Rathborne-Paxton called out after her, "*S'il vous plaît, arrêtez, mademoiselle. Je souhaite simplement passer du temps avec vous.*"

Nan gulped. It didn't matter how much time had passed or how long she had enjoyed her fame and her persona. Every time someone attempted to speak French to her, she felt as though she were treading on eggshells. She'd worked hard, studied the language as best she could in secret, and even traveled to Paris several years ago in an attempt to strengthen her ruse, but moments like these were the sort she dreaded.

She drew in a breath and attempted to calm herself. *Think, Nan*, she ordered herself. *You know the words. Puzzle it out.*

As soon as she was reasonably certain Mr. Rathborne-Paxton had said he only wanted to spend time with her, she schooled her expression into a smile, then turned to face him.

"You are very kind, *monsieur*," she said, focusing on her accent. That, at least, she could do competently. "But zees is not a good time, *non*?"

"It is always a good time for love," Mr. Rathborne-Paxton said, rushing to her and taking her free hand.

Nan yelped a bit in surprise and nearly dropped her script. Mr. Rathborne-Paxton backed off.

"Sorry," he said, back to being the charming, slightly bumbling nobleman that she'd come to know vaguely in the last few months. "That was far too forward of me. Please accept my apologies. It is just that circumstances in my life have changed a bit in the last few weeks, and I feel the time has come to—"

Nan gasped in the middle of his flowery, slightly embarrassing speech as she caught sight of an all-too familiar man stepping into the theater from the stage door at the far end of the backstage area. Montrose. The man had the Devil's own audacity to show up at the Concord Theater in the middle of the morning. She knew precisely why he was there as well.

"No apologies are needed, *monsieur*," she said, twisting her hand so that she could squeeze Mr. Rathborne-Paxton's. She maneuvered him so that his body blocked her from Montrose's view. "You are too kind. You are zee sweetest, zee most kind man who has—"

Her words dropped off as Montrose approached Mr. Abrams with a scowl. Nan didn't need to be close enough to hear what he was saying to know Montrose was demanding to know where she was. And blast him, but Mr. Abrams started to look around for her.

"Quickly," Nan whispered, grabbing Mr. Rathborne-Paxton's hand and dragging him off to the far side of the stage. She handed her script and pencil off to one of the younger stagehands, then ducked behind the fly curtains that had just been hung in the wings. It was a bloody shame that the entire stage was open with all of the scenery and fly curtains from the current production lifted high above them. There were very few places to hide.

"What is the matter?" Mr. Rathborne-Paxton asked, moving along with her. As soon as he glanced back over his shoulder and caught sight of Montrose, his entire demeanor changed. "Montrose," he hissed. He stepped up to Nan's side, resting a hand on the small of her back and keeping her body carefully concealed. "Do not worry, Mlle. D'Argent. I will keep you safe."

Those words should not have affected Nan the way they did. Something in her heart loosened and sang with relief. She'd been dodging Montrose for years, but his pursuit of her had increased in the last fortnight. If his had been a normal pursuit with the aim that most other men had in mind, she would have felt confident to deal with it. But Montrose didn't want her for her body. He wanted her for far more dangerous reasons.

"Quickly, in here," Mr. Rathborne-Paxton whispered as they drew near to a storage closet where unused props were kept.

"*Non.*" Nan shook her head, adjusting to hold Mr. Rathborne-Paxton's hand tighter. "Zere is no way out of zat room. We must go somewhere where we will be able to flee if we need to."

"Right," Mr. Rathborne-Paxton said, escorting her behind a newly-stretched canvas flat that stood drying off to one side. "Let me see...."

While Mr. Rathborne-Paxton glanced around, looking for someplace they could hide, Nan peeked around the edge of the flat to see what Montrose was doing. By the look of things, Mr. Abrams had pointed him toward her dressing room, but Everett had stepped up to talk to the villain before he could get there. Everett must have known she wasn't in her dressing room, but perhaps pretending as though he didn't want Montrose to go there was his way of distracting the man so that she could get away.

"Ah," Mr. Rathborne-Paxton said at last. "I know just the thing." He tugged Nan toward one of the narrow ladders that led up into the fly space. "Mlle. D'Argent, can you climb?"

"Can I climb?" Nan repeated the question incredulously,

her accent slipping just a bit. She'd grown up in the country. She'd learned to climb trees and scramble up the sides of barns and haystacks immediately after learning to walk. She'd had to climb up to help repair a roof or two in her childhood days as well. Once, she'd even had to climb on top of the schoolhouse to fetch the ball that one of the boys had thrown up there when he was trying to spoil the girls' game. "*Oui, monsieur*, I can climb," she said, pushing Mr. Rathborne-Paxton out of the way and ascending the ladder ahead of him.

As it turned out, Mr. Rathborne-Paxton's plan was a good one. Once they had reached the fly space, they were able to look down on the activity of the stage. Better still, the fly space was dark, and because the entire stage was well-lit as the new set was built, it was difficult for anyone below to see what was going on above them. Nan walked along the narrow path that led around the perimeter of the stage, keeping her back pressed as close to the wall as she could. To her surprise, Mr. Rathborne-Paxton grasped her hand at one point—not as a way to comfort her, but because he appeared to be afraid of heights.

She couldn't help but giggle a little, despite the danger of the situation. "You are scared, *non*?" she asked, grinning at him in the dim light.

"Poppycock," he said, a bit breathless. "Nothing scares me."

One of the stagehands who was working in the fly space toward the front of the stage dropped a coil of rope to the boards below with a loud clatter. Mr. Rathborne-Paxton stiffened and pressed all the way against the wall, as if he could grip it for support.

Nan started to laugh, but caught her breath a moment later as Montrose strode out onto the stage near the spot where the coil was dropped. He immediately began searching above him.

"We must move on," Nan hissed, pushing Mr. Rathborne-Paxton ahead of her.

Mr. Rathborne-Paxton nodded and rushed forward.

"I know she is here somewhere," Montrose said in a loud voice below them. "You cannot hide from me forever, Mlle. D'Argent." The way he said her name made Nan cringe. It was a horrible, dangerous thing when your worst enemy knew your biggest secret.

She and Mr. Rathborne-Paxton reached the far end of the stage and turned the corner to step into a particularly dark patch against one wall. They had the advantage of being almost completely concealed, but there was no place for them to climb back down that would go unseen by Montrose where he stood at the moment. Until Montrose left, they were trapped.

"You cannot hide forever, Mlle. D'Argent," Montrose called out again.

"I've told you, she isn't here," Everett said in his most bombastic voice, approaching Montrose as though the two of them were playing a scene. "She's gone to lunch with one of her admirers."

"A likely story," Montrose sneered. He turned to look as Patrick started toward him, balling his hands into fists and looking as threatening as he could.

That, of course, made Everett flush and fan himself. "Patrick, love, not now," he teased.

A few of the stagehands that Nan couldn't see laughed. She willed them to laugh on. Nothing diffused a man who believed himself to be a threat faster than being laughed at.

"Montrose is a blackguard," Mr. Rathborne-Paxton grumbled beside her. "The man should hang."

Nan's eyes went wide. "And what do you know of Montrose, *monsieur*?" she asked.

Mr. Rathborne-Paxton turned to her as though she'd just

returned home from a voyage abroad and had not yet heard the latest gossip. "He has declared war on my family, *mademoiselle*. He is in the process of destroying my father—though if you ask me, the man deserves to be destroyed—and he nearly ruined my brother Samuel and his new wife, Alice."

Nan winced and let out a low sound of understanding. "*Oui*, of course. 'Ow could I forget."

How *could* she forget? The London papers had been ablaze with rumors about Alice Woodmont—now Mrs. Samuel Rathborne-Paxton—the month before. Things in Nan's own life had been such a whirlwind during and since that time. Her agent, Mr. Brown, had signed her to three new advertising campaigns. Journalists were constantly pressing her for interviews about the close of one show and the opening of the new one. And on top of that, Montrose had climbed out of the pit of Hell that Nan was certain he lived in to accost her for money.

She sucked in a breath as several things fell into place in her mind. Montrose had made Alice Woodmont's life miserable, but the new Mrs. Rathborne-Paxton had slipped his trap and headed off to the country. Nan had assumed Montrose had heard about her new endorsement deals, and that that was why he had suddenly come after her for money. But the timing suggested that, because he'd failed to get what he wanted from one source, he'd turned to another.

"Mlle. D'Argent, you've gone pale," Mr. Rathborne-Paxton said. He seemed to forget his own fear as he turned to her, drawing her partially into his arms. It was far too intimate a gesture, but Nan found comfort in it. "Is there anything I can do?"

Nan bit her lip. "Perhaps?"

Mr. Rathborne-Paxton frowned at her answer. "You are concerned about Montrose. He wants something from you." His expression turned downright murderous.

"*Non*, it is not zat," she said, assuming Mr. Rathborne-Paxton believed Montrose *wanted* her. "I...he...zat is...." She bit her lip, scrambling for a way to explain that would not spill her secret.

Mr. Rathborne-Paxton waited patiently for her answer, his embrace growing slowly tighter. She should not have liked it as much as she did.

To keep herself from succumbing to the handsome and charming man in a way she knew would spell disaster, she forced herself to straighten and take a breath. "'Ow can I explain?" she began. "Montrose believes I owe him a great deal of money."

"Believes you owe him money?" Mr. Rathborne-Paxton asked, one eyebrow raised.

"He feels as though he is entitled to a portion of my earnings," Nan went on carefully.

Mr. Rathborne-Paxton shook his head, confused. "Why would he think that?"

"Many years ago," she said slowly, "he introduced me to Monsieur Jewel. Everett zen introduced me to Mr. Cristofori. Zee two of zem gave me my career and my fame." She paced as Mr. Rathborne-Paxton nodded in understanding. "Montrose believes he is entitled to a percentage of my earnings now."

"Because Montrose is strapped for cash and feels he must find it wherever he can."

Nan blinked at him, encouraged by the feeling they shared the same problem. "Do you believe so as well?" She cursed herself for letting her accent slip in her shock.

Fortunately, Mr. Rathborne-Paxton didn't seem to notice. "My brother, Sam, and his bride discovered that Montrose has financed most of his nefarious dealings on credit. He must always stay one step ahead of his creditors in order to continue his reign of destruction. But we believe he may have come to a point where his reach exceeds his grasp. The man is desperate."

Mr. Rathborne-Paxton's suppositions matched Nan's own. For a moment, her heart fluttered with excitement. She would cheer along with the rest of the crowd when Montrose met his downfall.

A moment later, a thought occurred to her that had her clutching a hand to her stomach. Montrose was the sort of man who became more vicious when he believed he was cornered.

"He will not leave me alone until he gets what he wants," she whispered.

Sure enough, as if to prove her words, Montrose shouted, "If you do not drag the woman out here immediately, I will make certain that this entire production, all of you, and this theater we stand in, are destroyed. You will all be ruined. Just tell me where Mlle. D'Argent is."

Nan must have made a sound or let her anxiety show. Mr. Rathborne-Paxton stepped into her again, closing his arms around her.

"Do not fear, my dear," he said, as romantic as any of the heroes Cristofori had ever written. "I will not let a single bit of harm befall you. You can put all of your faith and trust in me. Consider me your hero."

It was silly, given the situation and the moment, but Nan found herself smiling all the same. Perhaps Mr. Rathborne-Paxton was not the same as every other admirer who had ever clamored up to her with roses, demanding an autograph or a kiss. Granted, the man was a tad on the ridiculous side, but noblemen were entitled to be eccentric. And if she were honest with herself, she did rather like the fool.

"I must escape," she whispered, letting herself lean into him. If Mr. Rathborne-Paxton wanted to create a moment akin to the sort of scenes Cristofori wrote, then who was she to deny him that pleasure? "We must flee," she went on. "But we are trapped. 'Owever shall we untangle ourselves from zis situation?"

They stood so close, the heat of each of their bodies warming the other, that for a moment, Nan thought he might try to kiss her. It was a very real possibility as he leaned closer, gazing into her eyes with affection and desire. It was completely mad, but she was drawn to that desire. It wasn't as though she was some sort of virginal, fainting violet. She'd had her fair share of lovers over the years. She was not immune to the animal magnetism that some of her admirers had. Mr. Rathborne-Paxton might be good for more than simply evading Montrose.

Just when she thought he might swoop down to steal a kiss, he pulled back and said, "I have an idea."

"You do?" For the moment, Nan was willing to play the damsel in distress who required her hero to rescue her, mostly because she didn't have any ideas of her own.

"Yes," Mr. Rathborne-Paxton said, taking her hand and leading her quietly along the fly space until they came to one of the ladders.

"*Non*," Nan protested as he started down the ladder. "Montrose will see us."

"Not at the moment." Mr. Rathborne-Paxton nodded to the side of the stage where Montrose was now arguing with Everett, Patrick, and Martin. "He's distracted."

Mr. Rathborne-Paxton was right. They had a chance to get away, but only a brief one. As soon as Mr. Rathborne-Paxton was far enough down the ladder, Nan climbed down after him. The whole thing felt perilous in the extreme.

Once her feet hit the floor below, Montrose shouted, "This is preposterous! She is here somewhere."

Nan stifled a gasp—not just because Montrose broke away from Everett and the others, but because Mr. Rathborne-

Paxton grabbed her wrist and pulled her straight into one of the costume rooms just a few yards away from the ladder.

"But, *monsieur*," she protested as he shut the door, "we cannot 'ide where zere is no other means of escape."

"Oh, but there is another means of escape," Mr. Rathborne-Paxton said with absolute confidence, rushing around the racks of costumes and pushing things aside. He appeared to be looking for something, though Nan didn't have a clue what it could be. "There is always a means of escape when you are in disguise."

Despite herself, Nan barked a laugh. The fool didn't actually think they would be able to sneak out of the theater simply by donning costumes, did he? What a bold and charming idea that was.

"Here," he said at last, finding a long, red cloak with an exaggerated hood that Nan was certain had once been used in a Christmas panto of Little Red Riding Hood a few years ago. "Put that on."

Nan took the cloak, throwing it over her shoulders. "And you?" She lifted her eyebrows in question.

Mr. Rathborne-Paxton shifted through a few more costumes before his face lit with inspiration. He smiled from ear to ear, taking a costume with its hanger, and said, "This."

Chapter Three

Dean grinned broadly at the costume he'd plucked from the rack in front of him. He'd remembered the slightly militaristic suit whose breast was adorned with medals from an insipidly patriotic play that had been staged several years ago—not one of Cristofori's plays. It had been worn by the leading lady's uncle, and one of the chief criticisms of that play was that the character who wore that costume had born too much of a similarity to Sir Joseph Porter, KCB, from the Gilbert and Sullivan play *H.M.S. Pinafore*, which had been staged only a few streets away.

Dean had loved *Pinafore*, and he loved throwing on the pompous and overdone jacket with all its medals.

"You cannot be serious, *monsieur*," Nanette said, gaping at Dean as he buttoned up the front of his costume. "'Ow are we expected to escape Montrose's notice dressed like zees?"

"With style, *mademoiselle*, with style," Dean said, bursting into a grin as he caught sight of himself in the mirror.

Part of him knew the situation had teetered over into territory so ridiculous that it might have been considered surreal, but none of that mattered as Nanette burst into bright, amused laughter. He had made the object of his adoration laugh. He would face any villain, fight any dragon for that.

"If you say so." Nanette shrugged, then threw the red cloak over her shoulder with a dramatic flourish.

Dean spent a few more minutes searching for the hat that accompanied the costume he now wore. The best he could come up with was a shiny top-hat. Nanette had helped him search while seeking out accessories to aid the disguise provided by her own costume, which included a large fan that she could use to hide her face. Footsteps could be heard passing by the door to the costume room once or twice as they dressed, but no one entered the room.

That did not stop Nanette from gasping anxiously every time those footsteps were heard. Once, she even leapt to Dean's side, swaying close to him and resting a delicate hand on Dean's arm. The simple gesture had Dean's chest swelling with pride and affection, not to mention the determination to defend his fair lady to the death if necessary.

"Are we ready?" he asked once they were dressed and there had been silence outside the door for some time.

"We are ready, *monsieur*," Nanette said, the lilt in her French accent giving the words an exciting feel.

Dean moved to the door, cracking it to make certain no one stood between the costume room and the stage door that exited into the alley behind the theater. When he was certain their way was clear, he popped the top hat on his head, offered Nanette his arm, and when she took it, he opened the door and hurried into the backstage hall.

They made it to the stage door without difficulty. Dean grinned, congratulating himself for whisking his lady love to safety.

As soon as he opened the stage door and stepped with Nanette out into the sweltering, July heat of the alley, everything changed.

"Nanette! Here she is!"

"Mlle. D'Argent! Will you sign my program?"

"I've come to see your show every night, Nanette."

There were at least a dozen men and a few women lingering near the stage door, and the moment Nanette made her appearance, they all snapped to attention. Most of them appeared younger and relatively harmless, but the fact that they were there at all, and the eagerness with which they approached Nanette, had Dean immediately alarmed.

Nanette, however, seemed to take it all in stride.

"Ah, gentlemen, you are too kind," she said, slipping into some sort of character as she stood at the top of the small staircase leading to the alley.

The men gathered at the bottom of the stairs, as if waiting for their angel to descend.

"What is the meaning of all this?" Dean whispered, leaning close to Nanette's ear.

"Zey are followers," she murmured back with a shrug. "Zey are always here. But do not worry, zey are kind and harmless."

Dean doubted all of them were entirely harmless. He knew all about the men who flocked to catch a glimpse of Nanette after performances. He might have been one of them himself, on occasion. But seeing the number of men waiting by the theater in the middle of the morning, when they should have been at their places of employment or, in some cases, in school, was unnerving.

He was on the verge of telling them all off and whisking Nanette away when one the men called out, "My gosh, that's Prince Arthur!"

"Prince Arthur?" another answered. "Mlle. D'Argent is walking out with Prince Arthur?"

"It is Prince Arthur," a third gasped.

"Isn't Prince Arthur serving in Bombay at the moment?"

one of the men near the edge of the group asked in a quiet voice.

He was ignored. Dean grabbed hold of the giddy idea filling him and stood taller, puffing out his chest. "Do I look as though I am in India?" he demanded in his best imitation of a princely voice.

The men in the alley murmured and gaped at him, then backed up as Dean gestured for them to give him and Nanette space to descend the stairs. They did so with a slow, regal demeanor.

Out of the corner of his eye, Dean caught Nanette attempting to hide a smile. Just as it had in the costume room, that little show of amusement spurred him on to what he already considered to be the greatest theatrical performance of his life.

"I thank you all for your attendance on my...dear friend, Mlle. D'Argent," he said, standing as he had once seen Prince Arthur stand at an event at Buckingham Palace years ago. He attempted the haughty accent of the royal family as well. "I would also thank you to allow us a bit of privacy as we depart for an important engagement."

"Yes, Your Royal Highness," one of the men said, bowing low.

The others took their cue from him, backing up even farther and bowing low so that Dean and Nanette could pass through to the street. Dean kept his expression haughty and his shoulders back as he escorted Nanette past them, but he was certain he couldn't keep the humor out of his eyes as he peeked at Nanette.

"Thank you, gentlemen," Nanette called over her shoulder to her followers. "I can assure you, I will return later, and zen we shall have our fun, *non*?"

The gentlemen called their goodbyes to her and generally fawned over her from a distance as Dean and Nanette reached the end of the alley and stepped out to the street. One even exclaimed, "Nanette D'Argent is involved with Prince Arthur!"

As soon as they were out of sight of the followers, both Dean and Nanette burst into laughter. Nanette clutched Dean's arm tighter, which only increased his joy over the situation.

"I will not lie to you, *monsieur*," Nanette said as they picked up their pace, heading east. "Zat was zee most fun I have had in ages."

"I believe I could become quite fond of this theatrical life," Dean said, returning to his Prince Arthur posture. "I would make a rather good leading man. Mr. Jewel had better watch his back."

Nanette laughed, the sound filling Dean with warmth and desire all over again. "I do not think you should, 'ow do zey say, put your cart before your 'orse?"

Dean laughed, dropping his pompous posture and smiling fondly at Nanette. An hour ago, he was just another one of her followers. Now, through some miracle, he felt as though they'd crossed the barrier of friendship.

No, it was not a miracle, it was Montrose and the shared troubles they had with the bastard.

Dean's expression sobered. "I do hope you are satisfied with the way we've avoided Montrose," he said. "The man is a plague on humanity, and my family is struggling with all we have to stop him from dragging us under, as he has too many other noble families."

Nanette lost her mirth as well. "He is a bad man, Monsieur Montrose. Ruthless and cowardly together. Very few things frighten me, Monsieur Rathborne-Paxton, but Montrose's determination to extort money from me does."

"Please," Dean said, softness and affection seeping into his tone and, he hoped, his expression. "Call me Dean. I know it isn't appropriate, seeing as I am a prince and all—" Nanette's smile returned for a moment, and Dean's heart soared, "—but I would so like for us to be friends."

He would like for them to be much more than friends, but a man needed to start somewhere.

"Thank you, Dean," Nanette said, inclining her head to him as she did. "And you may call me Nanette."

"You are too kind," Dean said. He paused as they reached a street corner and turned to her to ask, "May I also treat you to lunch? Perhaps along the banks of the Serpentine in Hyde Park?"

Nanette's eyes went wide, and for a moment, she blinked rapidly up at him. "You wish to walk out with me?"

Dean's heart sped up as he caught the suspicion in her voice. And why would she not be suspicious of a man's offer to feed her. He'd just witnessed a dozen men clamoring after her attention for no reason other than that she was famous and the object of their fantasy. For all Nanette knew, he was no different than them.

He pivoted to face her fully, taking one of her hands in his. They'd rushed out of the theater so quickly that Nanette had not had an opportunity to don gloves, so the gesture felt even more intimate. "*Mademoiselle*, I know you may not see me as anything other than one of your followers, but please allow me to say that in my time assisting at the Concord Theater, I have observed you from afar, and I feel as though I know you, the true woman you are."

For some reason, his affectionate words killed the smile in Nanette's eyes completely. In fact, she appeared downright terrified for a moment, and her face drained of some of its color. "You...you know me?" she asked, her voice high and small.

"Yes, I believe I do." Dean smiled so that she would feel more at ease. "You are goodness and kindness personified. You are beauty and grace. I've seen how you interact with the stagehands and how you treat every tradesman as though they are your equal. You may have come from the finest ballet school in Paris, but you do not let that give you airs and graces. You are a woman above women, and I—" He stopped himself just short of making a silly declaration of love. Instead, he said, "I admire you immensely and wish very much that we could become better acquainted."

He flushed hot after his speech was done, worried that he'd made a sentimental arse of himself. Francis would scoff at him and shake his head. Sam would approve, however. Sam was forever going on about the ridiculousness of men being told to stifle their softer feelings.

Fortunately, Nanette returned to her easy, relaxed smile. "You, too, are kind and generous, *monsieur*." Her smile widened. "I would be honored to have lunch with you in Hyde Park."

Dean nearly laughed with relief, then turned to hail one of the cabs lined up and waiting for passengers nearby. "Thank you, Nanette," he said, deliberately using her name. "And while we're at it, we might think of ways that we can discourage Montrose from vexing you the way he has been."

Nanette lost her smile again as a cab pulled near and the driver hopped down to hold the door open for them. Dean gave the man instructions to take them to Hyde Park, and once they were safely tucked into the carriage and on their way, Nanette let out a breath and said, "I am afraid that zere is no simple way to turn Montrose away from pursuing me."

Dean frowned, mulling over the problem the way he spun the brim of the top-hat he'd removed when entering the cab. "You say that he feels you owe him for giving you your start in the London theater?"

"*Oui*," Nanette sighed, her shoulders slightly hunched.

"He feels as though zee introductions he made for me years ago entitle him to a percentage of my current income."

Dean's breath hitched mercilessly in his chest at her mention of income. Even though it made him feel just as much of a mercenary cad as Montrose, he asked, "That income is substantial?"

Nanette was silent for a moment, her head tilted down and her cheeks turning pink. "Zere is quite a bit of money to be made zees days, if one knows 'ow to capitalize on zee public's hunger for celebrity."

"Yes." Dean nodded slowly, his face heating as he thought of the trading card bearing Nanette's picture that stood on his bedside table. "I see your face everywhere, even in my dreams."

His silly comment served its purpose, and Nanette grinned bashfully. "It is a new thing, zis fascination with celebrities and using zere images to sell products. But zere is a great deal of money to be made from it. I earn more from zee agreements my agent makes with zee facial cream companies and zee biscuit makers zan I do from my salary at zee theater."

"Truly?" Dean's brow flew up.

But then, it made sense. Dean could conjure up a list of dozens of actors and actresses who had become famous on the London stage in the last century, but only a few who were known to be wealthy, like Nanette.

He blinked, then asked, "Agent? What is that?"

"It is a person who searches out opportunities for performers," Nanette explained. "Zere have been agents acting on behalf of writers, interacting with publishers, for decades, but it is only within zee past few years zat enterprising performers, such as myself, have sought out zee services of zees people for ourselves. And zee results have been good, *non*?"

"I suppose they have," Dean said. In fact, many things about the degree of renown Nanette had achieved now made sense.

"I predict zat in short order, every actor, singer, and dancer wishing to pursue a career will enlist zee 'elp of an agent to further zeir pursuits, even zough zee concept is quite new," she said with a nod.

"I think you are right," Dean agreed.

They reached Hyde Park a few minutes later, and Dean rushed to hold the carriage door for Nanette and help her down rather than waiting for the driver to do it. He paid the driver quickly, then helped Nanette arrange her red cloak so that it concealed her appearance somewhat, then escorted her into Hyde Park.

"There's a small café farther along that I and my brothers like to frequent," he explained as they walked.

Even with her concealment, it was clear that people recognized Nanette. It was hard not to when they walked past a small stand that had been set up to sell soaps, fragrances, and other toiletries, and Nanette's face was plastered all over them. Perhaps it was the size and openness of the park or the number of people who were there—or perhaps it was Dean's own commanding presence, or that of the costume he wore—but even though they smiled and waved, no one dared approach Nanette directly.

"I should not allow you to purchase my lunch, *monsieur*," Nanette said as they took the path that would lead them to the Serpentine.

"Nonsense, *mademoiselle*," Dean said with mock offense. "A gentleman always pays for his lady fair."

Nanette rewarded that comment with a broad smile. "*Oui*, but did you not tell me earlier zat Montrose is in pursuit of you and your family and that he has nearly bankrupted you?"

"I can still buy lunch," Dean laughed.

It was no laughing matter, though. Montrose's threats were very real. They were the whole reason he had summoned up the courage to walk out with a famous actress in the first place. Well, the reason he had allowed Lily and Martin to shove him into the situation. It was those reasons that caused him to charge forward, being blunt instead of finessing the situation.

"I wish to do more than buy you lunch, Nanette," he said, perhaps with a bit too much seriousness, as they passed a group of girls playing with their dolls on a blanket spread over the grass. Their nannies gasped, their eyes going wide, at the sight of Nanette, and they put their heads together to whisper.

"You wish to treat me to supper as well, *non*?" Nanette asked, a look of mock innocence in her eyes as she glanced to him.

Dean laughed, but his gut twisted a bit. He wasn't as much of a fool as people thought he was. He could see that she believed he wanted to bed her. And while yes, he did—who wouldn't with a figure as fine as hers and a spirit as vibrant—his intentions toward her went far beyond that. It hurt him to think she believe he was only after one thing.

"I wish to treat you to everything, Nanette," he said as earnestly as he could. "I know we have only just met, but I feel as though we have known each other for some time. We have been in each other's circle for months now. We share a common enemy. It occurs to me that the solution to both of our struggles with Montrose is to band together in...intimate ways."

"Oh?"

Nanette's single syllable answer to his halfway declaration did nothing to ease Dean's mind or settle his soul. There was something deeply guarded about Nanette and the way she watched him. Perhaps it was her talent as an actor, but Dean could not glean a single thing about what she might have thought of his attentions toward her. He was reasonably certain that she no longer saw him as just another admirer, but beyond that, he remained in the dark.

He would have to be far more open and blunter about his intentions and their reasons. He paused near a group of boys who were tossing a ball around and said, "The truth is, Nanette, my brothers and I have already devised a plan that we believe will thwart Montrose's intentions toward us."

"You have?" Nanette seemed surprisingly interested.

Encouraged, Dean went on. "Yes. In fact, it has to do with marriage."

He turned as he had on the street corner, before he'd hailed the cab, and reached for her hand that did not hold her fan. As he did, though, the ball that the boys had been tossing came sailing through the air and struck his top-hat right off his head.

Dean jerked at the sudden loss of his hat and turned to frown at the boys. They were all giggling, and one was doubled over with laughter, which convinced Dean they had aimed for his hat on purpose.

He stepped away from Nanette, rushing to retrieve his hat and the ball. As soon as he had the ball in his hand, he chucked it as hard as he could at the boys, scowling as he did. The boys yelped and scattered like bowling pins.

The ball sailed right past them and smashed into the side of a somewhat familiar-looking, well-dressed Indian woman who was seated on a stool, sketching the Serpentine. The woman cried out as her sketch pad and pencil box went flying, and she grabbed her arm where the ball had made contact.

"*Monsieur*!" Nanette gasped. "What have you done?"

"It was an accident, I swear," Dean said, appealing to Nanette, then rushing toward the Indian woman. "I am sorry, so sorry," he told the woman.

She recoiled as he charged at her, falling off her stool in the process.

To make matters worse, it was just Dean's luck that

Francis happened to be walking through the park at that moment, and he'd witnessed the entire scene.

"Dean!" Francis shouted. "What in God's name are you doing?"

Dean winced. Between his brother's fury, the Indian woman's upset, and Nanette's shock, he feared he had not only ruined his chances with Nanette, he'd branded himself no better than the wily boys who were still laughing uproariously as they fled the scene of their crime.

Chapter Four

The mishap unraveled so quickly that Nan didn't have a chance to warn Dean that the lovely Indian woman was sitting behind the boys before he threw the ball. She could hardly blame Dean for his momentary burst of temper—if that was even what it was. He seemed the sort who would have just as easily joined the boys in tossing their ball as attempt to knock off one of their heads with it.

The Indian woman was far less amused with Dean's childlike enthusiasm, though. Nan ran toward her, reaching out to help her right herself as, behind her, Dean was accosted by the new arrival on the scene. And if she was not mistaken, it was the same man who had been at the Concord Theater earlier, his brother.

"Francis," Dean answered the man's call with a nervous laugh, proving that Nan's assumption was correct. "Fancy seeing you here. What brings you to Hyde Park today?"

Lord Cathraiche—the title leapt to Nan's mind as she and the Indian woman stood—glowered as he marched up to his brother. "Never you mind why I am in Hyde Park. How dare you assault this woman in such an egregious manner?"

Dean frowned at his brother, then turned to the Indian woman. "Madam, I am deeply, terribly sorry. It was never my intention to—"

"I know what your intention was, sir," the Indian woman snapped. Nan's eyes went as wide as Dean's at the ferocity of her answer. "Do you think this is the first time I have been accosted without cause?"

"I...er...I am terribly—"

The woman stepped away from Nan and moved closer to Dean, practically breathing fire at him. "Do you think that because I am alone, because I am from a foreign kingdom, because I am a woman, it gives you the right to assault me?"

"No, madam, I do not think—"

Again, the woman cut Dean off. "My father sent me to London to be educated, sir, and I have learned more than my fair share about how Englishmen treat those who are foreign to their shores. My father is a king, and were we in Bengal, I would—"

"Miss Narayan, please forgive my brother's shamelessly bad behavior." Lord Cathraiche stepped in, interrupting the fiery woman's tirade. He shifted so that he stood by her side, frowning along with her at Dean. "He is—if you will pardon my callous speech—an arse."

Miss Narayan's eyes widened as she gaped at Francis. "You would dare speak to me in such a manner?" For the first time, Nan noticed the barest hint of a Hindustani lilt in her voice. She couldn't help but admire the way the woman had mastered a different accent—something she continued to struggle with herself.

"Forgive me, madam," Lord Cathraiche said with a slight bow, managing to maintain his composure impeccably, "but when it comes to my brother, Mr. Dean Rathborne-Paxton, only the rudest of words will suffice."

Nan clapped a hand to her mouth to stop from snorting

with laughter. Miss Narayan continued to scowl, but her stance and her eyes softened. Dean shuffled as though he didn't know whether to be offended or amused by his brother's words.

His brother. Nan's insides buzzed at the implications of the connection for her. Dean Rathborne-Paxton was the brother of the Earl of Cathraiche. She was a ninny for not realizing everything that could mean sooner. She was an even bigger fool for not catching on that Dean was the son of the Marquess of Vegas. The son of a marquess! And he'd just attempted to make love to her in the middle of Hyde Park, she was certain of it.

Nan's insides fizzled with excitement and calculation. The son of a marquess wanted to court her. Dean had intimated as much nearly from the start of their brief acquaintance. Dean understood Montrose and the threat he posed as well. He would not underestimate the power Montrose could hold over her, whereas other men might. And Dean had stated that his brothers had a plan to foil Montrose.

His *aristocratic* brothers. From an old, noble family. If she played her cards right, she could marry into the aristocracy. The public adored stories of women who raised themselves up, only to be rewarded with a place in the upper echelons of society. They would clamor to purchase items with her name and image on them. Her fortune would expand and be secure, but more than that, she would have the protection of a title, even if it was not her own or Dean's. Marrying a nobleman was precisely what she needed to shield herself from Montrose's machinations, and from the exhaustion of a life spent constantly in the public eye.

"Nanette? I say, Mlle. D'Argent, are you quite well?" Dean gently nudged her out of her thoughts.

"Hmm?" Nan answered, the sound a little too high-pitched and excited. "Oh, yes, do forgive me." She cursed herself a moment later for letting her accent slip. "Zat is, *oui*. My thoughts were, 'ow do you say, away with zee fairies for a moment." She stepped closer to Dean's side.

Lord Cathraiche and Miss Narayan were staring at her as well, but when Nan smiled at them, her face heated a little too much, Lord Cathraiche turned once more to Miss Narayan.

"Please allow me to treat you to a bit of tea to make up for my brother's lack of manners," he said.

Miss Narayan eyed him skeptically. "No thank you, my lord," she said. "Princesses can take care of themselves."

Nan caught her breath. She had missed something in her mercenary daydreaming.

"At least let me assist you in gathering your things," Lord Cathraiche said, moving to retrieve Miss Narayan's sketchbook.

"We'd better leave them before we get told off again," Dean muttered near Nan's ear, offering his arm.

"I believe you are right, *monsieur*," she whispered in return.

As soon as they were back on the path, heading toward one of the small cafés whose tables looked out over the Serpentine, she leaned close to Dean and continued in an excited voice, "Did she say 'princess'?"

Dean grinned at her, a bit of surprise in his gaze. "Were you not listening?" he asked.

"I was preoccupied," Nan said.

Dean laughed, glanced over his shoulder at his brother and a still irate Miss Narayan, then said, "Her father is the king of someplace in Bengal. Dashed if I can keep track of all those Hindustani kingdoms, but he's a raja. That makes her Rani Priya Narayan, not just plain Miss Narayan. Her father sent her to England, along with her brother, the future raja, to study."

Nan's heart beat even more rapidly in her chest. As they

reached the café and Dean helped her to a seat at a table facing the scene they had just left, she took a long, hard look at the way Lord Cathraiche continued to assist Miss Narayan. "Your brother seems quite taken with her."

Dean whipped around, his forehead creasing slightly as he stared at them. "Truly?" He made a curious sound, then helped himself to the place across the table from Nan. "I've always assumed Francis doesn't have a heart. Although, if he is as intent as he says on marrying—"

Nan leaned forward slightly, waiting for him to finish his thought. There was clearly more that he had intended to say, but he'd stopped himself. Now Nan wanted to know why. There was most certainly more to the Rathborne-Paxton family than met the eye.

More that she wanted to be a part of. The son of a marquess, the brother of an earl, and possibly, if what she thought she'd seen was correct, the future brother-in-law of a rani? Dean Rathborne-Paxton could very well be a gift from the heavens.

A waiter came to take their order, and as soon as they were comfortably ensconced with simple fare and sweet, milky tea, Nan stretched her hand across the table, inviting Dean to touch it.

"So, *monsieur*," she began, lowering her head slightly and glancing at him through her lashes in the most flirtatious manner she could manage. "What is zees about wishing to give me more zan lunch or supper?"

It was scandalous of her to encourage Dean the way she was. Some might see it as wicked of her to coax him into making more promises than he had intended so that she might secure herself a grander, safer place in society. But in the moment, Nan didn't care. She'd always been ambitious. More than that, she liked Dean. How could she not? Who else would look so dashing and at ease wearing a ridiculous costume laden with tin medals?

Dean's entire countenance lit like someone had turned up the footlights at the base of a stage. "I believe you know what I intend, my dear," he said in a tone that was too intimate for his intention to be mistaken.

"I believe I do," she said, leaning into the table. She flickered a glance to her hand, which still rested on the table between them in invitation.

Dean took the bait and slipped his hand over hers. It was scandalous for them to hold hands, without gloves, in broad daylight and in a public place, but the fact was not lost on Nan that the further she pushed things, the more Dean might be inclined to leap before he looked.

"I suppose it is ridiculous, to some degree, that I would pursue you in such a manner after such a brief acquaintance," he said. "But as I intimated earlier, before we were so rudely interrupted—" he grinned and glanced subtly over his shoulder, "—I feel as though we have known each other for a much longer time. And at the risk of painting myself as just another of your long line of followers, I have adored you for even longer than that."

Nan buzzed with excitement, but attempted to keep her expression calm. "You do me a great honor, *monsieur*," she said. "And *non*, I do not think of you as just another one of zose stage door Johnnies."

"Stage door Johnnies?" Dean repeated, a little too loud. Nan couldn't tell from his shocked expression whether he was insulted or amused by the term.

"It is what we call zose people who linger by zee stage door after performances," she explained.

"Well, the Devil take that," Dean went on, laughing, but looking a shade alarmed as well. "I am a greedy man, Mlle. D'Argent. I wish to keep you all for myself." His voice dropped to a seductive level, and he rubbed his thumb over her knuckles.

Even though she knew this was all just a game, that Dean had reasons for pursuing her that he had yet to reveal, and she was social-climbing by entertaining his pursuit, something in her thrilled at that simple gesture. And why should it not? Dean was handsome and charming. He had a way about him that drew Nan in. No matter who she pretended to be, she was not some innocent miss who shied away from such things. If it took kicking her skirts up to secure a different sort of life than she could ever have dreamed of, she would do what she must. With pleasure.

"Zere will always be admirers," she told Dean, surprised that she was compelled to be frank with him instead of feeding his fantasies of having her all to himself. That was a testament to how much she genuinely liked him. "Zey are part of my job. Zey are a necessity to any woman in zee gaze of zee public, *non*?"

"I suppose they are," Dean sighed, leaning back slightly and picking up his tea with his free hand. "If I had my way, I would have you all to myself so that we could get to know each other properly."

Again, Nan's heart fluttered a bit. The way Dean spoke seemed to hint that he understood they did not, in fact, know each other as well as they pretended, but that he wished to know her. And while that presented its own problems, it increased her warm regards for Dean.

"I should very much like to know you better too, Dean," she said, withdrawing her hand so that she could take up her fork and finish her lunch. "Perhaps we should arrange for another meeting? In more intimate surroundings?"

"I would like that very much," Dean said. He went so far as to wink cheekily at her over his teacup right before taking a sip.

They finished their lunch and enjoyed a stroll through Hyde Park. At first, Nan was anxious about Dean asking too many questions about her past and her family. He seemed more interested in what her life as a celebrated actress was, though. And about Montrose and his supposed claim on a part of her income. She answered as best she could, but spent most of her time turning the questions back on him.

"And zat is why Montrose is so determined to ruin your family?" she asked as they headed toward Hyde Park Corner so that they could find a cab to return them to the Concord Theater. "Because of some unknown sins of your father?"

Dean laughed humorlessly. "Not all of them are unknown. So far, Francis has uncovered gambling debts going back several years. There is some involvement with financing an opium operation as well. And it seems crass to admit it, but apparently, Father had a disturbing fondness for dog fighting as well."

"Is zat sort of entertainment usually something aristocrats enjoy?" Nan asked.

"No," Dean answered. "Which is another disturbing facet of the whole thing. We believe Father is guilty of a great number of sins we may never be able to trace because they are not the usual sorts of things our class gets involved in."

"I am very sorry for your difficulties," Nan said, her face heating. The way Dean spoke made her worry that he had some sort of prejudice against the working class. Too many members of the upper class did. Which made the secrets she carried all the more volatile.

"Don't worry about me," Dean said as they reached the street and he hailed a cab. "It is you I am concerned about. Montrose will not win, you know. I will not allow it."

Nan could only hope that Dean was right. She pretended to have complete faith in him and attempted to push Montrose out of her mind during the entire journey back to the Concord Theater. By the time they reached the theater and returned to the costume room to divest themselves of their borrowed attire, Dean even had her laughing again.

It was a bit of a shame that she had to say goodbye to him as everyone around the theater shifted from preparations for the new show to setting the stage for the one that was currently running. Different productions often overlapped in such a way, but Nan had been performing in *Love's Last Lesson* for so long now that she could have recited the lines in her sleep.

"This has been a lovely day, my dear," Dean said as they prepared to part near the stage door. He took her hand and squeezed it. "I do hope we can repeat it soon and often."

Nan noticed Everett step out of his dressing room several yards away to watch them with a slight smirk.

"I sincerely 'ope so as well, *monsieur*," she said, ignoring Everett to smile fetchingly at Dean. "I believe we have many beautiful days ahead of us."

"We do," Dean said with complete confidence.

He raised her hand to his lips. Nan's heart fluttered as his warm lips brushed her knuckles. A large part of her wished that he would kiss more than just her hand. Her thoughts and emotions were a jumble of ambition, affection, and anxiety, but she couldn't help but think that a good, solid kiss would ease every one of her worries.

When Dean let her go and left, winking as he did, Nan let out a sigh. She watched him until he stepped out through the stage door. It was as if she had everything she'd ever wanted—comfort, safety, renown, and love—within her grasp. It could all be hers, if she was willing to deceive a good man to have it.

As if he could hear her thoughts, Everett spoke up behind her. "That was lovely and romantic, Nan. Well done."

A nervous tremor shot through Nan's gut as she turned to

45

face her friend. "*Monsieur* Rathborne-Paxton is a kind and lovely man," she said.

Everett's grin widened as he followed her down the hall and into her dressing room. It was early for her to be at the theater for the night's performance, but there was no harm in preparing ahead of time.

"Does he know?" Everett asked, shutting the door behind him.

"Know what?" Nan asked, blinking innocently.

Everett laughed. "Come on, Nan. It's just us. And the door is shut. You can drop your mask."

Nan let out a breath and turned to Everett. "Of course, he doesn't know," she said in her natural, country accent. "I would be a fool to tip my cards this early in the game."

"So you are playing a game with him," Everett said, moving to sit on the edge of her dressing table with his arms crossed.

Nan had been friends with Everett for years. He was one of the only people who knew the truth about who she was. She trusted him with her life, so there was no point pretending anything with him.

"He wants to court me, Ev," she said. "I think he wants more than that. Can't you see what my life would be like if I managed to marry into a noble family? I wouldn't have to simper and fawn and run myself ragged all the time to keep my image pure. I would have a title, or at least a connection to a title, to do that for me."

"So, it's the comfort and security of an aristocratic life that you want," Everett said.

"It's the safety of having a place," Nan explained. "Having a position in society that is unassailable."

"Would you stop acting?" Everett asked.

Nan shrugged and turned to fetch her first act costume for the night's performance from the rack where it hung. "Perhaps. I could use a rest, as could you. We've been at this without stopping for years now."

Everett hummed. "Patrick and I have been talking about taking a trip to Italy. Italian boys are quite careless with clothing, or so we've heard."

Nan laughed and walked back to her dressing table with her costume. "Have a care that the two of you are not arrested for indecency."

"No one is arrested for indecency in Italy, love," he said with a cheeky wink. "That's why we want to go there."

"Your reputation could be ruined, then," Nan continued to tease him.

"As could yours, if word ever got out that you're just a sweet country girl from Shropshire and not a dazzling French ballerina." He spoke the last few words in a horribly over-exaggerated French accent.

Nan wanted to smile, but she couldn't. "No one is going to find out. No one can find out."

Everett's expression turned solemn. "Love, if you marry Mr. Rathborne-Paxton, you'll have to tell him. That's not the sort of secret you can keep from a husband." When Nan sent him a doubtful look, he went on with, "Patrick knows everything about me, even the things I wish he didn't know. That's what marriage is."

"You're not married," Nan told him.

"How dare you?" Everett clapped a hand to his chest in mock offense, but Nan could see that she'd genuinely irritated him by suggesting he and Mr. Wrexham weren't married.

"Sorry," she sighed, sinking into the chair beside the counter. "But what else can I do? I need to marry Dean for the protection and elevation his family's title can provide. And because Dean, too, is troubled by Montrose. He says that he and his brothers have a plan to defeat the man."

"Did he say what that plan is?" Everett asked.

Nan sagged a bit. "No, not yet. But I intend to ask him soon."

Everett hummed and nodded. "So, you feel you need to marry a man—a man who has not proposed yet, mind you— in order to wrap the mantle of protection that is his family's standing in the aristocracy around you. And don't think for a moment that I am ignorant of what marrying into the nobs will do for your career. But you also think that doing so will somehow protect you from Montrose?"

"Yes?" Nan said, wishing she felt more confident about it. "And...and I do rather like him."

Everett hummed as though she'd revealed more.

A moment later, he grew serious again. "Poppet, if you marry the man, you'll have to tell him the truth. And do you know why?" He rushed on to answer his own question with, "Because if you don't, Montrose will."

Nan sagged further. "I know."

Everett scooted closer to her, took her hand, and brought it to his lips to kiss it. "Well then, dearie, it seems you have a choice before you. Marry your handsome nobleman and reap the rewards of the upper classes—while being honest with him about who you really are—or let the whole thing go and keep the persona that has built your fame and fortune in place."

Nan sighed, staring at her hand when Everett let it go. The trouble was, she didn't like either option. All she could do was pray for a third to present itself.

Chapter Five

"Things are going swimmingly, as far as I'm concerned," Dean told Joseph the next morning, as the two of them sat down for coffee and a full breakfast. He wasn't certain where Francis was that morning, and Lord Vegas must have still been sulking in his room, as he'd taken to doing since his sons had shown signs of rebellion. But it hardly mattered to Dean. His youngest brother was a captive audience. "Mlle. D'Argent is quite taken with me, I believe."

"And what, pray tell, gives you that idea?" Joseph asked, staring at one of the several newspapers that were delivered to the family's breakfast table every morning. Joseph seemed to be in a surlier mood than usual, perhaps because he returned to the house even later than Dean had the night before.

"She walked out with me," Dean said, counting the reasons on his fingers. "She smiled graciously at me. She laughed at my jokes."

Joseph glanced up from the paper he was currently perusing with a look of shock. "Why would the woman do such a thing?" he asked. "You aren't even remotely funny."

Dean smiled broadly, a burst of affection for his brother filling him. Joseph was having the hardest time of all of them coming to terms with their father's duplicitous and hypocritical nature, but Dean could see that he was trying to keep a stiff upper lip. He was trying to remain loyal and friendly with his brothers, thus his joke.

"I am hilarious," Dean informed him with a stern frown. "You'd do best to remember that, young pup."

"Perhaps in your own mind," Joseph said with a slight shrug, returning to his reading.

"To Mlle. D'Argent as well," Dean went on, feeling pleased with himself, pleased with Joseph, and pleased with Nanette. "She has allowed me to call her by her given name."

Joseph peeked up at him, one eyebrow arched. "I question the morality of a women who allows a strange gentleman to address her by her given name."

"My dear boy," Dean said with a feigned air of imperiousness. "Firstly, there is nothing amiss in calling a woman by her given name. Secondly, is not the point of Francis's marriage scheme for us all to marry women of questionable morality?"

"No," Joseph was quick to correct him, "it was to marry women of astounding fortune but little social worth so that we might restore the family fortunes and ensure that Mama is well taken care of."

Dean grinned at his brother's use of the term "Mama" instead of the more formal "Mother" that the rest of the brothers had adopted. Joseph was twenty-one, but most certainly the baby of the family.

Dean cleared his throat and went on with, "Thirdly, I am not strange."

Joseph laughed out loud at that as he turned a page of his newspaper. The sound was music to Dean's ears. He'd hated seeing Joseph so unhappy throughout that summer, and even if the laughter was at his expense, he longed to hear more of it.

"What do you say?" he went on, hoping to make his dearly loved brother laugh more. "How would you feel about having a famous actress and dancer as a sister-in-law?"

Joseph snapped his gaze up from his newspaper and fixed Dean with a mock horrified look. It was such a delight that Dean would have endured whatever scandal the match would inevitably cause just to see Joseph happy again.

He would have taken the joke further, but Francis strode into the room a moment later—not from the direction of the staircase that led to their bedrooms upstairs, but from the front hall. His face was slightly pink and he carried the scent of the London streets with him, which seemed to indicate that he'd been out on some sort of errand.

"And just where have you been so early in the morning?" Dean asked in surprise, leaning back in his chair as Francis headed straight for his seat near their father's place at the head of the table.

Francis yanked out the chair and sat heavily, reaching for the coffee before their footman, Arnold, could reach it to serve him. "Landlords and housing agents are all blackguards and bastards," he grumbled.

Both Dean and Joseph stared at him in surprise. "What has happened?" Joseph asked.

Francis's expression passed through several levels of peevishness as he fixed his coffee. Dean noted that he helped himself to double the sugar that he usually used. "The flat I thought I'd secured for Mother," he said with a cryptic growl.

"What of it?" Dean asked. "I liked the sound of it when you described it the other day."

"Close enough to Mayfair to still be fashionable," Joseph agreed with a nod, "but not so close that Mama might encounter Father on accident."

"And not so expensive that we cannot afford it," Dean said, a bit more gravity in his voice.

Francis *humphed*. "That is precisely the problem," he said before taking a long sip of coffee. He winced, either at the taste or the temperature, then put the cup down with enough force to splash the otherwise pristine tablecloth. "They've refused to let it to us," he said.

"The flat?" Joseph looked surprised.

Dean knew that feeling. "There is a landlord in London who would dare to refuse to let a flat to the Marchioness of Vegas?"

Francis growled wordlessly, then said, "The man said our credit is not good. He said that he cannot go handing off valuable property to impoverished and embarrassed noblemen who will bankrupt him by failing to pay the rent he has asked for."

Dean and Joseph sank back in their chairs. Dean ran a hand through his hair. It felt very much like a weight had settled over his shoulders and pressed in on his heart. They'd begun to feel the sting of their father's bad dealings throughout the summer—tailors requiring their outstanding bills to be paid, Cook informing them they would have to change their usual menu to lower grocery bills, the unfortunate way they'd had to let a maid and a footman go, and the way Francis had been forced to sell two of their horses—but this was the first time they'd been denied something as substantial as a place for their mother to live.

"Mama must live somewhere," Joseph insisted, worrying the corner of the newspaper in front of him. "She...she wishes to return to London, does she not?"

Francis's frown deepened, and Dean sent his younger brother a sympathetic look. "She said she would be amenable to returning to London, with Aunt Josephine, under certain circumstances."

"Those circumstances are her own lodgings and an allowance that will allow her to maintain some of her social contacts," Francis said, then added in a mutter, "The ones who will have her, at least, after Father's disgrace."

A black cloud seemed to descend over the table as the three of them thought about their problems. Dean envied Sam for taking his new bride and Alice's son and decamping to Francis's estate near Winchester. Some might have seen it as retreating from the fight, but as far as Dean was concerned, after the way Montrose had menaced Alice to the point where she could have met with serious bodily and emotional harm, their little family deserved a reprieve.

The rest of them were stuck in London with all of their problems still. Except that they had the solution to their problems within their grasp. In fact, if Dean merely kept to the course he'd plotted for himself when it came to marrying wealth, only at a faster pace, they might be able to secure a flat for Mother immediately, if not sooner. The only thing that turned heads faster than money these days was celebrity.

It was an eerie coincidence that, at that moment, Joseph made a sound of surprise and said, "Good heavens, Dean. Your Mlle. D'Argent is involved with Prince Arthur."

Dean was grateful that he'd finished his coffee, otherwise he would have spit it across the table as he burst into laughter.

"What is this all about?" Francis asked, his ever-present frown as deep as ever as he craned his neck in an attempt to see what Joseph was reading across the table.

"It says right here." Joseph pointed to an article in the newspaper he was reading. "'*Mlle. Nanette D'Argent, darling of the London stage and the face of several lines of cosmetics and chocolates, was seen by several in the company of a man who is presumed to be Prince Arthur yesterday. Sources confirm that the prince was seen leaving the Concord Theater with the actress late yesterday morning.*'"

Francis scowled at Dean as he continued to chuckle, giddy

with delight. "Shouldn't you be outstandingly jealous and put out over this?" he asked.

"It was me," Dean said, then burst into laughter again. "It is quite a long story, but I was dressed in a princely costume as part of an effort to help Nanette escape the theater and Montrose."

"Montrose?" Francis's brow shot up, then fell into an even deeper scowl, if such a thing were even possible at that point. "What does that devil want with Mlle. D'Argent?"

Before Dean could answer, Joseph said, "The article goes on to say that the royal family is displeased with Mlle. D'Argent. They are calling it a vile bid for publicity, and they state that Prince Arthur is currently traveling home from India, and that he is not in England at all."

Dean's mirth extinguished in a flash. "Nanette isn't in serious trouble, is she?"

Joseph glanced up from the paper with an apologetic look. "It appears as though she might be." He handed the newspaper across the table to Dean.

Dean raced through the article, seeing it with different eyes. He scoured the other newspapers on the table as his brothers continued their breakfasts. There were more articles about the scandal of a famous actress dallying with the prince. Every article made it clear that the royal family was furious over the rumors, and that the future of Nanette's career could be in jeopardy if such rumors continued.

"I have to go to her," Dean said once he'd read the last article. He stood, pushing his chair noisily back from the table. "I have to save her from my own folly."

"And just how do you intend to do that?" Francis asked sardonically.

"By offering to marry her," Dean said, already on his way out of the breakfast room. "It is the best way to quash this rumor and solve our own problems in one action."

"But you've only barely made the woman's acquaintance," Joseph called after him.

Dean chose not to answer as he rushed to the front door to retrieve his coat and hat. He calmed himself by reminding himself that this was his intention all along, he was merely speeding things up a bit. He'd had that thought the moment Francis had mentioned the need for money to secure the flat for Mother, and this dangerous case of mistaken identity was just another reason for haste with his plans.

He took a cab straight to the Concord Theater, pushing his way through the crowd of followers waiting at the stage door. There were more of them than usual, and at least half of them appeared to be journalists of one sort or another. Dean ignored them, marching up the steps to the stage door and banging on it to gain entry.

"Hang on," one of the followers said, squinting at Dean. "That's him! That's Prince Arthur."

Dean twisted to stare at the man. He vaguely recognized him as one of the followers from the day before.

"That's not Prince Arthur," a newcomer—one of the ones who held a small notepad and looked very much like a journalist—said.

"It's not?" the first man said.

"I am Mr. Dean Rathborne-Paxton," Dean said, turning to address the group, as though he were on the stage instead of at the back door. "I am Mlle. D'Argent's beau. And no, I am not Prince Arthur. I was mistaken for the prince yesterday because of a silly costume I had donned. It was not intended to deceive anyone. Please send my deepest apologies to the royal family and inform them that it was entirely my fault and that Mlle. D'Argent bears no share of the blame at all."

Lily had opened the stage door while he gave his speech, and with a final, gentlemanly nod, he stepped through and practically slammed the door behind him.

"God, I hope that was enough to appease those jackals," he said, pressing his back against the closed door once he was inside.

"Celebrity, eh?" Lily said with a grave look. When Dean blinked at her, she shrugged and said, "Our lot endures it all the time. If you think what Nanette gets is bad, you should see the way they go after Everett. When they're not falling all over themselves to suck his cock, they're trying to have him thrown in prison."

Dean's jaw dropped at the audacious crudeness of Lily's speech. Equally surprising was his utter lack of upset in what she was saying.

Lily seemed to sense what Dean was thinking. She clapped a hand on his arm. "Why do you think Nanette is trying so hard to find something to do with herself other than being a famous actress?"

Dean stared at her even harder. "Nanette doesn't wish to be an actress anymore?" That hardly seemed likely to him. She was brilliant on the stage. He'd always had the sense that she loved it. Although how anyone could love the throngs of mildly threatening followers and hints that the royal family was upset with her because of a rumor was unnerving.

There was a certain spark in Lily's eyes that left Dean wondering if she was playing with him as she went on to say, "I think Nanette wants to be something very different than an actress. If you ask me, I think she wants to be one of those high and mighty society wives who cut ribbons at grand openings and give speeches on behalf of orphans and lepers, or some such."

Hope breathed through Dean, even though he was now certain Lily was leading him on for her own amusement. "And where is the indomitable Mlle. D'Argent?" he asked, craning his neck to look around her.

"She's not here," Lily laughed. "She doesn't have to be in

today. I can give you the address of her flat, though. Hardly anyone has that information." She winked as she spoke.

"Yes, yes, please," Dean said, his heart pounding against his ribs.

As soon as Lily gave him the address—which was not far from the theater, in a fashionable building close to the Savoy Hotel—Dean raced through the theater so that he could depart through the front door instead of battling with the followers and journalists in the alley again.

Nanette's flat was easy to find. He experienced a momentary, ridiculous thrill of riding an elevator up to one of the top floors. It was nonsense that experiencing that new conveyance could fill him with such excitement, but if one did not enjoy the simple pleasures of life, what was the point?

"Dean?" Nanette greeted him with a shocked look after he'd pounded on her door. "Whatever are you doing here, *monsieur*?"

"I have come to offer my sincerest apologies for the troubles I have caused you," Dean said, stepping into Nanette's flat as she moved back to let him in.

The flat was beautiful, but then again, Dean would have expected nothing less. It was furnished with several expensive, stylish pieces and decorated with tasteful art. From where he stood just inside the door, he could see that the rooms were large, with high ceilings. It was lit with electrical lights, which was as much of a delight to Dean as the elevator. He caught a glimpse of a small kitchen and a modern-looking stove through a doorway on one side of the main sitting room. A well-dressed maid with a deeply worried expression was busying herself there, apparently fixing tea.

Dean wondered why the maid seemed so upset until Nanette closed and locked her door, then paced anxiously in front of him.

"I did not expect to see you here today, *monsieur*," she said. "It has been a bit of a trying morning."

"The papers, I know," Dean said, rushing to her and taking her hands.

Nanette flinched at the action, eyeing him suspiciously. She continued to let him hold her hands, though. "Zere is always a danger when the gossip columns choose to pursue you," she said.

"I gather as much," Dean said, "And I fear it is entirely my doing."

"It is not your doing entirely," she said, relaxing a bit and sending him a warm, sympathetic smile.

Dean took that as a sign that Nanette would be open to his suit. "Oh, my dear, but it is," he said. "If I had not been so silly and pompous when we exited the theater yesterday, those —what did you call them? Stage door Johnnies? They would not have believed me to be Prince Arthur, and they would not have spoken to the newspapers. I have corrected their error, though, so you've no fear on that score."

"You have corrected zem?" Nanette blinked at him.

"Just now," Dean said, glancing over his shoulder at the door, as if they were all standing there. "I went to the Concord Theater first. Lily gave me your address."

"Did she?" Nanette arched one eyebrow, leaving Dean with the impression that Lily would receive a stern talking to later.

"She told me something else, my love," Dean said, throwing caution to the wind and tugging Nanette closer. "She told me that you have grown tired of a life in the public eye. She said you wish to be something else, someone else. That you wish to increase your standing in life." He grinned, breathing in the scent of her for a moment, before continuing with, "It sounded very much like some of the things we discussed yesterday."

"I...oh...." Nanette breathed shallowly, her cheeks going pink. There was deep, shrewd calculation in her eyes, though, instead of sentiment and overwhelm. Nanette was thinking. "I would like to be more zan what I was born to be, *oui*," she said at last.

Something about her statement was cagey, but Dean hardly cared. Nanette had her motivations and he had his, but that didn't mean they couldn't converge in one course of action that would benefit them both.

"I will be direct, my love," he said, taking a step back, but keeping a tight hold on her hands. "Nanette D'Argent, I wish to marry you. Say you will be mine."

Dean held his breath, forming all the arguments in his mind that he would need to counter Nanette's inevitable refusal. He had come to her with the proposal out of the blue, with no warning at all, but he was ready.

Which was why he was thoroughly shocked when Nanette said, "*Oui, monsieur*, Dean. I would be 'appy to marry you."

Dean gaped at her, hardly believing his ears. "You wish to marry me?" He expressed exactly the sort of surprise and doubt that he'd expected from her.

"*Oui*," Nanette said. "Do you find zat so surprising?"

In fact, he did. The tension in Nanette's smile as she gazed up at him seemed to hint that she was actually surprised as well. Something about that look, about the anxiety he could now feel vibrating through the room—especially as the maid in the kitchen looked out at them with round, astonished eyes —told him there was far, far more going on with Nanette than he was aware of. That feeling prompted him to a level of honesty that he never would have considered otherwise.

"I must be frank with you, Nanette," he said, taking a step back and letting go of her hands. He tried not to look sheepish as he said, "I am very fond of you. I have adored you since the moment I first laid eyes on you. And after yesterday, I find you to be as charming and amiable as I have ever found a woman to be." He paused, winced, then said, "I wish to marry you for your money."

Nanette blinked and reeled back slightly.

Dean was certain he had offended her. "I am sorry to be so blunt about it. I had not intended to be so open about my intentions, but I believe you deserve the truth. You know my family's struggles with Montrose. You know the sort of schemes Montrose executes against families like ours. Therefore, you must conclude that I and my family are in need of ready money."

"I...I do not know what to say." Nanette pressed a hand to her stomach.

"It is not for myself, though," Dean pressed on. "Please, you must believe me when I say that my need for money, and quickly, is not selfish." He began to pace as he went on with, "My brothers and I have been working tirelessly to secure a place for our mother. Mother was no part of Father's wicked deeds, but she is bearing the brunt of the consequences. We are attempting to furnish her with a home here in London where she can live separately from our father, but we've been refused any such respectable place because we cannot ensure payment of rent."

"Oh?" Nanette's eyes glowed with interest as she followed Dean's pacing. Dean could only hope that the light he saw there was also compassion.

He came to a stop in front of Nanette and said, "This is all for Mother. At least, the financial aspect. I wish to marry you for your money, and your renown, so that I might assist in securing a place for Mother. But, Nanette—" He took her hands again. "I do care for you," he went on in a soft voice. "I like you very much. I wish to marry you as a friend. One who could, perhaps, in time, become a lover and...and a beloved. After yesterday, I believe that is possible." He paused again, bristling with anxiety over the bright spark of calculation and consideration in Nanette's eyes. "Say you'll marry me?" His words came out sounding like a question and a plea. "Say you will be mine?"

Nanette took a deep breath. Dean was highly aware of the maid standing in the kitchen doorway, riveted by their scene.

At last, Nanette let out a breath. "Yes, Dean, I will marry you," she said. Dean was ready to shout for joy, but Nanette raised a hand to press her fingertips to his lips—a gesture Dean found incredibly arousing—and said, "You were honest with me, zerefore, I will be honest with you."

"Yes, love, of course," Dean said.

She opened her mouth, and all of the brightness and cleverness in her eyes turned into uncertainty and panic. Her mouth stayed open for a long moment as she endured some sort of inner debate. Dean continued to hold her hands, smiling at her, and willing her to see that he would always be on her side, that he would always support her.

Finally, she made a small, squeaking sound, then said, "I wish to marry you so zat I might gain the protection of zee upper class to keep me safe from scandals such as zee one zat could have happened zees morning. Lily was right. I wish to be something more zan a mere actress. I wish to be zee wife of a nobleman."

"Perfectly understandable, darling," Dean said with a smile. "And I do not hold that desire against you at all."

There was something else. He could tell in the anxious way she continued to hold herself. Her words had been honest ones, but Dean had the feeling she wasn't satisfied with something. He was desperate to know what it was, but sense told him that they would need to get to know each other much more intimately before she would spill all her secrets. And there was time for that.

"I shall inform my brothers that we are to have an addition

to our family," he said with a smile, raising her right hand to kiss it. "And I will inform the press of our engagement as soon as you would like."

That statement brought another wave of uncertainty to Nanette's expression. "Perhaps we could make some sort of announcement at zee party which will take place after zee last performance of *Love's Last Lesson*?" she asked.

"I think that sounds delightful," Dean said with a smile.

He wanted to kiss her. They were engaged now, so he could if he wanted to. He even leaned closer to her, staring intently into her eyes, begging the question with his heart.

Nanette leaned closer to him as well, but just when he thought their lips would meet, she turned away.

"Olivia, we must begin preparations for zee announcement," she told her maid, stepping away from Dean.

"Yes, miss," the maid said, dropping a curtsy and staring at Dean.

Dean let out a heavy breath. It did not matter. There would be time for the two of them to kiss and more later. He grinned from ear to ear, realizing that he'd just won the most important victory of his life. Nanette D'Argent, flower of the London stage, would soon be his wife.

Chapter Six

They had a full house for the closing performance of *Love's Last Lesson*. Nan was as sad to see the end of that particular play as the audience was, but seeing as Niall's new play, *The Marshall*, would be opening in just over a fortnight, everyone was willing to let *Love's Last Lesson* go. That was the way of life, not just of theater. One chapter closed and another began.

Nan smiled at that thought as she stood in the wings, watching the final chorus-only number at the end of the second act, just before she and Everett would return to the stage for their characters' final declaration of love, a stirring duet and dance, and the grand song and dance that was the show's happy finale. She felt as though she had the potential for her own happy finale right in front of her. Dean had surprised her—and shocked Olivia—with his proposal the other day, but as far as Nan was concerned, the timing was perfect.

Or perhaps her optimism about the transition her life was about to undergo was because she hadn't had a single whisper of a threat from Montrose in days. Perhaps the man had seen her with Dean. Perhaps he had heard of their engagement, even though, as far as Nan knew, only Dean's brothers and a few of her closest friends knew of it. She wasn't keeping the whole thing from her public on purpose, it was just that her heart was far more pleased with the prospect of marrying Dean than she'd anticipated, and she wanted something so tender and sweet, something that gave her so much joy, to remain hers and hers alone for the moment.

As soon as that thought struck her, Everett marched up behind her and murmured, "Well done, you," just as the chorus girls were twirled and lifted by their corresponding male chorus members out on the stage.

"Yes," Nan whispered back to him with a grin. "I think we both did a spectacular job with this show." It was probably dangerous of her to speak to Everett without her French accent when they were close to so many people, but everyone around them was busy, and she was too proud of herself and the coup she was in the process of staging to care.

Everett seemed to understand her thoughts, at least partially. He chuckled and inched closer to her, wrapping his arms around her from behind as they watched the dance number. "No, duckie," he whispered in her ear. "I mean well done for nabbing yourself a nob."

Nan snorted and swatted at his arm as it wrapped around her stomach. Everett was like a brother to her, and she was tempted to kick her heel into his shin to show him as much for his comment. They still had a dance number ahead of them, otherwise she would have done it.

"*Monsieur* Rathborne-Paxton is a fine and noble gentleman," she said, affecting her accent. "We two will be very 'appy together."

Everett laughed and leaned close to her ear. "Until he finds out who you really are."

Nan lost her smile and wriggled out of Everett's arms. "He

won't find out," she said, not quite able to meet Everett's eyes. "At least, not until I'm ready."

"So, you do intend to tell him the truth?" Everett asked, brow lifting.

Nan shrugged. "You were right when you said I'll have to at some point."

"But you'd like to wait until after you are Mrs. Rathborne-Paxton and after your dear, sweet, dim husband had already fallen in love with you," Everett said.

Nan frowned. "Dean is not dim. He is actually quite clever. He just chooses to approach life with brightness and enjoyment instead of plodding along, like most noblemen do."

Everett broke into a laugh that had the stage manager shushing them from the front of the wings. "You're falling in love with him," he said, lowering his voice dutifully.

A rush of heat filled Nan. Was she? If she were honest with herself, she didn't know what being in love felt like. She'd never been before, even though she'd had beaux. She'd even gone to bed with some of them. But love was something different. All she knew was that she'd been delighted when Dean had blurted out his proposal.

Delighted and afraid. Her house of cards stood on shaky ground, now more than ever, and a breeze was coming.

She was spared answering Everett's question when the chorus finished their number and it was time for their entrance. Nan snapped back into character, took Everett's hand, and the two of them sailed out onto the stage to perform their final, romantic scene.

They had performed the play so many times that Nan was able to fly through the scene. Her lines were so ingrained that they spilled out of her without much thought. That enabled her to glance up at the Rathborne-Paxton family's box. Sure enough, Dean was still there—his brothers with him—grinning at her as Everett declared his undying love to her. There was something fun and perhaps even silly about playing out a love scene with another man as her secret fiancé stared down at her. She rather liked it.

They moved from the scene to the final number of the show. She and Everett started off the song, along with a dance that Nan threw herself into with abandon. The chorus joined in, and before long, everyone was dancing and singing, and all felt right with the world. Niall Cristofori plays were well-known for their elaborate dance numbers and the fact that it took talented performers to carry them off. Nan loved dancing, loved singing, and at that moment, she loved life. She beamed to her adoring audience as the number ended and applause burst around her. There was nothing like the thrill of a thunderous applause after a solid performance.

The audience continued to applaud as the curtain closed and the cast quickly cleared off the stage. Nan moved to the back once she reached the wings, as the chorus members and minor players would take their bows first once the curtain opened. Everett stood in the wings on the other side of the stage so that they could approach each other as the final two to take their bows.

As she waited, one of the stagehands rushed up to her, handing her a huge bouquet of flowers. Nan made a sound of appreciation and drew in the sweet scent of the flowers, then picked up the card that was fastened to the stems.

As soon as she turned it over and read it, she wanted to throw the bouquet away from her as if it were poisoned. The card was written in simple, dark handwriting.

"I am running out of patience. You will give me the money I have demanded or all the world will know your secret."

It wasn't signed, but Nan didn't need a signature to know the flowers were from Montrose.

"Nanette," the stage manager hissed at her.

Nan raised her head in time to see Lydia, who played the

comic lead opposite Martin, step out onto the stage to take her bow. That meant Nan was next.

There wasn't time to throw away the flowers, or to turn and run from Montrose's threat. Nan swallowed hard and headed out to the stage, the card still in one hand. It took every last bit of her acting prowess to smile as she tucked the card back into the flowers, then sailed out onto the stage as the applause swelled. Shouts of "Brava!" filled the air, and most of the house rose to their feet as she met Everett in the center of the stage.

"What's wrong?" Everett asked, still managing to smile as though he were congratulating Nan. He turned forward to bow, received thunderous applause, then stepped back to her. He took her hand and kissed it, then escorted her forward for her accolades. "Where did those flowers come from?" he asked over the din of the crowd.

Smile as bright and broad as ever, certain there was panic in her eyes, Nan said, "Montrose," then curtsied and waved to the crowd as though it were the happiest day of her life.

She couldn't see Everett standing behind her as she curtsied over and over, waving as her audience cheered for her. She could see Dean, standing in his box, though. He cheered and applauded with the rest of them, but when Nan looked directly at him, her heart pounding against her chest, his smile dropped. Not only that, he tore away from the front of his box, saying something to his brother as he went, then disappeared at the back.

Nan wanted to cry in relief. He had seen her true distress. He had seen past her smile and her cheer to see something was wrong. She'd been right to tell Everett that Dean wasn't a fool. In fact, the more she knew the man, the more she believed him to be deeply perceptive.

Which was a problem in itself, but one she would solve another time.

Sooner than perhaps she should have, she stepped back and signaled to the stage manager to close the curtain. Everett supported her, taking one last bow as the heavy curtain closed to draw attention away from her. Some of the other members of the cast seemed put out by the action, but as soon as the curtain was fully closed and both Nan and Everett lost their cheery smiles, the rest of the cast seemed to catch on that something was amiss.

"What is it?" Martin asked, rushing in from Everett's other side. "What's wrong."

"It is nothing," Nan said, emphasizing her accent. Everett knew her secret, but no one else in the theater did. Except now Montrose was threatening to expose her to everyone if he didn't get his money. "I am feeling a bit woozy is all," she went on.

"Please let Nanette have some space," Everett said, stepping up behind her, resting a hand on the small of her back, and escorting her into the wings. "Lily, could you bring water to Nanette's dressing room?" he called out as he swept her through the wings and into the hallway of dressing rooms behind the stage.

Lily jumped to do as she was asked without question. Nan shoved the bouquet of flowers at the first chorus girl she passed, but tugged the card out at the last minute. If Dean was coming, she wanted to show the card to him.

Blessedly, Dean reached her dressing room almost immediately after she and Everett did.

"What is it?" Dean asked, racing straight to her. "What is the matter? Are you ill?"

Everett stepped aside with a curious look, allowing Dean to take his place. Dean grasped one of her hands and rested the other on the small of her back, similarly to how Everett had, as he helped her to sit.

"I...." Nan shook her head over her first, failed attempt to form her thoughts into words. Instead, she shoved the card into Dean's hand.

As Dean read Montrose's threat, Everett's Patrick appeared in the doorway. "Is something the matter?" Patrick asked. "Do you need help?"

Everett moved to Patrick's side, kissing him quickly on the mouth. "Montrose," he murmured.

Patrick closed one of his burly arms around Everett, as if he were the one who had been threatened.

A part of Nan longed for the sort of love and protectiveness that Everett and Patrick had for each other. When Dean threw the card down on her dressing table and tugged her into his arms for a comforting embrace, she was startled to think that she might actually have all of that within her grasp.

"I won't let him continue to threaten you like this," Dean said. "It's villainous in the extreme. Montrose will answer for the way he torments women in such a vile manner."

"Oh, *monsieur*," Nan sighed, leaning into Dean and letting him stroke her head.

The part of her that had worked so hard to make something of herself and that had struggled against all odds to be independent balked at the way she now let herself be weak. She was supposed to be clever. She was supposed to be a shining star of the London stage, beyond the reach of sorrow or hardship. But it felt simply wonderful to have a pair of strong arms around her at last.

She peeked at Everett to see what her friend thought of her lapse of fortitude, but Everett was busy burrowing into Patrick's arms and staring at his lover as though Patrick had hung the stars. It was a silly and overt display of affection, but somehow it made Nan feel better about relying on Dean. If the great Everett Jewel could allow himself to be made putty in his lover's hands, so could she.

"Thank you, Dean," she said, inching back enough so that

she could stare into Dean's eyes adoringly. "You have no idea what zees heroism means to me. For too long, I have been alone, dependent on myself. But now I have my own champion."

"You do, darling," Dean said.

For a moment, he stared at her lips as though he would swoop in and steal their long-overdue first kiss. More than anything, Nan wanted to kiss Dean until the two of them were breathless. Even if Everett and Patrick were standing right there and any number of theater people were glancing into the room as they passed by in the hall.

But then Dean pinched his face slightly and said, "What secret is Montrose threatening to expose?"

It felt as though Nan had been doused with ice water. "It is nothing," she said, pulling gently away from Dean's embrace.

"Are you certain?" Dean asked, his frown deepening. "Because if you're this frightened over a simple card, then it must be something."

"And I believe that is our cue to exit," Everett said in a whisper laden with teasing. He took Patrick's hand, nudging him out of the room, then stepped after him. "We'll see you at the Savoy for the party, duckie," he said with a wink before shutting the door behind him.

Nan's heart quivered and her knees felt weak over being left alone with Dean and her secret. She stepped away from him and sat heavily in the chair at her dressing table to begin removing her stage make-up.

"Darling?" Dean asked, moving to hover beside her. "What secret is Montrose threatening to expose?"

Nan scrubbed at her face with cold cream from a jar that bore her image, anxiety making her movements short and jerky. "It is a silly thing," she said, adding a nervous laugh.

She needed to tell him the truth of who she was. Dean would understand. He might even appreciate the joke of it all.

But she couldn't do it. Not just because she craved the protection Dean might be able to give her as her champion in her fight against Montrose, but because she liked him. More than liked him. She was fond of him. He'd proposed and she'd accepted. She wanted to be his wife. She wanted to share his bed and his life. She wanted to bear his name and his children. She'd hungered for all those things for a while in general without letting herself truly contemplate them, but now that she had Dean in her life, now that the vision of her future had a face and a laugh, a warmth and a feeling of kindness and safety, it would have killed her to let it all go.

"Nanette, you can tell me anything, I swear," Dean said, sinking to sit on the edge of her dressing table so that he was closer to her. "If you have some wicked scandal in your past, perhaps from your time in Paris, that the rest of the world does not know about, I swear, I don't care. I like you for who you are, wickedness and all."

The way he grinned and winked at her nearly broke Nan's heart. She couldn't imagine losing him now, not when she'd just found him.

"It was an affair," she blurted, cursing herself for lying, but unable to confess the truth. Not yet. "He was a patron of the ballet," she went on, transforming the story of an unimportant dalliance she'd had when she was first beginning to gain recognition as an actress into a far larger event than it had been. "He fancied me, and I allowed myself to be led astray. It was embarrassing."

Dean growled, and for a moment, Nan worried he was angry with her. Then he said, "Montrose is an arse for holding a little affair against a woman like you."

Nan wanted to burst into tears. Not only was Dean funny and kind, he was forgiving. She had the feeling he wouldn't hold any of her past lovers against her. But would he be able to forgive her for lying about everything that she was?

She finished removing her make-up and cleaning her face, then stood and faced him, stepping between his legs so that he couldn't stand from her dressing table. Once there, she rested her hands on the sides of his face and leaned in to touch her lips to his. It wasn't the first kiss she'd envisioned. It was barely a kiss at all. But it lit Dean's eyes like fireworks in the night sky.

"You are a wonderful man, *monsieur*," she said. "I am honored to be your fiancée."

"As I am honored to be yours," Dean said, a bit breathless. His breathlessness made her feel lightheaded, especially when he went on with, "And I will protect you, from whomever or whatever you need to be protected from. I swear it with my life."

Nan beamed at his promise. It was beautiful. She also wanted to weep. She didn't deserve a man like Dean, not with all the secrets and lies she was keeping from him. She needed to come clean, and the sooner the better.

But not yet.

"Come," she said, stepping back and taking his hand. He stood and allowed her to draw him toward the door. "We have a party to attend, *monsieur*. A party zat I believe will be quite interesting."

Chapter Seven

Why hadn't he kissed her? Really and truly kissed her, not the small peck Nanette had instigated. The moment had been right there, and Dean had let it slip away. For the life of him, he didn't know why. Nanette had certainly been willing. She'd gazed up at him with gratitude and affection, not to mention desire. Dammit, the moment would have been ideal for a deep, thorough kiss.

Except that something was wrong. As he helped Nanette into her coat, offered his arm, and escorted her out of her dressing room and down the hall to the stage door, he could feel the wrongness in his bones. They were at the beginning of their drama, and there were scenes that had yet to be played out.

It was Montrose, he told himself as Nanette was congratulated by a few, key patrons of the theater who had been allowed backstage to greet the principal players. Dean stood off to one side as Nanette was congratulated by a particularly enthusiastic society matron, fuming about the note Montrose had sent to Nanette. Montrose was the source of every one of the evils that had befallen him of late, and the man would pay for it. He felt as though they had the knowledge they needed to learn the best way to bring the man down, but he had no idea what to do with said knowledge.

"I do apologize, *mon cher*." Nanette swept back over to him after the matron was done with her, taking up Dean's arm once more and continuing to the stage door with him. Dean smiled at her use of the French endearment, and at her closeness as they walked. "It is zee life of a celebrity, *non*?"

"I suppose it is." Dean smiled at her as they reached the door. "I liked it when you called me *mon cher* just now."

"You are my darling," Nanette told him with a softness in her eyes. "At least, I would like for you to be."

"I am yours, my darling," Dean said in return, lifting one of her hands to kiss her knuckles.

It was a quaint, lovely moment, and it made his heart sing. But at the same time, that sense of wrongness was still there. It might even have grown. He didn't think that Nanette was being false with him and stringing him along. He might have been a sentimental fool, but he could tell when emotions were genuine. She wanted to marry him. So what was the matter, then? Was he somehow jealous of the affair Montrose was threatening to expose without realizing the depth of that jealousy?

A moment later, all thoughts were blasted from his head as he and Nanette stepped through the stage door and out into the alley. A crowd of admirers stood waiting for Nanette, and as she appeared, they burst into applause. The alley was well lit by men carrying lanterns—most of whom Dean recognized as stagehands and other men who worked for the theater, providing protection for the actors in moments like this one— so he was able to see every bit of adoration and desire in the eyes of those followers.

"Thank you, thank you," Nanette called and waved to the crowd. "You are too kind."

A few of the men rushed forward with their programs from the evening. Lily darted out through the stage door to hand Nanette a pencil so that she could sign them. Dean stood back and watched, astounded and flummoxed, as fifteen minutes dragged by with Nanette signing programs, having her hand kissed, and moving only a few feet toward the exit of the alley.

Such is the life of a celebrity, Dean thought to himself in echo of what Nanette had said earlier. Perhaps that was the wrong feeling he had. He could marry Nanette and make her his, but he would forever be required to share her with her adoring public.

"Why, if it isn't Prince Arthur!" the man who had misidentified him the other day called out, recognizing him as well.

"Prince Arthur?" someone else asked.

"Your highness, could I have your autograph as well?" The first man stepped forward, a cheeky grin lighting his eyes.

Despite himself, Dean burst into laughter and stepped around Nanette to take the man's program, saying, "I would be honored, sir."

"Is that truly Prince Arthur?" someone else in the crowd asked as Dean laughingly signed his name under Nanette's on the man's program. He also wrote, *She's mine, and don't you forget it.*

"No," someone else said. "He's just some man who's walking out with Nanette."

Dean fought not to wince. "I would have you know that I am more than just *some man*," he said to the followers in general, uncertain to whom he should direct his comment.

"He is much more zan zat," Nanette agreed with a laugh, taking Dean's arm. "Now, if you will excuse us, we 'ave a party to attend."

That seemed to be the cue for the stagehands to move in,

clearing a path so that Dean and Nanette could walk on to the street, then hurry along to the Savoy Hotel without being further accosted.

"It was never that bad when I was standing out there with the crowd, was it?" Dean asked as they crossed the street, then rushed the last few yards to the entrance to the Savoy.

"*Oui*," Nanette said, a bit of a sigh in her voice. "Zere have been times when it has taken an hour or more for me to leave zee theater. Zat is why zee stagehands where zere to 'elp tonight."

"I see," Dean said as an attendant held the door of the Savoy open for them.

He did see. He saw that his concerns were because of the life Nanette led. He saw that the anxiety that wouldn't loosen its grip on his chest was just a matter of the attention that Nanette received every time she stepped foot outside of the theater or her flat. That was it. That was what had him bristling with unease.

A tiny voice in the back of his head whispered that that wasn't it at all. Something else was going on. But damn him for not being able to put a finger on what it was.

"Ah, Mlle. D'Argent," a middle-aged gentleman in a fine suit that didn't seem to fit him right stepped forward from the people milling around the entrance to the ballroom, where the theater party was taking place. "You were splendid this evening as usual, Nanette."

Dean's eyes popped wide as the man boldly stepped forward and kissed Nanette's cheek.

He was about to protest the too-familiar behavior when Nanette laughed and said, "Thank you, Charles. I am so pleased you enjoyed it."

"Enjoyed it?" The man, Charles, laughed. "After a performance like that, I'm certain I can secure you a dozen more endorsement deals. You're going to be richer than this gentleman before long." Charles nodded at Dean as though the two of them were old friends in on a jest together.

Dean scrambled to put the pieces together. Charles must have been Mr. Brown, the agent Nanette had told him about. The man had the feel of a salesman about him. What tested Dean's patience and sent prickles down his back was the way he plucked Nanette off his arm, as though she were a can of fruit he needed to sell, and steered her toward a collection of men in fussy suits.

"Please excuse me, *mon cher*," Nanette said over her shoulder as Brown led her away. "I will conduct zees business, zen we will enjoy zee rest of zee party together."

"Of course, my darling," Dean said, trying to smile.

He watched Nanette like a hawk as Brown introduced her to the cluster of businessmen. That was the reason he felt as though everything were wrong. Nanette was a beautiful woman and a talented performer. She should not be passed around like a commodity. And yet, she seemed to take it in her stride, smiling and conversing with the businessmen with all the charm of a princess.

Dean could see a hint of tension in her jaw and around her eyes, though. He'd come to know her well in the last few days, or so he fancied. He'd come to know her well enough to see that she did not enjoy the business aspect of her celebrity as much as she might have let on. After what he'd witnessed at the stage door, he was beginning to think she didn't care for that sort of attention either, even though he'd had a moment of fun with it.

He didn't realize he'd been standing off to one side, alone and glowering, until the unexpected figures of Francis and Joseph swept up on either side of him.

"Calm down, Dean," Francis said with a smirk. "I don't think you're in any danger of being supplanted by that lot."

The comment was ridiculous enough that Dean laughed.

Laughter didn't settle the restless, questioning feeling inside of him, though.

"I'd no idea the life of an actress was so complicated these days," he confessed as Joseph handed him a flute of champagne. He was grateful for the gift and drank half of it in one go.

"Having second thoughts?" Joseph asked him.

Dean stared incredulously at his younger brother. "Certainly not," Dean snapped. "My heart belongs to Nanette now. I've already asked the question, and she's already said yes."

"But it hasn't been made public yet, has it?" Joseph asked. "You could still renege."

Dean glanced to Francis while gesturing to Joseph. "And who taught this whelp to have such a jaded outlook on life? Was it you?"

Francis laughed and clapped a hand on Dean's shoulder. "Don't mind him. He has yet to sip the sweet nectar of love."

"Like you have?" Joseph scoffed.

Francis turned an interesting shade of pink and cleared his throat, changing the subject. "I suppose these are the sorts of business dealings that have made Mlle. D'Argent's fortune?" He nodded toward Nanette.

Dean hummed in consideration. The feeling of wrongness pulsed within him so acutely that his feelings cracked through his resolve not to mind things.

"Something is wrong," he said to his brothers. "I cannot put my finger on what it is."

"What sort of wrong?" Francis asked.

Dean frowned and smoothed a hand over his hair. "Nanette received a threatening note from Montrose just before her curtain call this evening. She was deeply upset by it and required some calming down."

"Montrose," Joseph grumbled, as though the name itself were a curse.

"What did the note say?" Francis asked.

"Montrose is extorting her for money. He threatened to reveal her secret if she did not pay him," Dean explained.

Both Francis and Joseph jerked in surprise, turning to face Dean instead of studying the room, though Dean's eyes were still glued on Nanette.

"Mlle. D'Argent has a secret?" Francis asked.

"It's a trifling thing, really," Dean shrugged. "A past affair. Nanette is embarrassed about it more than anything. I suppose she doesn't want it to be made public."

"I doubt any woman would want her past indiscretions made public," Joseph said.

Francis seemed as troubled by the triviality as Dean was, which did nothing to ease Dean's mind.

"If she sees it as a small thing, as nothing more than an embarrassment, then why was she as upset as you imply she was?" Francis asked.

Dean wanted to curse loudly. His brothers were supposed to ease his worry, not increase it. His sense of wrongness grew, but he attempted to fight it away by saying, "I suppose that Nanette is not too fussed about the affair itself, seeing as it is over and does not appear to have affected her life. She must be anxious about the way knowledge of that sort would damage her marketability with the soap and biscuit people."

It sounded reasonable, but after speaking it aloud, Dean wasn't satisfied.

"At least we now know why she accepted your proposal so quickly," Francis said with a shrug, taking another sip of his own champagne.

Dean dragged his eyes away from Nanette as she laughed at something one of the businessmen said and looked at his brother. "Why? What do you mean?"

Francis swallowed his drink, then said, "As the wife of a nobleman, she would be able to avoid scenes like this. If those men wanted to offer her a contract to sponsor their products, they would have to come to her, or rather, come to you. They wouldn't be able to waylay her at parties."

"Our class does have certain privileges that comes with it," Joseph said, sounding uncertain how he felt about that.

Dean nodded in consideration. "True, true," he said.

But the sense of imbalance and off-ness didn't lessen one bit. Reason wasn't banishing suspicion at all.

He was spared thinking about it for a few moments as Francis suddenly laughed, then pointed at someone in the crowded ballroom. "Oh, look, Joseph. It's your wild western sweetheart."

Joseph immediately went rigid, glancing around the room as though someone had just told him a madman was on the loose with a pistol. "Good God, what is she doing here?" he gulped, turning red.

Dean spotted Miss Ellen Garrett striding toward them from across the ballroom. They'd first encountered the enigmatic young American woman at the reception for Sam and Alice's wedding, as there was some connection between Alice's friend, the Countess of Carnlough, and Miss Garrett's sister, Mrs. Lenore Mercer. As Dean recalled, Joseph had spent the better part of the reception arguing over the rights of women with Miss Garrett. He grinned now as Joseph shifted this way and that, searching for a means of escape.

He failed to find one before Miss Garrett reached them.

"Good evening, Lord Cathraiche," she curtsied to Francis in an appalling display of misplaced manners, then nodded to Dean. "Good evening, Mr. Rathborne-Paxton." Finally, she turned to Joseph and simply said, "Joseph," her eyes sparkling.

Joseph gaped and sputtered at her, going even redder than he already was. "You cannot address me as...we've had one conversation...where is your chaperone?" The question was issued as a demand.

Miss Garrett seemed completely nonplussed by the question. She glanced over her shoulder at the loud, jolly crowd in the ballroom, shrugged, and said, "Lenore and Phineas are in there somewhere. Phineas's brother, Lionel, and his friend David are here this evening, and Lionel was in the middle of a story about someone named Miss Flora when I spotted you. I simply had to come right over and greet you. And my, don't you look smashing this evening, Joseph."

Joseph made a series of tight, strangled sounds as he gaped at Miss Garrett, clearly out of his depth. Dean exchanged a glance with Francis as they both tried their best not to explode with laughter. Joseph had enough torture at Miss Garrett's hands without the two of them laughing at him and rubbing it in.

Turning to Francis brought Nanette back into Dean's line of sight just in time to catch Nanette glancing his way. There was something strained in her expression, more so than before, even though she was smiling. The way she looked at him made Dean feel as though they were an ocean away instead of just part of the length of the ballroom. He had to do something about it.

"Excuse me, gents, Miss Garrett," he said, handing his now-empty champagne flute to Francis. "It appears my lady needs me."

"Best of luck," Francis called after him.

Dean was tempted to call back that Joseph would need the luck, as he could hear Miss Garrett accosting him about why there were so many poor people in London when men like him lived in luxury, but he needed his wits for other games.

The businessmen had moved on to speak to other party guests, and Dean made it halfway to Nanette before an older couple swooped in and gobbled up Nanette's attention before he could reach her. Dean watched Nanette smile and curtsy graciously to the couple, indicating they were people of importance. He heard her sweet, false laughter ring out as well. Instead of warming him, like her laughter usually did, it chilled him.

He was only able to take one more step before Charles Brown stepped into his path. The man had the audacity to cup a hand around Dean's elbow and walk him off to one side, taking him even farther from Nanette.

"She tells me the two of you are engaged," Brown said without any pleasantries at all.

Dean quickly regained his composure and summoned all his authority to stare hard at the man. "We are engaged, sir. I think it would behoove you to begin seeing me as Nanette's husband forthwith."

Brown laughed. "I've no intention of getting in the way of whatever love affair you have going on. Mlle. D'Argent must be serious about this match, because she hasn't graced the scandal sheets with stories of any sort of affair for years. And that's good for business."

Dean was on the verge of replying to that when Brown rushed on with, "I want to keep Mlle. D'Argent good for business, sir. Which means you and I need to get a few things straight."

Dean widened his eyes at the man's audacity. "I beg your pardon?"

"You don't have to beg for anything," Brown said. "People like Mlle. D'Argent and Mr. Jewel are the aristocracy of the future. Your sort is teetering on the brink as it is. You're clever to marry your way into her shine, as it will keep you and your lot shiny long after your own light dims."

Dean could only gape at the man. There were no words for how the blighter offended him. This most certainly must have been the origin of his feeling of wrongness.

"Carry on with your marriage," Brown said, winking at Dean as though they were factory workers on their lunch break gossiping about the girls. "But rest assured, I will carry on with my business where Mlle. D'Argent is concerned. If you do anything to tarnish her image or destroy her appeal with the public, you'll have me to answer to."

Before Dean could get a word in, Brown clapped his arm, then walked away. All Dean could do was gape after the man in disbelief. What sort of a world had he stepped into by setting his heart on Nanette? He needed the money, yes. He adored Nanette, also yes. But he was beginning to wonder if he was truly prepared to be the defender and champion she needed.

Chapter Eight

She was losing him. That was the only thought that reverberated through Nan's mind as she smiled and laughed and gave the men who might employ her every reason to adore her. It was easy to win over industrialists and emperors of commerce. Her reputation and her face did that work for her. But as she stole yet another look across the packed, noisy, stuffy ballroom to Dean as he conversed with his brothers, the only thing Nan could think about was that she was losing Dean with her inattentiveness.

"I think you would be perfect for our upcoming line of floral perfumes, Mlle. D'Argent," Mr. Gracey—or perhaps it was Grimes, Nanette wasn't certain—said, smiling at her décolletage. "You are quite the flower yourself."

"You are too kind, *monsieur*," Nan smiled and posed for the man.

Inwardly, her heart squeezed over the way she'd addressed Mr. Gracey. "*Monsieur*" felt like a term of endearment that she had for Dean now. Using that word for another man felt wrong. Everything felt wrong.

She glanced across to Dean once more, only to find him

gazing back at her. He wore a smile, and it looked as though he and his brothers were now having some sort of jolly conversation with an expressive blonde woman, but Nan could see the uncertainty and, dare she name it, the hurt in Dean's eyes. She never should have let Brown carry her away from Dean when they'd entered the room. She should not have excluded him from what was, in effect, an impromptu business meeting. The short distance between them felt like a chasm of her own creation, and she hated it.

She was losing him, and, with a pang in her heart, she realized that losing Dean was the very last thing she wanted to do. It was far too soon to fancy that she loved the man, but she wanted to. She felt as though she could.

"I can see your attention is diverted, Mlle. D'Argent," Mr. Gracey chuckled, glancing to Brown. "I won't take up any more of your time. Go and discover who that dashing gentleman is."

"Very funny, *monsieur*," Nan laughed, touching the man's arm. "You do so amuse me."

She turned away all the same, though, glancing to Dean and feeling the pull toward him like iron filings toward a magnet.

Brown was a few steps ahead of her, and despite her forward momentum and focus, she was stopped by the august figures of Lord and Lady Campbell before she could take more than a few steps.

"An excellent final performance tonight, Mlle. D'Argent," Lord Campbell—whom everyone in London referred to as Lord Malcom for reasons Nan had never understood—said with a broad smile. "Katya, my lovely wife, and I enjoyed it immensely."

"We have been following the progress of your career from its start," Lady Campbell said, her shrewd eyes glittering with affection as she glanced to her husband. "I would venture to say that you are one of the greats of the London stage."

Nan had let her focus wander past Lady Campbell to where Brown had intercepted Dean as he'd tried to reach her. The compliment, coming from such an important woman, captured her attention, though.

"You are so kind to say so, my lady," she said, flushing with the praise and dropping into a curtsy.

Lady Campbell laughed, peeking over her shoulder to where Dean was now standing, seemingly flummoxed, as Brown patted his arm and walked away. Lady Campbell turned back to Nan. "It seems you have impressed others as well this evening."

Nan didn't know what made her say it, but she smiled at Lady Campbell and Lord Malcolm and said, "Monsieur Rathborne-Paxton and I have recently become engaged."

Lady Campbell and Lord Malcolm smiled and made sounds of congratulations.

"A fine choice," Lord Malcolm said. "For both you and Mr. Rathborne-Paxton. Life is never dull for a man who marries a wily woman." He sent his wife a grin that was shockingly lascivious, considering their advanced ages.

Lady Campbell laughed. "I can see I was correct about you and your ambitions, my dear." She rested a soft, wrinkled hand on the side of Nan's cheek, then said. "You'll go far. But now you should go to your man."

"Thank you, my lady." Nan dipped a small curtsy, resisting the urge to laugh as she stepped away from the elderly couple and headed straight for Dean. If she could cultivate friends in the aristocracy like Lady Campbell and Lord Malcolm, then perhaps she could shore up her position in society, even if Montrose followed through with his threats.

Her excitement and hope floundered as soon as she reached Dean, however.

"*Mon cher*, what is wrong? You seem upset," she said, taking Dean's hand.

Dean's expression flashed through several emotions, some of them distressing, before he schooled his face into a smile. "It's nothing, darling. I suppose I simply wasn't ready for the incidentals of your profession." He gestured toward Mr. Gracey and some of the other businessmen, who had moved on to the drinks table.

She was losing him, and for the first time, all the wealth and popularity that her celebrity brought with it wasn't enough to make up for the loss of something she wanted.

She gripped Dean's hand tighter, glanced around to make certain they weren't being watched—although she was always being watched—then started across the ballroom. To his credit, Dean followed her without question, his eyes sparkling with curiosity, as she headed for one of the doors that the hotel staff were using to bring food and drinks into the ballroom and remove empty trays. She glanced around one more time before pulling Dean into the bustling hallway that ran between the ballroom and the utilitarian rooms beyond.

"I am sorry," she said, drawing Dean several yards away from the door before turning to face him. "Zees is not what you had in mind by marrying me, I am certain." She lowered her head as she made her apology. "Would zat I could change things."

"Darling," Dean said in a voice that was softer than she deserved. He slipped his hand under her chin and tilted it up so that she was forced to gaze directly at him. "I do understand all of this. Truly, I do."

"But you should not have to be burdened with zee way I am," she said.

Her chest squeezed with affection for Dean. He smiled at her with such earnestness. Everything within her screamed at her to simply tell him the truth of who she was. He deserved to know the truth.

But she didn't want to lose him, and once he discovered how deep the lie she'd allowed him to believe about her was, she might never see him again.

As if he could read her thoughts, Dean frowned. "Something is wrong, darling. I've felt it all night. Something is amiss, and damned if I know what it is."

She had to tell him. He could not have opened the door for her to tell the truth more fully if he'd tried. She couldn't argue with herself that she would confess all when the time was right, because the time was near perfect at that very moment.

"It's Montrose, isn't it?" Dean glowered. Nan could feel the heat and tension of his fury with the man radiating from him. He inched back from her and rubbed a hand over his face. "That bastard is a blight on good society. I cannot wait for the day that someone brings him to his knees."

"He...he frightens me."

Nan winced as soon as the words were out of her mouth. Immediately, it was clear that Dean understood those three simple words as the explanation for everything that had her tied in anxious knots. She was a coward of the worst sort to let Montrose take the blame for her duplicity.

"He will not get away with it," Dean said, the fire of determination and, if Nan wasn't mistaken, deepest affection in his eyes. He stepped closer to her, clasping the sides of her face with a surprisingly tender touch, considering how obviously upset he was. "I swear to you," he went on, "I will not let Montrose harm one hair on your head. I have made a promise to you, and soon I will make a vow. I will protect you from him and from those jackals who see you as nothing but a product to be bought and sold. You are mine, and I cherish what belongs to me."

The agony of those sweet words was too much. Nan burst into tears. No one had ever said such sweet things to her or cared so much for her, other than her family. Even the paternal affection that her father had always shown her was nothing to the warmth and beauty of the way Dean pledged to protect her. Papa had known her for her entire life. Dean barely knew her at all, yet she could feel how genuine he was in his regard for her.

She had to tell him everything.

But if she did, he would hate her, and *she would lose him*.

"Don't cry, love," Dean said, moving with her as she slumped back to lean against the wall. "Yes, Montrose is a frightening devil, but he will not win. You have me as your champion now, and Francis and Joseph aren't particularly fond of the bastard either." His tone turned teasing, which caused Nan to let out a small, helpless laugh. "You no longer have to face this alone."

Her heart swelled so suddenly that it caught her breath. She blinked through her tears and glanced up at Dean. "You have no idea how much that means to me," she said, not caring that her accent slipped. She couldn't lose him. Dean was worth more than any endorsement contract, any leading role, anything.

Dean evidently didn't notice her flubbed accent. "You mean everything to me," he said, wiping away her tears with his thumb.

He leaned close to her, and Nan gasped a split second before his lips met hers. His lips were warm but firm, and even though his kiss began as mere encouragement, it quickly deepened into something pulsing and passionate. She swayed into him, parting her lips to let him in and moving her hands to grip the front of his jacket.

Dean was encouraged by her movements. He increased the ardor of his kiss while adjusting so that he could embrace her fully. His passion turned to a conflagration as he moaned deep in his throat and kissed her as Nan had never been kissed before. His tongue sought out hers, teasing and coaxing her. She was helpless to do anything but meet his thrusts with sighs and teasing of her own. It felt like a glorious prelude to everything that could happen between the two of them.

All too soon, Dean inched back, drawing in a sharp breath and blinking at Nan in amazement. "My darling, you are glorious," he said, his voice hoarse.

"Not as glorious as you," Nan said, dizzy with desire. Not only did she not want to lose Dean, she wanted to give him everything she had. She wanted to take him home and explore every bit of the possibility that throbbed between them. "Come with me—"

She was cut off before she could finish her wicked invitation as one of the waiters cleared his throat sharply beside them. She and Dean leapt apart as the poor, young waiter blushed and shuffled, looking mortified.

"I'm terribly sorry, Mlle. D'Argent, but Mr. Brown is looking for you," the young man said.

In an instant, Nan was back in character, smiling graciously at the man. "Thank you, kind sir. I will deal with Mr. Brown immediately."

Dean looked deeply disappointed by her statement. Nan grasped his hands, holding them tightly and gazing up at him with all the desire she felt in her eyes. "I must see to whatever business Monsieur Brown has for me," she said. "I will make it as swift as possible. You know where my home is, *non*?"

"I do," Dean said, the fierce light of desire coming into his eyes.

Nan treated him to her wickedest smile. "Meet me zere in one hour. We will have zee rest of zee night together, you and I."

Dean drew in a breath, then raised one of Nan's hands to

his kiss-reddened lips. "I will count every second," he said, eyes gleaming.

"Until zen," Nan said, giddy with expectation.

She peeled away from Dean, leaving him standing in the hallway as she made her way back to the ballroom. She spared one final, naughty glance for him before clearing her throat, taking a deep breath, and walking back into the ballroom.

Within thirty seconds, she wished she had turned to run in the other direction. The party continued to swirl with color and noise and every manner of scent from the bodies packing the room. The mood was still light and celebratory. Everett was inching toward the small stage where the orchestra played a waltz, clearly intending to take over and probably sing one of the ribald songs he was known for. Brown noticed her from where he was standing in conversation with yet more businessmen who seemed interested in her.

But it was the solitary, lurking figure of Montrose—only a few yards away from her, by the corner of one of the refreshment tables, dressed in such a dark and simple manner that he blended in with the background—who had her gasping.

She started to turn and run back toward the door to the hall, but Montrose moved quickly and caught up with her.

"Might we have a word, Mlle. D'Argent?" he asked.

Without waiting for an answer, he rested his hand at the small of Nan's back and whisked her away to one of the darker corners of the ballroom. Nan was forced to smile and nod to the people who glanced to her in question, pretending as though nothing were wrong. If any of them so much as looked threateningly in Montrose's direction, she was certain Montrose would bring the entire party to a screeching halt so that he could shout the secret of her identity through the room.

"What more could you possibly want from me, Montrose?" she asked as though the two of them were laughing about how well the final night of *Love's Last Lesson* had gone.

"You know very well what I want from you, Mlle. D'Argent," Montrose said as they came to stop in the shadows of the corner. There were several huge, potted palms and a few smaller plants arranged in a way to hide the instrument cases of the orchestra members. The room had been decorated specifically to draw attention away from that corner. "I want the money that I am due," Montrose said.

"You are due nothing," Nan said, though without the determination that she wanted her voice to have. In fact, she sounded frightened and small despite her best efforts.

Montrose chuckled, almost as if she had told a droll joke. "Now, now, Nan," he said, using her real name easily. "We both know what you stand to lose. I daresay you've made my job even easier in this last week by creating the greatest liability of all for yourself."

Nan tilted her chin up, pretending she didn't know what he was talking about. Her kiss-pink lips betrayed her, though.

"How do you suppose Mr. Rathborne-Paxton would react if he knew that his delightful, French fiancée, the famous Nanette D'Argent, was, in fact, simply Nan Silvers, crofter's daughter, from Shropshire?"

"Please, no," Nan whispered, not bothering with her accent. "I...I love him."

"That, madam, is your problem, not mine." Montrose nodded solemnly. "Also your problem is the matter of the ten thousand pounds you owe me."

"Ten thousand pounds?" Nan yelped, clapping a hand to her throat. "That is much more than you demanded before."

Montrose shrugged. "I have the ability to ask for more, now that the penalty for your noncompliance is more than simply a ruined reputation."

Nan gaped at him. The man was vile to use something as precious as the new love she felt for Dean to ruin her.

"I will give you one week, Miss Silvers," he said, his mouth pulling into a tight smile. "If you fail to deposit ten thousand pounds into my bank account within one week, the public will know your secret. But more importantly, your dear fiancé will know it as well. I do not think you wish to see that happen, do you?"

Nan swallowed hard. There was no point in answering him, no point in begging him to reconsider. Montrose had her cornered, and there was nothing she could do about it.

"Good evening, Mlle. D'Argent," he said with a final, mocking bow, then turned and strode off with a smile.

Nan stood where she was for a moment, reeling. She could hardly draw breath into her lungs. The room seemed too loud, the perfume of the ladies in attendance too cloying. Everything she feared could happen was now an absolute certainty.

A couple of middle-aged sisters whom she knew to be the daughters of an earl looked as though they might approach her to give her comfort, but Nan was beyond comforting. She snapped her back straight, smiled, and pretended with everything she had that nothing was out of the ordinary as she walked through the room, heading toward the nearest exit. She ignored every kind word and question about her health and state of mind. She even ignored Everett when he spotted her and attempted to reach her instead of mounting the stage.

As soon as she reached the door, she bolted, dashing out to the street and hurrying as fast as she could to her flat, stopping for nothing.

"Olivia," she called out desperately as soon as she threw open her front door. "Fetch my traveling bag. I'm leaving immediately."

"Where are you going, ma'am?" Olivia asked, flying into motion from where she had been tidying up in the kitchen.

"Home," Nan said, racing into her bedroom to begin pulling clothes from her wardrobe.

"To Shropshire?" Olivia asked, stunned. She headed straight for the cupboard in the corner, retrieving Nan's bag.

"Immediately," Nan said, fighting back tears. "I...I need to speak to my mother and father."

She didn't realize why she felt the pull to return to her parent's house so strongly until she spoke the words. Remembering her father in the way Dean had showed so much kindness to her earlier had caused something within her to long for home and the steadiness of her parents. And after the terror Montrose had instilled in her, she couldn't think of anything but rushing into her father's and mother's arms and being encircled in their safe embrace.

"What about the show, ma'am?" Olivia asked as she helped Nan to pack. "The new show, I mean. Won't they need you for rehearsals?"

Nan sniffled, grabbing a handkerchief from the whirlwind of her packing. She blew her nose and dabbed her tears before saying, "You will have to go to the theater tomorrow to tell Mr. Cristofori that I have taken a short leave of absence. I am certain he will understand."

"And what of Mr. Rathborne-Paxton?" Olivia asked with more caution.

Nan had known Olivia her whole life. They'd been a few years apart in primary school. Olivia was the younger sister of one of her childhood friends, and when Nan had announced her plans to go to London to seek her fortune, Olivia had begged to go with her. Bringing Olivia along was something Nan had never regretted. Not only was Olivia one of the few people she could trust to keep her secret, her friend was not afraid to speak her mind when it was called for.

Nan winced and slowed her packing for a moment. She

had to think quickly, to make decisions that could have a deep impact.

"If he inquires after me, tell him that I have been called away home, to Paris, for a family matter," she said. "It's close enough to the truth. He may not make any attempt to see me at all, though."

That was another lie. In her heart, she knew that Dean would be on her doorstep, wondering where she was, as soon as he discovered she was gone. In fact, only then did she remember that she'd told him to meet her right there, at her flat. She gasped and sped through her packing with careless abandon. She needed to be gone before he arrived.

"Tell him...tell him I am sorry and that we will speak when I return," she said, close to bubbling over with tears.

She would have to speak to him and face the music eventually. She could only hope and pray that her father and mother would help her figure out how—if she even had the courage to tell them the entire story to begin with.

Chapter Nine

Dean's heart soared as he climbed the stairs in Nanette's building to make his way to her flat, velvet-covered box in hand. He'd taken a bit longer than an hour to make it to their rendezvous—more like two hours—as he'd dashed home first to retrieve a pair of earbobs belonging to his mother as a gift for Nanette. Part of him felt a tad guilty for taking his mother's jewelry when she wasn't there to ask, but seeing as Mother had packed up and taken nearly everything with her to Shropshire, Dean figured that the bits and pieces that had been left behind were fair game.

Or else they were false gems. In which case, he hoped Nanette would find the gift amusing and forgive him for the deception. There was nothing quite so pitiful as false gems masquerading as something of real value.

His heart and his high spirits stumbled when he reached Nanette's flat and knocked on her door, only to have his knocks ignored. He frowned, glanced up and down the hall for a moment to make certain he had the right flat, then knocked again. Still nothing. He leaned close to the door and listened, but there was no sound at all from the inside of the flat. In a bold effort to determine what was going on, he tried the door handle, but it was locked.

Dean frowned and rocked back to stare at the door. A creeping sort of anxiety gripped him—that Nanette had been false with him and that she didn't really want him at all—but he pushed that away. Their kiss in the hallway of the hotel had been magnificent. Nanette had clearly wanted him, as he wanted her. There had to be some other explanation why she was not at home now.

She must still be at the Savoy. Relief passed through Dean as the thought occurred to him. It was entirely likely that Nanette hadn't been able to get away from the party as easily as he'd assumed she could. Perhaps Brown had continued to push her at businessmen and potential employers. Or perhaps the theater people had begun carousing and Nanette had joined in on the fun. Dean smiled as he strode back down the hall and descended the stairs. He wouldn't mind a little further carousing himself, as long as he ended up in Nanette's bed by the end of the night.

But the party at the Savoy was over by the time he arrived at the hotel. It was the small hours of the morning by then, and bleary-eyed hotel staff were the only people left in the ballroom as they picked up discarded champagne flutes, gathered bits of uneaten treats from corners where guests had dropped them, and swept up other flotsam and jetsam abandoned by the party-goers.

"Pardon me, but you haven't happened to see Mlle. D'Argent of late, have you?" Dean asked the nearest hotel worker as he stood in the ballroom door.

"No, Mr. Rathborne-Paxton," the young man said, thankfully recognizing him and not believing him to be one of Nanette's followers. "She left the party early, not long after you did."

Dean frowned, thanked the man, and turned to leave.

The worry he'd shoved aside earlier returned in full force. He left the hotel, wavered uncertainly on the dark, London street for a moment, then decided to check the Concord Theater, just to be certain Nanette hadn't returned there for any reason.

All he found when he reached the Concord was that the theater was locked up tight. He received a few propositions from ladies of the night as he lingered by the mouth of the alley leading to the stage door—and one colorful offer from an alarmingly young man who described acts he'd be willing to do that were as disturbing to Dean as they were intriguing—but he ignored them.

The only thing left to do was to return to Nanette's flat for one more attempt to find her. But once again, he was disappointed to find the flat door locked and no answer to his repeated knocking.

At last, just as he had given up and started back along the hallway to the stairs, confused and dejected, he came suddenly face to face with Nanette's maid, Olivia.

"Olivia?" Hope rushed through him at the sight of the wan and exhausted maid. "Thank God. Do you know where Nanette is? I feel as though I've searched half of London for her, and that when we'd made plans to meet this evening."

Olivia stared warily up at him. There wasn't a hint of surprise in her large, blue eyes. An itching sensation broke out down Dean's back. The woman knew something, he was certain of it.

Olivia cleared her throat and stood a little taller. "Mlle. D'Argent has been called away suddenly," she said. "She has been informed that her family needs her at once. I've just come from seeing her off at Euston Station."

Dean's shoulders dropped in a combination of short-lived relief and deeper confusion and disappointment. "She said nothing to me about family being in trouble."

Olivia glanced down, wringing her hands. "It was unexpected, sir."

Dean frowned, rubbing the back of his neck. "Did she... did she leave any messages for me? Did she say anything at all?"

Without looking up at him, Olivia said, "She was in a great deal of hurry, sir."

Dean blew out a breath, feeling a bit lost. He was unwilling to lie to himself and say it didn't hurt that his beloved fiancée, a woman he had just kissed passionately, had departed London in an instant, without a word to him. He stopped short of believing it was cruel on Nanette's part. He had no idea what sort of problems his beloved had rushed off to solve, and for family at that.

Another thought struck him, and he frowned even harder. Had Nanette ever mentioned family to him? Surely, she must have family in the French countryside, or perhaps in Paris itself.

"If you please, sir," Olivia said, shaking him out of his thoughts.

Dean sucked in a breath and moved out of the maid's way. "Yes, forgive me. You look knackered. Go and have yourself a good rest. I am going to...." He let the words drop. He didn't know what he was going to do.

With a final, kind nod for Olivia—which was returned with an anxious, wary look—Dean headed on, descending the stairs at a slower pace. He breathed what was intended to be a cleansing breath once he reached the street and raised a hand to hail a cab, but no matter what he did, that feeling of wrongness that he'd had earlier in the day loomed large in his thoughts and feelings.

It didn't let up once he got home, undressed, and climbed into bed. It wouldn't let him sleep, no matter how late the hour and how exhausted the whole evening had made him. He eventually drifted off to a small degree, but his sleep was restless and dreamless, and when he awoke, the same questions continued to swirl around him: where had Nanette gone, and why had she left in such a hurry without informing him?

By the time he dressed in fresh clothes and dragged himself downstairs to join his brothers for breakfast, he was just about ready to blame Montrose for everything.

"The party last night was not *that* good," Francis told him with a smirk as Dean flopped into his chair and reached for the pot of coffee on the table.

"It was dreadful," Joseph grumbled without glancing up from the newspapers he pored over.

"You're just saying that because Miss Garrett argued you into submission on the subject of suffrage," Francis teased him. He turned back to Dean and said, "You should have seen it. That American firecracker talked circles around Joseph. Joe lapped the whole thing up, though. For a moment there, I thought he would unman himself right there in the middle of the ballroom."

"Francis!" Joseph snapped, turning scarlet. "Even you must have some sense of propriety. I would never do such a thing. I was not in the slightest way aroused by Miss Garrett's outspokenness."

Dean didn't even have to look at his brother to know Joseph was lying. He wasn't in the mood to grin or tease, though.

Francis noticed. "What is the matter, *frater*?"

There was no point in hiding anything from his brothers. "Nanette was called out of London on a family matter. She left in the middle of the night, without leaving a note for me," Dean said.

"Is it the fact that she's gone that bothers you or that she did not inform you of her whereabouts?" Joseph asked.

"How do you know where she went and why?" Francis added.

"Her maid, Olivia, told me when I went searching for Nanette at her flat." Dean left out the detail that they'd arranged a tryst, even though his brothers would have understood.

"Do you know when she's coming back?" Joseph asked.

Dean shook his head and took a long swig of black coffee. "No," he answered before taking a quick second. "The whole thing is an utter mystery."

Francis's expression hardened. "Are you certain Montrose isn't involved?"

"That thought had occurred to me," Dean confessed. "But Olivia was certain that Nanette had gone to her family. I've no reason to doubt the maid's veracity."

Francis and Joseph both hummed and frowned in sympathy, but they had even fewer answers than Dean had. There was a long pause as the three of them got lost in their own thoughts, freeing Dean to tuck into his breakfast.

"Perhaps the timing of this is good after all," Francis spoke after a few minutes, as though he were already in the middle of another thought. "If your fiancée is not in London at present, then it will be less of a burden for you to leave yourself."

Dean snapped his eyes up from where he'd been concentrating on his eggs and stared at his brother. "Are you suggesting I leave London too? When Nanette might return and wonder where I am?"

Francis let out an impatient breath, then said, "Someone needs to go to Aunt Josephine's house to fetch Mother back to London."

Dean blinked at him. "Whatever for?"

Francis surprised him by smiling. "Those arrangements for the flat we've wished to let for Mother are all in place now. I do not know whether it was the landlord relenting and agreeing to honor our credit or the hint I'd dropped that you would soon be wed to Mlle. D'Argent, but the way has been opened for Mother to have a home in London again. I thought that it would be wise for one of us to go to Shropshire ourselves to give her the good news, to make certain she is thriving with Aunt Josephine, and to assist her in packing her things and returning to us."

"And you want me to do this?" Dean asked.

"You are the ideal candidate," Francis said.

Dean thought about it as he chewed on a piece of toast. Francis might have a point. As loath as he was to leave London when Nanette might come back and ask for him, his mother was more important. He missed her dearly. Mother might even have some bits of sage advice about how to approach a woman like his intended, and how to make her happy. And a change of scenery was always a good idea.

"I suppose I have no choice but to do your bidding, *primogenitus frater.*" He shrugged. "I'll go."

Of course, departing for a county on the other side of the country was not something Dean was able to accomplish in one day. It took him two days to arrange everything that needed arranging, to pack, and most importantly, to check in at the Concord Theater to make certain Nanette hadn't returned without informing him. It was a bit of a relief to discover that she hadn't. Niall Cristofori was only mildly concerned that his leading lady had left town and would be missing rehearsals for his new play, but seeing as there were two weeks before the play's opening night and Nanette was a consummate professional, he wasn't as worried as Dean was over her absence.

And Dean was worried. His worry only increased over the days when he and Nanette weren't together. His sleep continued to be restless—so much so that he ended up dozing through most of the journey to Shrewsbury as the train rocked him with its steady rhythm. In a moment of madness, he'd searched Euston Station for Nanette, as if she might be there, until he realized that trains bound for France did not depart from Euston at all. Olivia must have been mistaken when she'd mentioned the name of that station during their middle of the night meeting.

What surprised Dean the most was the overwhelming sentiment he felt when he stepped off the platform in Shrewsbury and found his mother and Aunt Josephine waiting for him.

"Mother, you look so well," he said, breaking into a wide smile and crossing the distance from the platform exit to where his mother and aunt stood in the heart of the station.

His mother did look well—perhaps better than he'd ever seen her look. Gone was the cowed, wan appearance that she'd had for as long as Dean could remember. She stood taller now and had more color in her complexion. Her hair was styled softly, with a pert hat affixed to the top, instead of pulled back in the modest style Lord Vegas preferred. She wore a gown of summer yellow accented with flowers instead of the dowdy brown or black that Lord Vegas insisted she wear. The result was that she looked at least ten years younger than the last time Dean had seen her and entirely refreshed.

Best of all, she held her arms out openly to Dean, drawing him into a hug of the sort that they had rarely been allowed to indulge in, thanks to Lord Vegas's stern rules about displays of affection. Dean actually groaned with happiness and relief as his mother embraced him, feeling like the child he'd once been, craving his mother's affection and receiving it at last.

"You look well yourself, darling," his mother said as Dean released her from their hug and moved to kiss his Aunt Josephine's cheek. "Though perhaps you could do with a bit of sleep."

"I must confess, I have not been sleeping well as of late," Dean said, feeling as sheepish as a child confessing to stealing an extra tart at a picnic. He shifted and offered his mother his arm, extending his other elbow so Aunt Josephine could take that one, and nodded to the porter who had his bags to follow them out to the street.

"I have always tried to impress upon you boys the importance of sleep," his mother said. "It improves one's constitution far more than the nuisance of frequent prayer and fasting that Lord Vegas always demanded."

Dean noted the steel in his mother's voice as she spoke of her husband. He had never really noticed before that she referred to the man to whom she was wed as "Lord Vegas"—just as it had never occurred to him that he and his brothers referred to the man in the same way sometimes instead of as "Father"—but now that his heart belonged firmly to Nanette, he couldn't imagine calling a spouse by any other term than an endearment.

No sooner had the thought of Nanette crossed his mind than he caught sight of a woman across the street and several dozen yards down who was the spitting image of Nanette. So much so that he blinked and stared. The woman had Nanette's dark hair and lithe build, but she was dressed in simple, country clothes. The woman was with an older woman who was clearly some sort of farmer's wife. They each carried baskets for shopping, and almost as soon as Dean noticed the doppelganger, they turned away and continued across the street on their errands.

A moment later, his attention was pulled firmly back to his mother as she said, "I have heard about your engagement, Dean," in a voice laden with disapproval.

Dean swallowed and steeled himself to be told off. "Nanette is wonderful, Mother," he insisted. "She is kind and clever, and she is the most beautiful woman I've ever known, save for you and Aunt Josephine, of course." He sweetened his words by kissing first his mother's cheek, then Aunt Josephine's as they stood waiting for a carriage to pull its way through the crowd of cabs waiting for passengers in front of the station.

His mother hummed as though she disapproved, though her cheeks glowed pink after the kiss. "She may be kind and clever, but Joseph's letter said she is an actress, sir."

Twin feelings of outrage that Joseph would tattle on him and giddiness at the easy way his mother joked with him—something she had never been allowed to do under Lord Vegas's rules—filled Dean.

"Did Joseph also inform you that he has caught the attention of a wild western American cowgirl?" Dean added, letting go of his mother's and aunt's arms to help the porter load his things into the carriage as it stopped for them.

"What nonsense is this?" his mother said, following after him.

Dean would have cowered at the unusually stern tone of her voice if he weren't so busy laughing at Joseph's expense. "You need to ask him about it yourself when you return to London."

"And if I have no intention of returning to London?" his mother asked.

Dean nearly fumbled his traveling bag. He spun to his mother, eyes wide. "But of course, you will return to London. Francis has sent me here to fetch you home. He said you were eager to come home and he's secured a lovely flat for you in a fashionable neighborhood."

"Where I will be snubbed for that man's crimes and treated like a social pariah," his mother said as Dean handed her, and then Aunt Josephine, into the carriage. "Your brother wanted me to be eager to return to London. I never told him that I was."

He climbed in after them and said, "I thought you would want to return to the excitement and bustle of the city."

"Excitement and bustle are precisely what I have fled from, my dear boy." His mother patted Dean's knee as she spoke.

The carriage jerked into motion, lurching Dean's stomach. "But...but we would so like to have you near us again."

"Being near to you boys means being near to *that man*." His mother frowned. "You and your brothers have no idea how Lord Vegas has wronged me. Nor do you have any idea of the humiliations I will face over things that have yet to come to light."

Dean arched an eyebrow. "What things have yet to come to light, Mother? Does this have something to do with Montrose?"

His mother pressed her lips together and took both of Aunt Josephine's hands when they were offered. "We shouldn't speak of such things," Aunt Josephine said in a whisper.

Dean opened his mouth to say more, but thought better of it and shut his mouth again. Aunt Josephine was a widow and a woman of the world. Her husband had been a bit of a bad sort, and she had been forced to deal with scandal and heartache as well. If Aunt Josephine thought his mother should be spared from something, he would do well to listen to her.

He glanced out the carriage window as he gathered his thoughts, but instead of his mind settling, it flared into a different sort of turmoil as he spotted the woman who was a dead-ringer for Nanette again. The resemblance was keen enough that he stared for a moment. The woman had the same build as Nanette, but, blast it, she was turned mostly away from him as she and the older woman with her haggled over a cut of meat in front of a butcher's shop.

"Darling, do pay attention," his mother said, drawing his focus to her and away from the haggling woman. "I've no intention of returning to London, and you can tell Francis that as soon as you yourself return."

Dean let out a breath, forgetting about the lookalike. Nanette was in France. The woman there in Shrewsbury merely resembled her. The world was filled with millions of people, and it was entirely feasible that some of them looked the same.

"I will not give up so easily," he told his mother. "I won't leave Shropshire until I've convinced you to come home."

"Excellent," his mother said with a cheerful smile. "That means we will have a long, happy visit, then."

Dean laughed at the way his mother had so expertly turned the conversation. Perhaps he would enjoy spending some time with this new, unencumbered version of her. Even if his heart did long for Nanette and worry about her so much that he was seeing her in the faces of random country girls.

Chapter Ten

"To tell you the truth, Mama," Nanette said as she and her mother left the house of a family friend of theirs in the small town of Sutton, near Shrewsbury, "I will always be a country girl at heart."

"Is that so?" her mother said eyeing her sideways, a doubtful grin pulling at her mouth.

"Yes, it is." Nan nodded for good measure. "London is all well and good," she went on, feeling unaccountably awkward as she began her argument. "I enjoy dining out and the shops. I have quite a few friends there now too. And it is lovely sometimes, when the rain washes away the smoke and soot and makes everything so shimmery and beautiful."

"But?" her mother hummed, her grin widening and her eyes sparkling with mirth.

They turned a corner, walking past a cobbler's shop—her mother waved to her friend, the cobbler's wife—and continued on toward the high street. The town was close enough to Shrewsbury to be thriving and busy, but far enough away to still have a country feel. Nan knew it like the back of her hand. The place still felt like home...to a degree.

"But nothing," Nan said, her voice overly bright. "London has its charms, but I just know that my heart truly belongs in the country, here, with you and Papa and the family."

She didn't know why she was so breathless as she spoke, or why she felt as though she were telling a small fib. Or perhaps a large fib. Shropshire was her home. It was a part of her. It should be far easier to accompany her mother on a morning call than it was to affect a French accent and persona for her followers in London.

Which did nothing to explain why it felt like such a stretch to walk at an easy pace by her mother's side, or why the simple blouse and skirt she wore didn't seem to fit her as well as the elaborate gowns she wore in London.

"You are a treasure, Nan," her mother chuckled as they paused in front of a greengrocery so that her mother could pick through the vegetables in baskets out front. "And you are an exceptionally talented actress," she added, her mouth twitching.

"I have worked hard to excel at my craft," Nan said, throwing her shoulders back and assuming the posture she did while she was on the stage. "I have learned from the very best that the London stage has to offer, after all. I am not one of those actresses who gives herself airs and pretends as though there is nothing more she can learn from the talented performers she works with. And I am always careful to heed the advice of the directors I work with. Mr. Abrams is particularly astute in his—"

Nan stopped in the middle of her justifications when she noticed her mother laughing at her. More than laughing, her mother seemed downright tickled by everything she was saying.

Nan blew out a breath, her posture sagging. "You weren't talking about my profession," she said.

"No," her mother laughed, patting Nan's arm, then

leaning over to give her cheek a kiss. "I most certainly was not."

Her mother moved on, leaving the greengrocer and continuing down the street to peer into a baker's shop.

In the back of her mind, Nan was aware that someone had stepped out of the greengrocer's as she and her mother walked on, and that said person remained nearby, but as she was used to London—where hundreds of people were packed in together on every street and could not help but live practically on top of each other—she dismissed it.

"I am not acting when I say that I enjoy the country, Mama," she insisted as her mother's eyes grew excitedly at the sight of a tray of buns on the other side of the window that were still steaming from the oven. "This is my home. This is where I was brought up. You and Papa and everyone else still call this place home."

"Yes, we do," her mother said, straightening and facing Nan. She patted Nan's cheek this time. "You might have been brought up here, but this is no longer your home, dearest. You have grown beyond the small comforts that Sutton, or Shrewsbury, or Shropshire in general, can provide. You are a city girl now. You are Nanette D'Argent, darling of zee stage," she said in a poor imitation of Nan's accent. "Not humble Nan Silvers anymore."

"That isn't true, Mama," Nan protested crossing her arms in front of her. "And I resent the implication that I...that I no longer fit with my own family." The sudden thought made her sad, and her tone switched from offended to sorrowful in the middle of her sentence.

"Dear Nan." Her mother leaned in to hug her, even though she was carrying her shopping basket. "How I love you. And I am delighted that you are happy to be home. But you know as well as I that this is merely a visit. You are not here to stay."

Her mother moved on, looking through the window of the seamstress's shop beside the bakery as she did.

"What if I have no choice?" Nan asked in a small voice. "What if something were to happen and...and I was exposed as a fraud and had to come home?"

"A fraud?" Her mother laughed. "Darling, you have just proven to me that you are an exceptional actress. You are clever as well. I have full confidence in your ability to invent yourself anew, if circumstances should call for it. You know I was not in favor of your French ruse when you first proposed it to your father and me."

"I needed something that would set me apart," Nan argued. "Papa agreed that it would be a lark. And we were both right. The only reason anyone ever looked twice at me during an audition was because I was supposedly French."

"And yet, I can see the whole thing exhausts you, my dear," her mother said, smiling back at her.

"I am tired," Nan sighed, leaning against the side of the building. She lowered her head and stared at her hands. They were soft with elegantly-shaped nails. They were not the hands of a country girl. "I thought I was close to something that would allow me to rest from the trials and travails of leading a public life," she went on, trying not to feel morose about the situation she found herself in but failing. "I thought I'd found something wonderful and beautiful, something I've always wanted."

Her mother grinned at her. "This wouldn't have anything to do with the beau you hinted at yesterday, would it?"

Nan's face heated. She'd only been brave enough to hint to her mother and father about Dean so far. They'd guessed that there was someone special in her life, but when they'd pressed for details, she had remained cagey. But how could she raise her family's hopes by telling them she was engaged to the son of a marquess when she might very well lose Dean the moment he discovered the truth about her?

Just thinking that question squeezed Nan's chest to the point where she couldn't breathe. She raised her fingertips to her lips without being aware of the action, remembering the way Dean's lips had felt against hers and the way his tongue had tasted. She remembered his free and easy laughter, the way he had been so quick to rush into silliness with her. She remembered the way he had pledged to be her champion against Montrose. For the first time in a long time, she had felt as though she wasn't alone against the crueler forces of the world.

"Nan, dear," her mother pulled her out of her thoughts, "if you have found someone to love and who loves you in return in London, even if he is one of those wicked theater people you are so fond of writing about in your letters home, your father and I will not think less of you."

"It isn't that," Nan mumbled, still glancing down, even though she stood straighter.

In the back of her mind, as a distant afterthought, she sensed that whoever had followed them from the greengrocer's had stepped nearer.

"Is it the feeling that this beau, whoever he is, will take you away from us permanently?" her mother asked. "Because if that is your worry, if you ran away from London to nestle in the bosom of your family out of the fear that you might lose us, you needn't worry. Children grow up and discover lives of their own. Sometimes that means moving to a new, bigger place. Your ambitions have always been bigger than your origins, Nan."

"It isn't that either, Mama," Nan said, dragging in a long breath and facing her mother as bravely as she could. She needed to tell her mother everything. That was why she'd come home, after all. She needed to tell her father about

Montrose as well, but she hadn't known how to start that conversation either. "The truth is, Mama, the man I mentioned yesterday isn't just my beau. He is...he is...we are engaged."

Instead of her mother being shocked that she would engage herself to a Londoner, a man she had never laid eyes on, her mother seemed delighted. "Oh, Nan, that is wonderful. I had so hoped that you would find someone who loves you, even with your dazzling career."

"There is a greater problem, Mama," Nan went on, desperately overheated with the shame and anxiety of her confession.

"A problem?" Her mother frowned. "Is he honest? Has he treated you poorly? Is he someone you should be ashamed of?"

"No!" Nan yelped. "Far from it. He is the most wonderful man I've ever known. He is funny and kind and intelligent. And...and he is the son of a marquess."

Her mother gasped, her eyes going wide. Then she burst into laughter. When Nan frowned at her, she said, "Engaged to the son of a marquess in London, and she thinks that she could be content with the life of a country girl?"

Nan crossed her arms and frowned. "It is not funny, Mama. I am in a terrible pickle because of it all."

"And what pickle might that be, oh beautiful, talented, famous daughter of mine who is soon to marry into the upper class?" Her mother continued to laugh.

Nan was so irritated with her mother's mirth that she blurted, "He believes me to be French. He thinks I am Nanette D'Argent." Her mother sobered in a hurry. "He does not know who I truly am."

Nan thought she would get an earful from her mother for that truth, but the moment took a far more terrifying turn when Dean's voice spoke behind her, saying, "He knows the truth now."

Nan couldn't breathe. She couldn't think for a moment. She was utterly frozen to her spot with horror and disbelief. When she finally did have the courage to whip around, only to find Dean standing just a few yards away from her, his expression one of shock, her body began to shake uncontrollably.

Several things suddenly fell into order. She hadn't imagined seeing Dean step out of the train station in Shrewsbury the other day. She hadn't felt so desperately guilty for fleeing London without giving him a proper explanation that she'd fancied spotting him in the window of a carriage that passed as she and her mother had purchased meat for a roast. Dean must have been the one who stepped out of the greengrocer's and followed her and her mother—followed and overheard the entire conversation.

Nan opened her mouth, desperate for something to come out that would explain everything Dean must have just overheard. Nothing at all came out, though. Not even air. Dean had heard everything she'd said to her mother since the greengrocer's. He'd heard her speaking without her accent. He'd heard her talking about her life at home and her life in London. Of all the times for her to speak openly with her mother about the predicament she found herself in, she had to speak when Dean was standing nearby, listening.

There was no point in pretending to be Nanette anymore. The game was up, and there was nothing she could do about it.

"What are you doing here?" she managed—somehow—to ask, her voice high and shaky.

"My...my mother has been staying with her sister, my Aunt Josephine, the dowager Countess of Dorrington, at her estate nearby. I've been sent to fetch her back to London,"

Dean said. The only good thing about his reply was that he sounded as gobsmacked as Nan felt.

The two of them stood there, gaping at each other. Nan couldn't feel her hands or her feet.

"I...I can explain," she blurted, even though she absolutely could not.

"Dean!" a matronly voice called from across the street. "Dean Rathborne-Paxton, what in heaven's name are you doing accosting poor girls on the street?"

Nan felt as though time were moving too slowly as she turned to see a beautiful, older woman in a stylish, summer outfit marching across the street and up to Dean's side. Nan could see the resemblance at once and knew the woman was Dean's beloved mother.

What surprised her was the strangled sound her own mother made as she dropped into a deep curtsy. "Lady Vegas," her mother said with utmost deference.

Nan's mouth continued to hang open as she fought to understand the awkward situation she'd stepped into. She was at a complete loss. All she could do was gaze desperately at Dean, praying that he didn't hate her and that he would have the first idea of what she should do to salvage the situation.

Making matters even more surreal, her mother grabbed her sleeve and tugged at it, silently ordering Nan to curtsy to Lady Vegas. There was nothing Nan could do but curtsy as humbly as she'd ever curtsied. To her potential mother-in-law.

"Mrs. Silvers," Lady Vegas said, nodding to Nan's mother with exactly the sort of gracious manner that a woman of her standing should use when addressing a crofter's wife. The fact that Dean's mother knew who Nan's mother was came as both a surprise and a deep source of terror to Nan. "Who is this attractive young person?" Lady Vegas asked, as though nothing were out of the ordinary.

"This is my daughter, my lady. Nan Silvers," Nan's mother answered dutifully.

"Silvers," Dean whispered, barely audible, then made matters worse by adding, "D'Argent."

Nan wanted to sink into the ground and disappear. She peeked up at Dean only to find that he'd made the connection. "*Argent*" was French for "silver". Dean stared hard at her, as if trying to gauge exactly how awful Nan was. Nan wished he would glare at her outright instead of looking at her with a baffled, slightly hurt expression.

"This is my son," Lady Vegas went on—not unkind, but certainly feeling as though she were far above Nan and her mother. "Mr. Dean Rathborne-Paxton."

"How do you do." Dean nodded to Nan's mother, his manners perfect, then turned to stare intensely at Nan. He nodded again and said, "Miss Silvers," as though nothing were out of order.

Except that everything was out of order. Nan felt as though lightning would strike her out of the blue at any moment, and if it did, she would deserve it.

"My son is here to convince me to return to London," Lady Vegas said.

Nan's mother drew in a sharp breath. Her gaze flashed from Lady Vegas to Nan to Dean, then her eyes widened with understanding. Understanding and panic. She pressed her lips tightly closed, as if she were too terrified to say another word. Nan could feel that she would catch hell as soon as her mother felt free to speak again.

"Dean," Lady Vegas said, turning to Dean with a somewhat irritated look, "what has taken you so long? Josephine and I have been waiting at the café these several long minutes."

"I...er...." Dean worked his mouth silently for a moment before glancing back to Nan and fumbling, "Miss Silvers forgot one of her purchases at the greengrocer's. If she

LET'S FACE THE MUSIC AND DANCE

would care to accompany me back, I can show her where it is."

"Purchases?" Nan's mother said.

Panic squeezed in around Nan. "Yes, thank you, that would be delightful," Nan said quickly, before her mother could reveal too much to Lady Vegas. She turned and all but ran back in the direction of the greengrocer's before her mother could say more.

Within seconds, Dean had caught up to her. He didn't say a word, merely marched by her side, until they were able to duck into the greengrocer's shop.

"What in blazes is going on here?" Dean hissed as soon as they were safe inside the shop and out of the view of the mothers.

"Dean." Nan gulped, pressing a hand to her stomach. "I can explain."

"Can you?" Dean's voice rose to an octave that was unbecoming for a man. He cleared his throat, leaned in closer to her as one of the shop's patrons stared curiously at them, then repeated, "Can you, Nanette?"

Nan winced. Not only that, her face pinched and crumpled until she was in danger of sobbing.

She pulled herself together with a few steadying breaths, then said, "I didn't mean to deceive you. I've been Nanette for so very long, and I had no idea I would meet you or that I would...." Her throat closed up before she could confess that she loved him. It came as a surprise even to her, and she felt herself in danger of passing out at the sentiment.

"I...I don't know what to say," Dean stammered, moving his hands restlessly at his sides, as though he felt he should make some sort of gesture, but didn't know what that was. "You're not French."

"No," Nan said. She blinked, wondering how bad the revelation could get.

"And I suppose that means you're not from Paris either," Dean went on.

Again, Nan held her breath, but this time for other reasons. Dean didn't seem to be as horrified or angry as she supposed he'd be. In fact, he mostly just sounded surprised.

A moment later, Nan questioned whether she would really get away with everything scot-free. Dean's confused expression turned to a sharp frown. He shifted his weight, crossing his arms over his chest, and asked, "If you are not Nanette D'Argent and you are not from Paris, would you kindly explain to me who the devil you actually are?"

Chapter Eleven

I t *was* Nanette—or rather, Nan Silvers—whom Dean had spotted in Shrewsbury, he was certain of it now. He'd come into Sutton to treat his mother and aunt to tea in the local café as a means of convincing his mother to return to London, and he'd spotted her again, with the same older woman who had been with her in Shrewsbury. For several, long moments, he'd stared through the window of the café, ignoring his mother's and aunt's conversation, convincing himself that what he was seeing was not an apparition, but his fiancée.

He'd excused himself from tea, inventing an excuse to hurry across the street on an errand. He'd been certain Nan hadn't seen him, so he'd taken cover in the nearest shop, the greengrocer's, in order to observe her further and listen to her conversation.

Several things had become immediately apparent to him. Nan was not French. For a moment, he considered that perhaps she was merely rehearsing an English accent and that the older woman was helping her. That notion had flown straight out the window as soon as he'd heard the topics of their conversation. He'd heard quite a bit—likely more than Nan would have ever wanted him to know.

A thousand thoughts had roiled through him as he'd caught up with her, called her out for whatever game she was playing, and then been treated to yet another shock by discovering his mother seemed to know her. At least, his mother knew Nan's family. It felt as though he'd stepped straight into the middle of one of Niall Cristofori's plays without realizing it.

Now, as he and a fretful Nan stood just inside the greengrocer's, garnering more looks from other patrons of the shop than he would have liked, Dean's thoughts and feelings were as diverse and scattered as the goods for sale around him.

"If you are not Nanette D'Argent and you are not from Paris, would you kindly explain to me who the devil you actually are?" he asked.

He was furious with her for deceiving him. No, no he wasn't. He was merely hurt that she hadn't confided in him. No, it was not that either. He was worried for her and whatever reason she might have for pretending to be someone she wasn't.

He didn't know what he thought or felt.

Nan wrung her hands in front of her, glancing down and biting her lip, distress in her eyes. "I am the same woman you have always known," she said in a hesitant voice, looking up at him through her long lashes.

Dean swallowed. Damnation, she was still the most beautiful thing he'd ever seen. False though she'd been, there was something frightened and needy about her that made him want to rush to her aid and be her champion. Still.

"I am Nan Silvers. I was born and raised nearby. I am the daughter of a prosperous crofter," she went on.

"My mother seems to know as much," Dean said, straightening a bit. His heart longed for her, but he crossed his arms and stared flatly at her all the same. "Apparently, my mother knows more about you than I do."

"I am sorry, Dean," she said, swaying toward him.

A moment later, she pulled back. Hesitancy lined her face, almost as though she didn't know whether she had a right to address him by his given name anymore, or at all.

She took a breath and went on. "Lady Dorrington is your mother's sister, is she not?"

"She is," Dean said with a nod, wondering what his aunt had to do with anything.

"My family has been tenants on Lord Dorrington's land for many generations," Nan said.

Dean's brow inched up. His fiancée was the daughter of his late uncle's tenant? The tangle of class was more than he could think about at the moment.

"I've always had a talent for acting and singing and dancing," Nan went on, lowering her head again and flushing. She bit her lip before continuing with, "I have always been ambitious as well. There was a play when I was just out of primary school. I performed as the lead. A journalist from London was traveling though and attended the performance. He said I was talented and pretty enough to have a career on the London stage."

Dean arched a brow. It was as likely as not that the man, whoever he was, had said as much in order to get Nan to lift her skirts for him. Dean was suddenly seized with horror at the idea that perhaps she had done just that.

Nan seemed to read his mind. "He was not saying those things to lure me to bed," she told him, censure in her voice and a touch of indignation sparking in her expression.

She'd spoken a bit too loud, and a middle-aged woman with a shopping basket one aisle over gasped, scowled, and marched out of the shop.

Nan sighed, rubbed her forehead, and gingerly turned

back to Dean. "I took a chance and followed his advice, traveling to London. I brought Olivia with me. I have been friends with her older sister since childhood. We supported each other, both taking employment in shops and such whenever we could find it. Olivia was wonderful to allow me to go to auditions and the like. But I was just another country girl with dreams of the stage.

"It wasn't until I became bored at work at the shop one day that it occurred to me to pretend to be French," she continued, lowering her voice a bit, perhaps in shame. Her expression flashed back to sheepishness—which did strange things to Dean's heart that it likely shouldn't have. "There was a customer, a French woman, who was so high and mighty. She offended all of us shopgirls egregiously. So I adopted her mannerisms to amuse the other girls." Nan shrugged. "It stuck. I increased the amount of commission I earned in the shop threefold. And then I tried out the persona when I went to an audition. It was only for a small part in an inconsequential production, but I got it."

"I admire your cleverness," Dean said carefully, his emotions still a bundle of contradictions, "but how does one go from jesting with fellow shopgirls to gracing the stage of the Concord Theater as a counterfeit Frenchwoman and gaining a dozen endorsement deals in the process?"

Dean expected more shame and sheepishness. He was surprised when Nan's expression turned frightened.

"Montrose," she said. She paused, then shook her head. "No, Montrose was only part of the story. He frequented the shop where I worked. He was aware of my transformation from simple country girl to Frenchwoman. I was surprised when he attended the performance I'd been cast in. I was more surprised when he invited me to attend a party with him as Nanette D'Argent."

Dean's eyes widened in surprise as well. "I did not think

Montrose was at all interested in...." He was at a loss for how to finish his thought. From what Alice had told the rest of them, Montrose had explicitly told her he abhorred anything sexual.

Nan winced a bit. "He was not interested in that way. I believe, knowing what I know of the man now, that he had hoped to use me as an instrument to fool and bring down his enemies. He could in no way have known I would meet Everett Jewel at that party."

"Everett Jewel?" Dean blinked. The story was beginning to take shape in his mind.

Nan nodded. "We got along right from the start. We ended up singing a duet that night, and the party guests loved it. Everett and I talked quite a bit into the night. He said he wanted to introduce me to Niall Cristofori, which he did shortly after." She paused for a moment, studying Dean as though trying to determine whether he was still angry with her.

Dean was so absorbed in Nan's story that he didn't notice some of the patrons inching closer to listen in on the conversation. When one of them said, "I saw Everett Jewel at the Concord Theater in London two years ago. He was quite dashing," Dean frowned.

"Yes, he is rather good," he answered the woman, then reached for Nan's arm.

He cupped her elbow and escorted her out of the shop and away from the small audience they'd gathered. His mother and Mrs. Silvers were still conversing where they'd left them, and he could only hope that the two didn't notice him and Nan leaving the greengrocer's. He steered Nan around the corner, into the alley between two shops.

"I take it Jewel and Cristofori together launched your career," he said.

"They did," Nan nodded, seemingly anxious to have been

dragged out to an alley, as if Dean were a thief who planned to rob her.

"Do they know your secret?" he asked. The moment the words left his lips, the note that Montrose had sent to Nan on the closing night of *Love's Last Lesson* came to him. It made sense now.

Nan bit her lip and twisted her fingers together. "Everett knows," she said. "No one else does."

Dean hummed, nodded, and leaned back to study her. He didn't have the first clue what to think about Nan now. She'd been false with him—and everyone else in London and the world—from the moment he'd seen her. She'd become engaged to him without whispering a word. She'd let him kiss the same lips that told lies every time they opened.

But then, why would she tell him something so integral to her career and her persona when they had, in fact, known each other for so short a length of time? When would she have had the opportunity to explain everything, as she was explaining now?

"You would not have let me lead you to the altar and joined our lives together forever without telling me the truth, would you?" he asked, arching one eyebrow.

"I—" Nan hesitated, her mouth staying open as her eyes danced with uncertainty. Dean was more than a little uncertain as she failed to answer the question immediately. "I panicked," she admitted at last, her shoulders dropping. "Everything happened so quickly between the two of us. You wanted me to be Nanette. That was who you were so enamored with. And with Montrose's threats, I rushed into something that I believed afforded me some protection from his machinations. I...I was frightened."

Dean's heart nearly burst in his chest as he realized she was still afraid. It seemed so incongruous and wrong in so many ways. Nan was strong and graceful. Whether she was French or not, she'd taken London by storm. He'd always known her to be powerful and fascinating. She was no less fascinating, now that she'd revealed the truth. In fact, if he were honest with himself, Dean admired her all the more for pulling off something so daring.

Before he could tell her as much, Nan glanced up at him again and said, "I know you must be furious with me for lying. I cannot imagine what you must think of me right now. I have deceived you. I will not be false anymore. I rushed into an engagement with you because I believed that your status as the son of a marquess might provide me with protection, should the truth ever be revealed. I...I had hoped that I might be able to keep my fame and commercial endorsements while also slipping out of the public eye, so that when the inevitable happened, the blow would be softened." She lowered her head to stare at her hands. "I am sorry. I will understand fully when you cast me aside, and I would not fault you, should you choose to reveal the truth to all."

Dean's already aching heart felt as though it might shatter at Nan's contrite speech. He wanted to be angry with her. He wanted to huff and pout over the way she'd wounded his pride and played him for a fool. Except, he didn't think she had played him for a fool. He had been the one who pursued her, after all. Who she truly was would not have been of any consequence to him if he'd stayed in the wings, painting scenery and admiring her from afar.

Furthermore, chances were that she was not the only performer who had invented a story for themselves. He couldn't even say that what she'd done was unusual. She was a woman of fire and strength who had grabbed hold of an impossible dream and actually achieved it. The truth only made Dean admire her more.

"I am not going to cast you aside, Nan," he said in a quiet voice, inching closer to her.

Nan snapped her gaze up to him. "You're not? After all the lies I've told you?"

Dean shrugged, moving close enough to her that he could reach for her. "I do not believe you have ever told me a direct lie." He paused, tilted his head to the side, and said, "Well, perhaps that story about a former lover Montrose wished to expose. That wasn't the secret he threatened to reveal, was it?"

"No." Nan lowered her head for a moment. Dean rested his hands on her arms and could feel her trembling slightly. "I believe you know what secret he plans to reveal if I do not give him the money he's asked for." She looked up at him again.

"Well, he can't have it," Dean said, managing a small smile. "That money is mine now. That's why I'm marrying you, after all."

It was a terrible joke, all things considered. Nan blinked up at him, surprised by the statement.

"You still wish to marry me?" she asked breathlessly.

"Yes," Dean answered with a shrug. "Because you are still beautiful. You are still clever and talented. And you're still wealthy and famous." He grinned impishly as he spoke. He failed to add the biggest reason he still wished to marry her. He wasn't certain he could even admit it to himself. It still felt too soon to say that he loved her out loud.

"Oh." Nan blinked, seemingly shocked. "I would have thought—"

He didn't wait to see what she would have thought. He drew her fully into his arms and slanted his mouth over hers. The end of her sentence became a moan of pleasure and relief against his mouth as he traced his tongue over her soft lips, coaxing her to let him in. She complied easily, sliding her arms around him and meeting his kiss with equal ardor. Dean didn't care what she called herself or how she spoke when he felt the rush of desire fill him. It wasn't just his lust for her, it was the way she clearly wanted him as well. That powerful, pulsing feeling made everything else—

"Dean! What is the meaning of this display?" his mother's shrill voice snapped Dean from the amorous haze he'd fallen into.

He and Nan both gasped and leapt away from each other. They spun to face not only Dean's mother, but Nan's as well, and Aunt Josephine. The three women gaped at them as though they were in the middle of something much more scandalous than a passionate kiss in an alley between two shops.

"Mother, I can explain," Dean said with a nervous laugh. He threaded his fingers through Nan's, holding her hand.

"You have been in Shropshire for no more than two days, and already you are defiling village girls?" Aunt Josephine asked, horrified.

"Actually, no." Dean felt his face grow hot as he nodded to his aunt, then turned to Nan. "As it happens, Miss Silvers and I are very well acquainted from London."

Nan grasped Dean's hand that held hers with her other hand. "It's true, Mama," she told her startled mother. "Mr. Rathborne-Paxton is the fiancé I told you about."

Nan's mother sucked in a breath. "You are engaged to Mr. Rathborne-Paxton?" She broke into a smile.

"You are engaged to a crofter's daughter?" Dean's mother demanded, gaping.

"Nan might be a crofter's daughter, Mama," Dean said, falling back on the way he'd addressed his mother as a small child, "but she is also one of the most celebrated actresses on the London stage."

That statement did nothing to appease his mother. She groaned as if Dean had told her Nan was the scullery maid at Buckingham Palace and pressed her fingertips to her forehead. "Smelling salts. Josephine, I need smelling salts."

Aunt Josephine yelped and began searching in the purse she carried with her.

"Mother, there is no need for such dramatics," Dean said, frowning in irritation. "Nan is a lovely woman, and she is exceedingly popular in London."

"So was Lady Chatterley," his mother moaned. Dean wasn't amused with that either. "How can you bring so much more disgrace on our family when we are already laid low?" she went on, her dramatics rivaling Nan's. "First, your brother marries his...his *mistress*—" she hissed the word as though it were foul, "—and now you are seeking to marry an *actress*?"

"Mother, really." Dean sighed impatiently. "I am certain that once you have the opportunity to know Nan better, you will find her as charming as I do."

Dean glanced to Nan as she gave him a hopeful smile. He could see that she didn't think she was out of the woods yet, though, particularly when his mother went on.

"I cannot stand another upset today. Dean, you will come along at once. We will discuss this matter at home." She snapped her fingers to indicate that Dean was to leave Nan and go with her.

Dean's brow shot up to his hairline. He had never known his mother to be so forceful or determined. It was a paradoxical joy to watch. For most of his adult life, his mother had been brought to heel by Lord Vegas. It had turned her into a ghost of the woman she had once been. But that woman had returned, and it seemed to Dean as though her will had doubled. He loved it. It was the most encouraging thing he had seen in ages, even if his mother's energy was set against him.

He glanced between his mother and Nan, knowing he didn't have time to explain why his mother's transformation was so wonderful and why it meant that he had to obey and go with her. All he could do was let go of Nan's hand and say,

"We will speak later. I have much to tell you. We have so much to discuss."

"We do," Nan said, letting him go with just enough reluctance to warm Dean's heart.

"Son," his mother said threateningly, gesturing for him to come to her side.

Dean burst into a smile despite the command. Or rather, because of it. It was absurd for him to be so happy all of a sudden when everything had looked so bleak just an hour before. A part of him was still hurt that Nan had kept him so much in the dark, particularly when she'd left London several days before, but another part of him understood. They had time. Everything could be sorted out. And best of all, his mother was in the process of demonstrating just how much the country had agreed with her.

"Until later," he called to Nan over his shoulder as his mother dragged him away like a boy a third of his age.

"Goodbye." Nan raised a hand and waved to him, an astounded smile on her face.

"You will not see that woman later," Dean's mother huffed, exchanging a look with Aunt Josephine. "You will cease to consort with women that far beneath your station at once. You will find yourself a well-bred woman of your own class, a woman of reputation and regal bearing, and you will marry her."

"I am already engaged to Miss Silvers, Mother," Dean said, putting little effort into the argument. He wouldn't win it with a few words, that much was certain.

As if to prove his point, his mother huffed. "We shall see about that," she said, tilting her chin up. "We shall see."

Chapter Twelve

"So, am I to understand that my eldest daughter is engaged to be married to the cousin of Lord Dorrington?" Nan's father asked that evening, as Nan sat at the kitchen table with her mother and father after her younger siblings had gone to bed.

Nan's mouth opened to answer, but she paused to consider before she spoke. She supposed that was true. Dean must have been the cousin of the current Earl of Dorrington, Lady Dorrington's son. Realizing that brought the vast difference between her and Dean's social standings into greater focus.

"Yes, Papa," she answered at last, a little stunned herself. "That is true."

"Has he interfered with you?" Her father leaned back in his chair and crossed his arms. "Is that why he's marrying you?"

"Richard," Nan's mother hissed. "You should not speak of such things with your own daughter." She squirmed a bit, then continued with, "Men of Mr. Rathborne-Paxton's class have no need to marry a girl when they've...you know." She nodded to Nan.

Deep embarrassment of the sort that could only come through discussing one's love life with one's parents washed over Nan. "No, Mr. Rathborne-Paxton has not interfered with me," she told her parents, crossing her arms and, admittedly, behaving with the sort of petulance she would have had a decade before. "He has only ever kissed me." Although he would have done quite a bit more the night of the closing night party, if Montrose hadn't derailed things.

Her father snorted as though he wasn't convinced. "But he wants to marry you," he said. "He actually *wants* to."

"And what is so very wrong with that?" Nan asked, tilting her chin up defiantly. "I have made quite a name for myself, Papa. I live in a luxurious flat in a sought-after neighborhood in London. My image graces many a product, and I have reaped the financial benefit of those endorsements."

"Yes, I know," her father said, raising his voice. "I am forever running into my daughter's face when I peer through the shop windows of everyplace in Shrewsbury. It's indecent, it is."

"Richard," her mother scolded again. "Nan is the reason we were able to send Albert away to university. You've not said no to the money she sends home."

"Aye, and I've not kept a cent of it for myself," her father went on. "It's all gone to the children." He looked at Nan again. "But what if you do marry this cousin of an earl? Will any of us be welcomed in your house? Will we be welcomed at Dorrington Hall if you take up residence there?"

Nan caught the gist of the problem immediately. Her father was worried about more than whether Nan's imagined purity had been spoiled. She could see in the stubborn line of his jaw and the spark of hurt in his eyes that he was afraid Nan would be out of their grasp forever. The chasm between their place and the place she would have if she married Dean was wide indeed.

Nan stood and leaned over the corner of the table to kiss her father's cheek. "I will never let go of you, Papa. I will never distance myself from any of you. And if you knew Dean the way that I do, you would see that he will welcome you into our future home with open arms."

Her words sounded pretty, but there was more speculation and supposition in them than she had ever managed to fit into such a short statement before. Would Dean embrace her simple family? Would he want the tenants of his cousin staying in the guestrooms of his house? Would he order her to sever all ties with her family?

Did she truly know the man she was engaged to at all?

"I think it is time for me to retire for the evening," she said, stepping back from the table.

She didn't want to step away from her father. She'd come to Shropshire to consult with him about Montrose, but in the confusion of everything else that had happened, and considering how busy he'd been with work since her arrival, she had yet to bring the topic up. Now, with the truth about her engagement to Dean revealed, she doubted her father would want to talk about anything else.

"Yes, dearest," her mother said, getting up to hug her and kiss her cheek. "You go to bed and rest your pretty head." She patted Nan's cheek. "We will discuss this more in the morning. But I, for one, am proud of the way you've brought yourself up in the world." She took a step back and regarded Nan with a sigh. "My Nan, the daughter-in-law of a marquess and the cousin-in-law of our own Lord Dorrington. Who could have imagined?"

No one, Nan thought to herself as she kissed her mother goodnight and turned to head upstairs to her bedroom. No one at all, least of all herself, could have imagined the wild twists and turns that her life had taken since she and Olivia had scraped together all their funds to purchase train tickets to London. She never could have dreamed she would meet with so much success, or that that success would prove to be so terrifying.

Because, whether she'd had the time to consult with her father about it or not, the threat of Montrose continued to loom over her. The circumstances of her travails with that devil had not changed one bit, even though everything else in her life felt as though it were in complete upheaval. She still had a secret that Montrose had threatened to expose. She had only a handful of days to meet the deadline that he had set for her. Everything—from her career to her fortune—hung in the balance.

But perhaps not her relationship with Dean. As she undressed and washed up, then donned her nightgown for bed, she contemplated how strange it was that the thing that could have formed her greatest loss was, in fact, the one thing she potentially felt confident in. Dean hadn't rejected her outright that morning. He'd said he wouldn't. And he'd kissed her. Hope welled in Nan as she carried her lantern to the table beside her bed.

Then again, Dean had obeyed his mother, Lady Vegas, a marchioness, and left with her when she'd called him. Lady Vegas had expressed her disapproval in no uncertain terms. She might have been a woman, but Nan would be a fool to think a marchioness had no power over her sons, or their choice of brides. It was particularly worrying, considering how short a time she and Dean had been engaged, or that they'd known each other. One snap of her fingers, and Lady Vegas could unravel everything.

Nan sank into her bed, willing herself not to think about it, but finding she could think of nothing else. The facts were the facts. She was, at best, a middle-class country girl with pretentions in Lady Vegas's eyes. Dean could have his pick of the debutantes of London—or rather, he could have his mother's pick. And if Montrose carried through on his threat and exposed the truth about her, there was no possible way Lady Vegas would allow the marriage to go forward.

That thought brought her very near to the edge of tears when a tapping at her window jolted Nan from her misery. She gasped and pulled her bedcovers up to her chin, shrinking away from the window directly beside her bed.

Her gasp turned into a cry of surprise a moment later as Dean peeked through the glass. As she recognized him, he broke into a smile that was so filled with joy it was comical. She couldn't help but laugh as she rolled over and knelt on the bed so that she could push the window open.

"What are you doing, you daft man?" she asked in a loud whisper. She poked her head out the window and glanced down at the ladder Dean had set against the side of the house and climbed. "If my father catches you, he'll have your hide."

"He won't catch me," Dean whispered, nudging her back and climbing through the window. "The house is dark downstairs. The only other light is from a room on the other side of the house."

Her parents must have gone to bed. Their room was at the direct opposite end of the house from Nan's room. The house wasn't large, though. If she and Dean were too loud, they would be heard.

As soon as Dean was all the way through the window, he turned to close it. "I had to speak with you. I was not satisfied with the way we left things this morning," he said as he fastened the latch, then turned to her.

"Your mother does not approve of me," Nan said, addressing the problem head-on.

"No, she does not," Dean said, shifting to kneel on the bed with his knees touching hers. He reached for her hands. "She does not know you, though. Once she does, I am certain we will be singing a different song. This is merely the end of Act One. We shall triumph at last in Act Two."

Nan grinned at his metaphor. Her heart fluttered in her chest, but sentiment was squashed by sense.

"You do realize that we find ourselves in an impossible position, do you not?" she asked him, sitting on the bed. Dean mirrored her position, though he looked ridiculous doing so while fully dressed. "We are divided by class and birth. We are hampered by secrets and threats."

"It sounds like the perfect recipe for a dramatic, happy ending," Dean said with a smile.

Nan sighed, running her thumbs over his knuckles as they held hands. She shook her head, but couldn't help smiling as she did. "Real life is not as smooth as the stage, Dean. There are so many forces working against us that I question whether—"

She stopped and bit her lip. She couldn't bring herself to say she questioned whether it was a good idea that the two of them were involved. She wanted Dean. She wanted him now more than ever. Deep down, she suspected she needed him desperately for the storm they were about to sail into.

Instead of finishing her sentence as she'd planned to, she said, "I question whether there are more things we need to do to ensure our safety and happiness."

"But of course there are things we must do to ensure it all," Dean said, still unerringly confident. "We must defeat Montrose, for one. Do not think I have forgotten about him."

"I haven't forgotten about him either," Nan said. "But everything that happened this morning with your mother is simply the overture to what all of London will say once Montrose spills my secret."

"Not necessarily," Dean said, his smile brightening. "I rather think they will all react the way I have."

Nan arched one eyebrow. "And what way is that?" she asked.

Dean scooted closer to her. "They will understand the lengths to which you have gone to grasp the life you wished for yourself," he said, holding her hands tighter. "They will admire your inventiveness and the clever way you have convinced everyone of your ruse. They will see it as proof that you are a consummate professional and simply the greatest actress to ever grace a stage with her presence."

Nan felt her face heat as she glanced away from Dean, smiling. "You are too kind and much, much too generous. People don't like to be fooled. It makes them feel stupid, as though they are being laughed at."

Dean grew suddenly serious. "I have been laughed at my entire life," he said. "For being clumsy, for failing to appreciate the things that my peers find interesting, for wishing to spend my time with imaginative sorts that society does not approve of. I have learned to ignore the clamor of a society that wishes to dictate every last thought and deed depending on class and birth in order to reach for the things that I truly want."

Nan's heart felt as though it might grow too big for her chest. She didn't think Dean realized it, but those were precisely her feelings on life as well. She wanted something different than what she'd been born into as well. No wonder she'd felt such an instant connection with him. It convinced her to fight for him, even though all the world seemed to be against them.

The emotion was so powerful within her that she couldn't express her agreement with him in words. Instead, she surged into him, throwing her arms over his shoulders and bringing her mouth to his in a kiss that spoke more than words ever could.

It was an impulsive, sentimental action, but Dean responded as though it had been his intention to kiss her all along. He moaned deep in his throat, sliding his arms around her waist and pulling her closer. Nan answered his moan with one of her own, shifting her legs so that she could straddle his thighs and lean closer to him. His mouth was heavenly on hers, and she opened to him without question, letting him draw her tongue into his mouth. She liked the way he invited her to take a more aggressive role in their kiss, as if he was not afraid of her desire or her eagerness to express it.

And she did feel desire for him. So much of it. It was madness that women were taught to suppress their desire, as though it were something shocking and shameful. Quite the contrary, desire was a wonderful thing. It prompted her to kiss Dean harder, to learn the shape of his lips and mouth with her own, and to run her hands along the buttons of his jacket before unbuttoning them so that she could bring his heat closer to her own.

"Darling," Dean murmured, his eyes glazed with wanton fire.

"Yes," she answered the question he hadn't asked. Consequences be damned, she wanted Dean. She wanted this lively, unusual, heroic man to be hers, now and for always.

His job was easier than hers. She was already in her nightgown, and when she'd moved to straddle him, the thin fabric had bunched around her waist. All he had to do was burrow his hands under it to slide them up her sides to her breasts. Nan sucked in a breath, her fingers faltering as they worked through the buttons of his shirt and pushed his jacket from his shoulders. She mewled and quivered as he rubbed his fingertips over her nipples to coax them into stiffness, then sighed into him as he cupped her breasts and squeezed.

"Yes," she repeated as she leaned into him to steal another kiss. "Yes, yes, yes." She kissed him deeper with each word, tugging the hem of his shirt out of his trousers with the last one.

Dean growled and pinched her nipples lightly. "Absolutely."

They were less than a minute in, and Nan knew that Dean was likely the most skilled lover she'd ever been with. How else could he have her throbbing with need so swiftly? She hummed her approval as he slanted his mouth firmly over hers and pushed her to her back. The fire took hold of her quickly, and she scrambled to push his suspenders down over his arms before working the buttons of his trousers loose.

The whole time, Dean hiked her nightgown higher and higher, until he'd exposed her stomach and breasts. She had only just pushed his trousers down his hips and freed his erection when he moved down her body, out of the reach of her hands, to rain kisses across her breasts. There was nothing she could do but sigh and arch her back and drink in the glorious sensations he drew out of her.

He focused on one breast, dragging his tongue over her sensitive nipple, then blowing on it. Nan shivered as the pleasure of it shot straight to her core. She had to stifle a cry when he closed his mouth over her nipple and sucked. It was as though there were a direct conduit from her breast to her sex. She squirmed with desire, spreading her legs wider for him.

He took up the invitation enthusiastically, skating a hand up her thigh to touch the wetness that had flooded her. He groaned at that sensation, playing his fingers over the hot flesh of her sex before plunging two inside of her. It was impossible for Nan to swallow the cry that wanted to escape from her at that blessed invasion. She arched into his mouth, which had switched to her other breast, and pushed into his hand, letting him know she wanted all of it.

He made everything even better and brighter, if that was possible, by drawing his fingers out of her and using her wetness to slide his touch around her clitoris. Nan was well aware of the magical properties of that part of her, but with

Dean touching her, the sensation was that much more glorious. She gave into it, forgetting to swallow her cries as her body coiled tightly, ready to explode.

He took his hand away before she did, though, leaving her panting and thrashing against her bedcovers. He moved to kiss the pout from her lips that had formed over being denied, laughing as he did.

"You are a wild minx, Mlle. D'Argent," he said, imitating her French accent.

"Fuck me," she panted.

Dean laughed, a look of shock and amusement lighting his face. "Where did you learn that sort of language, minx?"

He didn't wait for her answer. Instead, he kissed her again, then shifted so that he could kiss and lick her stomach. Nan couldn't decide if she wanted to laugh or moan or complain as he dipped lower and lower, teasing her navel, then stealing her breath entirely as he grew closer and closer to her sex.

She gripped the bedcovers and nearly wept with pleasure as he made his way between her legs. He held her thighs firmly apart so that she couldn't move them, then brought his tongue to her entrance. The combination of pleasure and restraint was devastating, and she could barely catch her breath as he thrust his tongue into her over and over.

The sounds she made turned frantic as her body flew back to the edge where he'd left her before. "Please, please," she gasped, trying to wriggle, even though he held her still.

"I *am* fucking you, darling," Dean said, his voice rough with passion. "You failed to specify which part of me you wanted inside of you."

He was the most infuriating man she'd ever known.

"Cock, you fool. I want your cock." She couldn't help but laugh at the ferocity of her demand and the ridiculousness of it. Particularly as their conversation had left her teetering near the brink without finding satisfaction again.

"One thing first," he said, as though they were on a shopping excursion and he needed to visit one final shop before heading home.

He returned to her sex, drawing his tongue up over her sensitive flesh until he reached her clitoris. Nan thought she might die or come out of her skin as he circled and licked it, teasing and sucking now and then, and generally driving her wild with need.

He didn't stop, thank God. He pleasured her until the coil that had tightened in her core shattered into wild, pulsing throbbing. It was absolutely the best orgasm she'd ever had, and she moaned recklessly at how wonderful it felt. It just kept going and going as well as Dean encouraged it. Nan felt as though she was in serious danger of leaving her body. But that would have been a shame, seeing as her body felt so wonderful.

Dean was breathing heavily, his shirt damp with sweat, as he finally pulled away from her and repositioned himself above her. His trousers were down around his thighs, and he didn't hesitate even slightly as he pushed inside of her. Nan shuddered as her orgasm throbbed again at his invasion. He was large and hot, and he knew just how to thrust in her to draw her pleasure out. She wanted all of him, so she pulled her legs up to allow him to drive deeper, and so that she could dig her fingertips into his arse, encouraging him.

He liked what she was doing, as evidenced by the way he pounded into her.

"Yes, oh, God, yes," she gasped, encouraging his enthusiasm.

The bed creaked with his movements, and she couldn't control the sounds that she made in rhythm with his thrusts. The whole thing flew quickly to a head, and Dean cried out as he spilled inside of her. Every muscle of his body tensed and then relaxed against her, and she wrapped her arms and legs around him, thanking him, praising him, and giving herself to him fully. It was probably a terrible thing that he hadn't pulled out to complete, but then again, if his mother or her father needed a reason to grudgingly approve of the match—

Her thoughts were cut abruptly short in the very worst way as her bedroom door flew open, banging against the wall so hard that Dean jolted, even though his energy had just left him. As if her thoughts had summoned him, Nan's father stood in the doorway, glowering as though the Kaiser had sent in troops and it was his sole duty to defend his family.

"How dare you, sir?" he bellowed.

Nan hid her face against Dean's shoulder. She truly had never been so embarrassed in her entire life.

Dean scrambled back as fast as he could while panting, sweaty, and in a state of partial undress. He was gentleman enough to shield Nan's body from her father and to help her cover herself and slip under a blanket before anything else. Once he was satisfied that she was covered, he tugged his trousers up and held them closed with one hand as he stumbled off the bed, nearly falling over his own feet, and stood, facing Nan's father.

"I can explain, sir," he said, his eyes wide and round, without a single explanation in them.

"Ohh," Nan's mother squealed from the hallway. "That's Mr. Rathborne-Paxton. That's her fiancé."

"I don't care if he's the bloody King of Spain," her father boomed. "Get out of my house this instant, you cur. I should fetch my rifle."

Nan scrambled out of bed, standing by Dean's side and reaching for his hand. "He truly is my fiancé, Papa," she said. "And I'm sorry, I—"

"Get out of my house at once," her father continued to shout.

Crying sounded from somewhere down the hall, and

Nan's mother scolded, "Richard, you've woken the young ones. What will they see if they come out?"

"They'll see nothing," Nan's father shouted. "Because this louse will be out of the house or dead or both by the time they crawl out of the bed."

"If he's going, then I'm going with him," Nan said, deciding in the moment. "You throw Dean out and you throw me out as well."

Her father turned furious and hurt eyes on her. "Then so be it," he grumbled.

"Richard, you don't mean that," Nan's mother gasped. She turned to Nan and said, "He doesn't mean it."

Nan was certain her father would regret his rash order in the morning, but in the moment, not only was he serious, but Nan would have done anything to get away from the embarrassment of being caught by him.

"We will be gone in five minutes," she said, whipping around to fetch her traveling bag from beside her wardrobe.

"Good," her father said. He nodded, then stormed back into the hallway.

"He doesn't mean it," Nan's mother said, her face wide with panic.

"I know, Mama," Nan said, throwing a robe over her shoulders, "but I need to go anyhow. I'm too embarrassed to stay."

Her mother looked like she might cry, but she nodded instead and dashed down the hall after Nan's father.

Dean rushed to close the door, then returned to Nan.

"Are you certain this is what you want?" he asked, fastening his trousers and tucking his shirt in. "I...I could attempt to reason with your father, if you'd prefer."

Nan shook her head. "I can't stay here anymore. Not after that." She sent him a red-faced, shame-filled look. "I regret nothing," she insisted, "but one does not recover quickly from having one's father walk in on them while—"

"Say no more," Dean said, his eyes wide with empathy. He finished straightening his clothes and started to help Nan pack. "We can go to Aunt Josephine's house. There are plenty of rooms for us there."

Nan froze, snapping to face him. She said nothing, though. If her parents were angry with her for what she'd done, she couldn't imagine how furious Dean's mother and aunt would be. The alternative was to travel all the way back to Shrewsbury to find a hotel, or to ask for a room at the pub right there in Sutton. She did not feel up to either at the moment, especially not as she would probably be recognized.

"To Dorrington Hall, then," she said with a sigh.

She just hoped that whatever they found there was not as much of a disaster as what had just happened.

Chapter Thirteen

I t had been worth it. Even with the mortification of being caught in the throes of passion—or at least the afterglow of the throes of passion—by Nan's father, it had been worth the risk of climbing up to Nan's bedroom and possibly being rejected to taste the sweet wonder of the bliss they'd shared. Perhaps it was trite of him, but now that he'd held Nan in his arms, kissed her, possessed her, and felt her body's shudder as she'd come for him, there was no possible way their drama would end with anything other than the two of them becoming man and wife and living a long and happy life together.

"Mother will come around to see you as the wonderful woman you are," Dean whispered to Nan as the two of them crept up the stairs of Dorrington Hall to his guestroom.

It was the dead of night, his mother and aunt had long since gone to bed in a different part of the house, and even the servants had retired from their endless, daily labors by the time they'd returned to the estate. The hall boy had let them in, and they'd made their way upstairs with only the light of a single candle to guide them. Dean found it all rather poetic. Even if all he had was a tiny light of hope to lead him, he would help Nan defeat Montrose and find her place in society.

Nan seemed to be able to sense his thoughts. "You are a great deal too cheerful for a man who has just been chased out of a crofter's house in the middle of the night under ignominious circumstances," she murmured as Dean opened the door to his room in his aunt's house.

Dean chuckled as he drew her into the room, putting Nan's traveling bag down and lighting a lamp with his candle. "I am not nearly happy enough for a man who has everything he wants right here in his grasp," he answered.

As soon as he lit the lantern, he blew out the candle and discarded it, then stepped over to Nan and drew her into his arms for the sort of kiss he should have given her, if they'd been left alone to enjoy the aftermath of their lovemaking.

Nan laughed and pushed away from him playfully. "You are daft, Dean Rathborne-Paxton."

"Madam, you wound me," Dean said with a dramatic sigh.

Nan laughed harder. Dean would never tire of the sound, even though she shook her head.

A moment later, her expression pinched. "You think too highly of me," she said, lowering her eyes. "You've built me up in your mind to be someone and something I am not."

"Nonsense," Dean said. He slid a hand under her chin and lifted it so she would look at him. "You are a strong, talented, and beautiful woman. I have admired you from afar for a long time, and now I am privileged enough to love you up close."

Nan sighed and lowered her head again. "Have I not proven to you that I am much less than everyone assumes me to be?"

Dean's heart hurt for her. Optimism had always come easily to him, but he could see that wasn't the case with Nan. She had every reason to be anxious, he knew. Her life as it was now constituted a monumental gamble. Montrose was on the verge of calling her bluff. Dean wasn't fool enough to believe there wouldn't be consequences if Montrose followed through on his threats.

"The woman I have fallen in love with is not the glittering French actress," Dean said in a soft voice.

Nan snapped up to meet his eyes, sucking in a breath. "You love me?" she asked quietly.

"I do," Dean confessed. "I love the witty, determined woman in my arms. The woman who had the power and determination to make more of herself than anyone could have expected of her. I do not care if that woman speaks with a French accent or a Shropshire one. She is wonderful."

"Oh, Dean." Nan let out a heavy breath and threw herself at him, wrapping her arms around him and leaning her cheek against his shoulder. Her body felt heavy with exhaustion against his, and Dean supposed it was not only the exhaustion of the evening, but that of the last several years of Nan's life.

"Come on, love." He inched away from her, steering her toward the bed. "We need to sleep. It's been an eventful night, and chances are it will be twice as eventful when Mother discovers that you've spent the night under the same roof as her."

Dean was absolutely correct in his assumption that his mother would have something to say about Nan's presence at Dorrington Hall.

"Is she here to entertain us with a song and a dance?" his mother asked, eyes wide and back rigid with affront after Dean escorted Nan into his aunt's morning parlor late the next morning.

Dean pressed his lips together for a moment and fought to maintain his composure—and to remind himself that he loved his mother, she was a good and fair woman, and her reaction was merely a product of her class. And perhaps too much time spent under Lord Vegas's thumb.

"No, Mother," he said. "My fiancée has had a bit of a spat with her parents. I thought it would be better for her to reside here for the time being. And this way, the two of you can come to know each other better before the wedding."

Aunt Josephine, who sat by his mother's side on the sofa, made a sound of dread and swayed a bit as if swooning. Dean sent her a flat look. Who was the more dramatic actress now?

"I do not wish to know this woman," his mother said, less dramatic, but more imperious. "And you will not be marrying her."

"I *will* be marrying her, Mother, and you would like Nan very much, if you would only sit and talk with her for a while," Dean said. "The two of you have quite a bit in common."

His mother looked affronted. Nan appeared doubtful. Dean wondered why women could not just see sense and accept the decisions that the men around them made.

"You are very kind to show me hospitality, Lady Vegas, Lady Dorrington," Nan said with perfect grace, including Aunt Josephine as well. "I will be forever in your debt."

"You most certainly will not, child," Dean's mother said. She made a disgruntled sound, shifted slightly as she sat, and stiffened her back with an entirely different emotion as she frowned at Dean. "If it is marriage you wish, you should have told me. I have friends in London with daughters who are far more eligible than this...this actress." Before Dean could argue, his mother went on with, "At least, I once had friends in London. Heaven only knows what those women think of me now. Perhaps they think I am the sort of woman who would have an actress as a daughter-in-law." She let out a small sob and sank in on herself.

Dean was left with his mouth hanging open, no idea what

to say or do. His instinct pulled him in two directions. He was desperate to defend Nan as the woman he loved, but his heart also bled for his mother and the horrible situation Lord Vegas had put her in. It seemed he would not be able to make everyone happy.

"Suitability is not something one should build a marriage on," he said, his feelings getting the better of him. "Father was a suitable match, and look how that turned out."

He gestured to his mother, who snapped straight, glaring at him with hurt and offense.

Dean backtracked, shrugging. "Alice is in no way suitable as Sam's former mistress, but the two of them are blissfully happy now, as I plan to be with Nan. And we've yet to see what sort of inappropriate brides Francis and Joseph come up with to complete the scheme."

A tense sort of silence fell over the room. All three women stared at Dean.

"Whatever do you mean by that?" Aunt Josephine asked.

Dean instantly felt as though he'd dug himself into a hole, and there was no way out but to confess all.

"It is part of Francis's plan to thwart Montrose and the threats he has made to destroy our family," he said, speaking quickly to get it over with. "Montrose cannot ruin something that is already ruined. He already has all the family's money, it is true. That is why Francis devised a plan for the four of us to marry brides who are as wealthy as they are reprehensible to society."

"I beg your pardon?" Nan turned to stare at him incredulously. "*Reprehensible*? I thought I was merely unusual."

Dean's face heated, but he was in too deep to stop now.

"Sam married his mistress, and as you know, that caused quite a stir in the gossip columns. I...well, I have adored Nan from afar for quite some time, but you must admit, it is beyond the pale for the son of a marquess to marry a French actress." He winced as he felt three sets of indignant glares focus on him. Which was why he rushed on with, "Joseph has a particularly garish American cattle baron's daughter sniffing after him, so that might come to pass. I do not know who Francis has in mind. Perhaps that lovely Indian princess we saw in Hyde Park. You know how he is always discreet about everything. But you can be certain she will be both as rich as Croesus and as shameful as...."

He let his sentence fade off as he glanced from his mother's furious look to his aunt's indignation to Nan's resentment.

"So, you engaged yourself to me because I was the most shameful option available?" Nan asked, her voice hoarse with emotion.

"No, darling, of course not." It was a bit of a lie, but Dean wanted it to be the truth. "I engaged myself to you because I adore you. You know that."

"And because of the fortune I have made as a result of my career," Nan added, crossing her arms.

Dean rubbed the back of his neck. "Yes, well, that too. But you knew—"

"A career that is shameful," Nan continued, driving her point home without mercy. "And that could be in very real danger of exploding in my face, thanks to Montrose."

There was nothing Dean could do but say, "Yes?" making the single word sound as uncertain as possible.

Nan *humphed*, then uncrossed her arms. She turned to Dean's mother. "My lady, I am very sorry to have importuned you. I believe it is time for me to return to London." She glanced to Dean. "Immediately."

With a final nod to Aunt Josephine, Nan turned and marched out of the room, her head held high.

Dean shoved a hand through his hair as he watched her, then turned to his mother. He glanced back at the empty doorway once more before returning his focus to his mother.

"It seems as though leaving London was not the wisest decision I could have made," his mother said. "While I am livid with your father and wished to cool the hatred I feel for the man and his many, many betrayals, it appears as though I have made a mistake in leaving you boys alone."

"We are doing as well as could be expected under the circumstances," Dean said, wondering if that were true. He glanced to the parlor doorway again. "I need to go after her."

"You need to listen to your mother and do as she says," his mother said, raising her voice.

Dean glanced to her. "Perhaps, Mama," he sighed. "But I am a grown man now, and my primary concern at the moment is my fiancée."

He nodded to Aunt Josephine, then pushed himself into motion, leaving the room.

"Dean," his mother called after him. "Come back here this instant. I am not done scolding you."

A brief smile crossed Dean's lips as he strode on, catching up to Nan on the stairs. It was truly wonderful to see his mother alive and strong again. If not for Nan, he would have reveled in the way she had rediscovered her backbone. He would have let her order him around and everything, just to glory in the freedom she had found separated from Lord Vegas.

"Do not say anything to me," Nan stopped him from speaking once they were at the top of the stairs. "I am returning to London, and I will not hear any argument to the contrary."

"I was not going to argue, darling," Dean said, laying his subservience to her on thick. "I am merely going to come with you and see that you are delivered safely to your flat."

Nan eyed him sideways as they neared his guestroom. He

schooled his face into a perfect, comical mask of obedience and contrition, rather like a puppy.

Nan's mouth twitched as if she wanted to smile. Instead, she blew out a breath and shook her head. "You do beat all," she sighed as she pushed open the door to his room.

They packed up their things and headed for the train station in Shrewsbury. Neither had much to say, both because Nan appeared to need the time to gather her thoughts, and because they had yet to make it past the exhaustion of the trip. Dean was grateful when they took their seats in the first-class compartment Nan paid for, and when the train pulled out of the station and made its way to the picturesque countryside.

"I am exceedingly vexed with you," Nan said at last, once they'd left Shropshire and the turmoil they'd found there behind.

"As well you should be," Dean said with a nod. "But that does not alter the circumstances we find ourselves in now."

He knew she wanted to take charge of the conversation and the situation, but he wasn't about to have that.

"I am sorry that you are offended by the bald truth of my reasons for marrying you, and my brothers' reasons for choosing their brides, but I was honest with you from the start," he began.

Nan's mouth had been open and ready for some sort of retort, but she closed it and sank back against her seat, crossing her arms and frowning at him. "You humiliated me in front of your mother."

"Darling," he said, attempting a roguish grin, "I humiliate *myself* in front of my mother—and the rest of London—on a regular basis."

Nan's face pulled as if she were trying to hide a smile again. She looked away from him and out the window as if to marshal the strength to remain angry.

Dean went on. "It may seem like a bitter pill to swallow

now, but I promise you that we will build a wonderful, happy life together. I will stand by your side through thick and thin. I do not even mind if I stand in the wings of your grand performance, as long as I am the one who holds you close at night, once the curtain has closed and all of those stage door Johnnies, as you called them, have gone away empty-handed."

Nan glanced back to him, still fighting the tender emotions Dean caught flittering through her eyes.

"No matter what happens, I will be your rock and your champion," Dean went on. "When the truth comes out, I will shield you from the worst of the blows. I will build a new life for you with my own two hands, if that is what it takes. Fame and fortune or no, you will be the happiest woman on this earth for the rest of your days."

He smiled at the end of his speech, impressed with himself. If Cristofori ever needed someone to help him write his plays, Dean fancied himself up for the job.

Better still, Nan stopped trying to hide her smile or her affection for him.

"I do not know if you will make me the happiest woman on the earth," she said, her arms still crossed in front of her, though her posture held more sass now than anger, "but I will certainly be the most entertained."

Dean smiled broadly. "That is all I could wish for, my darling."

They grinned at each other in silence, enjoying each other's company. Dean was loath to break that warm feeling, but it was necessary.

"Montrose will not let up simply because we have found happiness in each other," he said. "In fact, I would wager that he will increase his attacks."

Nan's smile dropped. "I know," she said quietly.

"Therefore," Dean went on, "I think it will be necessary for you to employ the same tactic that my brothers and I are using as we marry women whom...whom society might take some getting used to."

Nan arched an eyebrow at him. "And what tactic is that?"

He knew his suggestion would be met with resistance, but he made it anyhow. "You need to come clean about who you really are. First. Before Montrose blabs to all of London."

"No." Nan shook her head vehemently. "I cannot do that."

Dean scooted forward, resting his hand on Nan's knee as she sat on the seat opposite him. "Darling, I think you must. You must be the one to control this information. If you reveal yourself as who you are, there is a chance the public could be charmed. They might see it as another role you have played. You could even make up a charming reason why you have done it."

He paused, watching Nan's face intently as she turned away from him and stared out the window.

"If you allow Montrose to break the news, he will turn it into something deceptive and seedy. Your reputation may never recover. This is why you need to do it."

He could tell from the way Nan's face pinched that she knew he was right. He might have been a fool most of the time, but he was not stupid. In fact, if he did say so himself, it took a man of exceptional intelligence to play the fool without coming off as foolish.

He let Nan sit and stew for a while before prompting her with, "Nan?"

Nan squeezed her eyes shut, then opened them and puffed out a breath. "I do see the necessity of revealing all," she said quietly. She dragged her eyes to meet his, hopelessness and anxiety radiating from her. "I have worked so very hard to achieve what I have. It may not mean much to others, but my success means a great deal to me."

"I know, darling, I know," Dean gestured for her to come sit on the seat with him.

Nan did, pulling her body reluctantly from its position and leaning heavily against Dean once she was on the seat with him. He put his arm around her and held her close, but he could still feel the tension and reluctance in her body. She was fighting an internal war, and in truth, he couldn't blame her. She truly had accomplished a miracle, and it was blisteringly unfair for her to be forced to give that up.

"Allow me to try one last thing," she said, glancing up at him. Her gaze was sad and trusting and full of inspiration all at once. "I have one last idea that might mean Montrose loses his power over me. Please, let me try that one last thing."

"Of course, darling." Dean dipped down to kiss her forehead. "If you think it might spare you giving up Mlle. D'Argent, then give it a try." He smiled, his heart full of pride in her.

"*Merci, monsieur*," Nan said in her French accent. "You are too kind."

Dean laughed and held her tighter. Whether Nan was able to remain Nanette D'Argent or not, whether her career vanished once the truth came to light or she was able to remain on the stage, Dean was certain that there would never be a dull moment in their lives together. He was happy that they would have a life together.

Chapter Fourteen

Revealing the truth was the very last thing Nan wanted to do. Even though, deep down, she knew that Dean was right. The only thing Montrose had to use against her to extort the money he needed was the truth of her identity. Just one thing, but it was a large and looming thing. Logic and reason said that, if he could no longer hold the threat of discovery over her, he would abandon his war against her to search after an easier target.

But revealing all risked destroying Nan's entire life as she knew it.

"I do hope this plan of yours works, darling," Dean murmured as he leaned close to her ear while escorting her onto the bare stage at the Concord Theater.

Rehearsals for *The Marshall* were in full swing, even though the show would not open for another ten days and the sets had yet to be fully constructed. The entire cast was there for a full rehearsal, though, and the majority of the stage crew was there, building or painting set pieces. Even Niall Cristofori was there, and he had brought his paramour, Lord Selby, with him.

Nan took a deep breath in the remaining moment before all of her friends, her theatrical family, noticed that she'd returned. She pressed a hand to her stomach. In a very real way, the plan she'd developed to save herself from public discovery was far more terrifying than anything Montrose could do to her.

"This has to work," Nan whispered—in answer to Dean, but mostly for herself. "I cannot watch everything I've built for the last five years fall to pieces around me."

Lily Logan happened to be carrying a load of paint across the stage at that moment, and she glanced up and spotted Nan. Her broad smile alerted some of the other stagehands to Nan's presence, and that brought the attention of everyone on the stage to her.

"Nanette, you're back," Everett called out from the far end of the stage, where he was standing with Martin Piper and Mr. Abrams.

There was no getting out of it now. It was this last-ditch plan or the equivalent of a public execution for Nanette D'Argent.

"I'm right here with you," Dean murmured as he let go of Nan's hand and nudged her forward.

Nan turned to give him one last, desperate smile before squaring her shoulders, taking a deep breath, and walking into what felt a bit too much like the unknown.

"*Oui,*" she announced, throwing her arms wide and pretending to be the bold, confident, French actress that she'd built her life on for the past five years. "I have returned. I missed zees place so very much, and I missed all of you even more."

"You were gone for less than a week," Everett teased her as he crossed the stage to embrace her. Once he had her firmly in his arms, he whispered, "And how is Shropshire?"

"It was lovely," Nan said, beaming and pretending he'd

asked her how Paris was faring these days. "I had quite zee relaxing journey 'ome."

"I thought you went home because there was some sort of family trouble," one of the stagehands standing near her said, scratching his head in confusion.

Nan's heart shuddered in her chest. There it was. That was the signal that the orchestra was warming up and her drama was about to unfold. The people closest to her were already asking questions, and her story no longer fit together.

"Ah, yes," she said, keeping her accent, but deliberately using the word "yes" instead of "*oui*". "Zat is something I wish to speak to you all about."

She headed toward the front of the stage, where Cristofori and Lord Selby stood. There was no better place to address her friends. She felt as conspicuous as though she were hitting her mark while completely undressed, though, and as soon as she stood near Cristofori and Lord Selby, she turned back and focused on Dean.

Dean gave her just the sort of encouraging smile she needed. She could do this. She could come clean to her friends in order to save herself from being forced to admit the truth to all of London. This would work.

She cleared her throat and pressed her hands to her stomach. "As some of you may know, I have come under threat lately from zee man known as Montrose."

Most of the assembly of cast and crew that had gathered to listen to her returned her statement with looks of sympathy, and some with anger on her behalf.

"We won't let the bastard touch you," Lily called out, sounding like a ferocious lion.

Several of the others made sounds of agreement.

"I thank you so much for your kindness." Nan touched a hand to her chest over her racing heart. "Zee fact of zee matter is, Montrose has demanded money from me. Quite a bit of money. He has determined zat he and he alone is responsible for my rise to fame and fortune. He is taking all zee credit for my accomplishments, and he demands zat I compensate him accordingly."

Several growls of outrage and sounds of disapproval rang through the assembly.

"That's ridiculous," Mr. Abrams said, stepping forward. "Anyone who has worked with you knows that you've risen to fame on your own merits."

"Absolutely," Cristofori agreed. "I have cast you as the leading lady in my last few shows because of your talent, not because Montrose told me to."

Nan tried to breathe a sigh of relief. It was the reaction she'd hoped for. But there was still more to come.

"Zee problem is, Montrose believes he has zee perfect means to blackmail me into paying him," she went on. "He has threatened to expose a massive secret about me which will surely ruin me."

Everyone seemed to be holding their breath, waiting for her to go on.

"My last 'ope of saving myself, and of saving you all, my dear, dear friends, from becoming a target of zat man's wrath, is to prove zat Montrose was not, in any way, responsible for my career."

"Well, he wasn't," Everett said with a shrug. "We all know that."

There were more sounds of agreement from the cast and crew.

"I will need you all to swear by it," Nan said. "I will need each and every one of you to speak up for me and to assert zat Montrose had nothing at all to do with my success."

"Of course," Martin said. "We will always speak up for you, Nanette."

Everyone agreed, nodding and calling out words of encouragement.

Nan began to feel better, until the same young stagehand who had called her out for saying she was relaxed when a family emergency drew her away said, "Hang on. What secret has Montrose threatened to expose?"

"Is it as bad as all that?" one of the new chorus girls asked.

A strange sort of tension filled the air. Several of the cast and crew glanced around at each other, or at Dean, as if waiting for someone else to be the first one to ask the next question.

Nan also glanced to Dean. There was no getting around things now. It was time to come clean to the people who mattered the most to her. Dean's smile of encouragement gave her the strength to go on.

"Zee fact of zee matter is...."

She paused, pressing her hands to her stomach again. She lowered her eyes and took a deep breath. She couldn't look at the people she'd betrayed for so long as she made the confession.

She cleared her throat and started again without her accent. "The fact of the matter is, my name is not Nanette D'Argent. My name is Nan Silvers. I am not from Paris. I did not train with the Paris Ballet. I've only ever been to France once. I'm the daughter of a crofter in Shropshire, and I was born and raised in a small town near Shrewsbury."

Absolute silence followed. Nan couldn't draw in a breath. The tension was killing her. She waited for the shouts of derision and the harsh words. Someone would start hissing at her or ask her to leave the theater forever at any moment, she was certain.

But no, the silence went on. When she couldn't stand it any longer, she lifted her head slightly and peeked up at the cast and crew.

Most of them stared back at her with varying degrees of sympathy and compassion. Some were even smiling. Everett Jewel, damn him, had a hand over his mouth and was laughing.

Nan was at a complete loss. Shouldn't they be furious with her? The only thing that grounded her was the fact that Dean looked just as flummoxed as she felt.

Finally, when Nan felt as though she might crawl out of her skin, Cristofori took a step closer to her and said, "Nan, we know."

Nan blinked at him, not certain she'd heard him right. "I beg your pardon?"

Cristofori's mouth twitched, and light danced in his eyes. "We know. We've always known."

"Right from the start," Martin said as he stepped up to her other side.

Nan gaped at them both, then turned to Everett. "Did you tell them?" she demanded, barely able to squeeze the words out.

"No," Everett said, continuing to laugh. "I didn't have to tell them."

"We knew who you were before I hired you for that first show," Cristofori explained. "You'd performed in smaller shows in London and nearby. The world of the theater is a small one. I recognized you in an instant during that first audition."

Nan couldn't believe what she was hearing. She glanced around. Everyone was grinning at her now, but they were not unkind grins. She didn't know whether to laugh or to hide her face in embarrassment.

Dean started toward her from the other side of the stage, no longer content to let her make the confession on her own. He was the one who asked the question on her lips. "If you all knew from the start, why didn't you say something?"

Everett's laughter burst out, and he shook his head. "Nan was having too much fun. And she was dead right about the persona appealing to the public."

Cristofori shrugged. "Why interfere with something that was working well?"

"You knew?" The question popped out of Nan with more ferocity than she'd intended. "You knew and you didn't tell me that you knew?"

Everett wedged his way around Cristofori to hug Nan, even though she was rigid with shock in his arms. "Honestly, darling, we thought you knew we knew."

"You didn't know we knew?" Lydia, who played the comic secondary lead in most of Cristofori's shows, asked, blinking.

"I didn't know," Nan wailed.

She pushed back from Everett, losing her balance a bit. Dean caught her just as she burst into laughter. At last, she could see the humor of the situation. With that, a massive weight was lifted from her shoulders.

"You know. You all know," she said. She covered her mouth with both hands and glanced around at her smiling, supportive theater family. A moment later, she gasped. "This is wonderful. You all know my secret, so you can help me to thwart Montrose's plans to blackmail me."

"Of course, we can," Mr. Abrams said, beaming at her like she was his favorite daughter. "We will do whatever you need us to do to keep you out of Montrose's clutches."

Nan's joy at that statement was immediately cut short when the sharp voice of Montrose himself called from the back of the stage, "Then I shall be forced to bring down every one of you."

A gasp echoed across the stage, and the clustered chorus members stepped aside to reveal Montrose. Nan would have laughed at the perfect, theatrical timing of his entrance if it didn't represent something so horrific.

Montrose stepped slowly forward, his back stiff and his head held high. He was dressed impeccably, as usual, and still wore his coat and top hat. He held a shining, ebony cane with a silver claw on top as well. As he walked, he looked down at everyone. Some of the younger chorus members jumped out of his way, as though he would strike them with his cane.

Montrose marched all the way up to the cluster where Nan stood before Cristofori pulled himself to his full height and said, "You won't touch Nan. She's one of us, and we will defend her."

"Then you will be defending yourself as well," Montrose said with a shrug, as though he didn't care. "I have no qualms about bringing the rest of you, and this production of yours, to its knees along with Miss Silvers." His smile as he spoke was cold as ice.

"And what could you possibly do to us?" Everett said, inching forward and crossing his arms to glare at Montrose.

It wasn't so much the picture Everett made as the way Patrick strode forward from where he'd been watching off to the side to stand menacingly behind Everett. Patrick could have snapped Montrose in two without breaking a sweat.

Montrose laughed at the show of support as though he'd never seen anything funnier. "You ask what I could do to you?" He gaped at Everett, then at Niall and Martin and Mr. Abrams as though they were pitiful. "One word in the right ear, and I could have half of you arrested for gross indecency and sentenced to three years of hard labor." He focused on Cristofori. "Do you think theatergoers of London would deign to pay good money to see the work of a catamite?"

"Is that the best you can do?" Everett asked, apparently still borrowing courage and strength from his lover.

"Oh, far from it," Montrose said, sending Everett a sneer. "I could purchase the mortgage of this theater and call in your loan. I know the names of every actor and crewmember who works here," he went on, raising his voice and turning to the nervous assembly that now hung on his every word. "I know your landlords and your daytime employers. I could have every one of you evicted and sacked. You'd all be out on the streets."

A murmur went up from the chorus as Montrose turned back to Nan and Dean.

He made a face at Dean as though he smelled bad, then said, "I am already well on my way to ruining your family, so you are beneath my notice."

Rage flooded Nan, but strangely, Dean merely smiled back at Montrose. "We'll just see about that, shall we?"

Montrose's sneer turned into a narrow-eyed look of loathing. He ignored Dean, turning back to Cristofori.

"Are you really willing to risk your reputation and that of your key players for this bit of skirt? Are you willing to pay the price for defying me?" he asked.

"Frankly, yes," Cristofori said, crossing his arms and glaring right back at Montrose. "I think you should leave my theater. Patrick?"

For the barest of moments, Montrose's arrogant snarl faltered. It was the only ray of light in an otherwise dismal situation. Nan's insides churned with the knowledge that her last-ditch effort to save herself had resulted in the potential ruination of everyone she held dear.

"You have until the opening night of this show," Montrose said, turning to go as Patrick crowded in on him. "That is ten days until I expect the money I have asked of Miss Silvers be deposited into my account." He paused, even though Patrick stepped in closer, then said, "And I expect fifty-thousand pounds in my account from the coffers of this theater, Mr. Cristofori, or this new play of yours will be the biggest flop London has ever seen."

"Move along, you," Patrick growled, shoving Montrose at last. "No one here is interested."

Montrose let himself be shuffled along, but he sent Nan one last, victorious grin. He clearly thought he'd backed her into a corner that she couldn't get herself out of.

As soon as Montrose was gone, she let out a soft wail and collapsed against Dean. "What have I done?" she asked, tears springing to her eyes.

Dean comforted her with a hug, but it was Everett who said, "Nothing, duckie. You've done nothing at all."

He sounded far too nonplussed, considering what had just happened. Nan straightened in confusion and turned to him. Everett looked as carefree as ever. Strangely enough, Cristofori did as well.

"Montrose's threat has no teeth," Cristofori said.

"But...but he threatened to expose you," Dean said uncertainly.

Everett laughed. "Do you think most of London doesn't already know I take it up the backside on a regular basis?"

"Everett, be good," Patrick's deep voice scolded as the man walked back to join the discussion.

"Yes, darling," Everett said, batting his eyelashes at Patrick as though he had brought the moon back with him.

Nan didn't know whether to smack Everett for his carelessness or whether he had a point.

"All of England knows about me and Blake already as well," Cristofori said with equal nonchalance, turning to wink at Lord Selby. "That revelation will come as a surprise to no one, and it hasn't hurt us in the past."

"Well, not much," Lord Selby murmured.

Nan took note of the fact that Lord Selby didn't look as casual about the potential of exposure. Martin didn't seem as carefree about it either.

"Edward is still an MP," he mumbled, almost to himself. "He's been searching for an opportunity to step down so he can do less public work, but that opportunity has not presented itself yet."

"I can't lose my place at the boarding house," the young stagehand called out, looking panicked. "It took me ages to find that place to begin with."

A few of the others looked anxious as well.

"I didn't accept this part so it could ruin me," one of the chorus girls said. She took a step forward and addressed Cristofori. "I'm sorry Mr. Cristofori, but I quit."

As she turned to go, a few of the other chorus members turned away and walked off as well. So did the young stagehand. Nan's heart sank as she watched them go. Their numbers were not so great that it would interfere with the production—as much as she hated to admit it, chorus members were easy to find, and the ones who left would be replaced before the day was done—but the precedent was worrying. Montrose's threat might be a serious one after all.

"Stop worrying, darling," Dean told Nan, pulling her back into his arms. "You've an entire family here who will stand by you, come what may."

"He's right," Everett said, sliding into Patrick's arms the way Nan was held by Dean. "Who cares about that horrid old man anyhow?"

Nan cared. She cared very much. It was bad enough that she was in danger, but now the people she cared about were in trouble too.

"This isn't going to be solved right now," Cristofori said with a sigh. He clapped his hands together. "We're still in rehearsal. This show goes up in a fortnight, and despite what Montrose says, it's going to be our greatest triumph yet."

The remaining cast and crew cheered him, then rushed to take their places.

Nan let Dean lead her back toward her dressing room so

that she could fetch her script and join the rehearsal. She couldn't keep the wariness from her face, though.

"I cannot help but feel this could still end very badly," she confessed to Dean once they were alone.

"Perhaps it will," Dean said. "But it might not. You have so much support here at the theater, and you have my support as well."

Nan smiled up at him, letting him hug her. "So, you still wish to marry me?"

Dean laughed. "Of course I do. Wild horses couldn't keep me from it."

"What about your mother?" Nan asked.

Dean smiled and leaned down to kiss her. "Mother is all the way in Shropshire. What can she do to interfere with my impending nuptials from there?"

Nan tried not to wince at the question. Questions such as that had a way of answering themselves, and the last thing she needed with Montrose poised on the brink of destroying everything she loved was a woman who neither liked nor approved of her.

Chapter Fifteen

Dean was so proud of Nan that he could have burst. She had marched boldly out onto the stage and confessed her secret to the people who mattered the most to her, conscious that they could have rejected her.

Of course, Dean wasn't surprised that the theater crowd already knew everything about her. Not one bit. The entire reason that he spent so much of his time at the Concord Theater was because actors and the like were such a jolly, accepting bunch.

"Mother cannot do anything at the moment," he told Nan, kissing her lightly. That was the other thing he enjoyed about theatrical sorts. They did not so much as blink when he kissed his beloved in public. "Why don't you come over to our house and join us for supper tonight?" he suggested, holding Nan's hands and kissing her knuckles on each. "I know Francis and Joseph would love the company."

"And your father?" Nan arched one eyebrow.

Dean snorted. "Father has fallen into the habit of taking his meals at his club of late. Though how he can show his face there after everything is beyond me. Then again, much of the villainy that Montrose has uncovered and is dangling over Father's head has yet to be revealed to society, even though all of London knows *something* is amiss. Montrose has merely bankrupted us for now and continues to squeeze Father's balls with the threat of revealing the rest."

"What a colorful image that paints," Nan said with a smirk. She grew serious again before Dean could answer. "That seems to be the way Montrose operates, though. He parcels out just enough destruction up front, then uses the rest to turn the thumb-screws and keep you dangling until he's done with you."

Dean hummed. It seemed Nan truly was in the same boat as the Rathborne-Paxton family after all. Which made it all the more perfect for her to join the family through matrimony.

"Alright," she said with a smile. "I will join you all for supper tonight."

"I will count every moment until we meet again," Dean said, deliberately over-dramatic, as he kissed both of her hands once more. "Until then, my love, *adieu!*"

"*Au revoir, monsieur,*" Nan said, fully French again, as Dean pulled away from her.

Dean chuckled, his heart feeling light despite the turmoil that Montrose had caused earlier. Unlike Francis or Joseph, he was an optimist. Yes, the threats that Montrose posed to both his family and to Nan were dire and dangerous. But he was confident that they could overcome the threat and defeat the man. They were not engaged in the battle alone. They now had the entire complement of the Concord Theater on their side. Who could triumph against such an army?

His mood remained buoyant as he spent the rest of the day accomplishing errands before returning home. He paid a visit to the family solicitor to gauge the current situation of their finances—which were not good. He met up with Francis at their club—which they could barely afford anymore—and inquired after the progress furnishing the flat for Mother. Progress was being made there. Then he set out on his most delightful errand of all, arranging for a license so that he and Nan could marry as soon as possible.

He was bubbling with positive energy and excitement by the time he returned home. He had just enough time to dress for supper, then to await Nan. He was very much looking forward to having her across the table that night, and once the thought of having her there to dine with them every night took hold, he began to sort out in his mind where the two of them would live once they were married. They would have to stay at Rathborne House at first, but with Lord Vegas living there, it wouldn't be ideal. Nan's flat was lovely, but there was something uncomfortable about a gentleman moving to—

His rambling thoughts were cut short three steps into the front hallway of Rathborne House, just as he was handing his hat off to Flynn, when his mother's voice called out to him from the formal parlor, "Dean Emanuel Frederick Rathborne-Paxton, you will come into this room this instant and explain yourself!"

Dean felt as though he had walked straight into a brick wall while someone had simultaneously poured a bucket of ice-cold Thames water over his head. He sent Flynn a terrified look. Flynn returned it with a serious, wide-eyed look of doom. There was nothing Dean could do but slink his way into the parlor, as if he'd been caught causing mischief.

It was worse than he could have guessed. Not only were his mother and Aunt Josephine in the parlor, taking up an entire sofa and looking like avenging empresses as they did, Francis and Joseph were also there, standing like terrified attendants at either end of the sofa. The looks they sent Dean as he entered the room were a dead-giveaway that they were all in deep trouble.

On top of that, Lord Vegas was also in the room. And for

a change, the man looked nervous. He sat in his favorite chair, but rather than looking as though he were holding court from a throne, the chair almost dwarfed him. His face was pale, which made the lines of his age stand out all the more, and his usual stiff-backed posture was tense and brittle, as though he might snap at any moment.

"Explain yourself," his mother demanded as Dean inched his way into the room.

Dean glanced to Francis for help. He wasn't certain what his mother meant by her curt command. Francis's eyes shone with a moment of panic and warning, but Dean could not figure out what was meant by that either.

Dean cleared his throat. "Well, Mother, I have returned late because I've been out all day, running errands," he began.

"No, not that." His mother brushed away his words with an irritated look. "Explain your current state of engagement to that crofter's daughter."

"Oh. That." Dean cleared his throat again, shifting on his spot, as though he were a small boy again.

He peeked at his father, curious as to what the man thought of his wife's sudden show of strength. Lord Vegas looked utterly out of his depth, as though he felt he should take charge of the situation, but didn't know how.

Dean took in a breath and focused on his mother again. "I am not certain what there is to explain. Nan and I are engaged to be wed."

His mother made an impatient sound. "I will not have it," she said. She glanced to Francis. "This wicked plot of yours to marry out of spite will cease at once."

Lord Vegas leaned forward, frowning. "What plot is this?"

Dean suddenly understood the alarm in Francis's eyes. "Er, we are doing as you requested, Father," Francis said. "We have and are seeking brides of vast fortune to repair the family coffers."

Lord Vegas narrowed his eyes, but before he could reply, Lady Vegas said, "So this is your doing?"

Lord Vegas pulled back, almost as if he would disappear into his chair. A moment later, he shook his head and sat straight once more. "Montrose has attempted to ruin us. I simply asserted my authority as the boys' father to demand they use the tools at their disposal to remedy the situation."

"Oh, so *Montrose* is to blame?" Dean's mother asked, her voice rising in pitch and volume. "And I suppose *Montrose* is the one who wasted all of his money in gambling hells? *Montrose* was the one who squandered his fortune on opium and brandy?"

Dean's brow shot up. He hadn't realized his father was involved with *taking* opium, even though he'd heard rumors about him selling it. But then, he had suspected all along that Mother knew more about the situation than he and his brothers did.

His mother went on. "*Montrose* was the one who lured innocent young women to his bed with promises of redemption?"

Joseph winced at that one. Dean and Francis merely blinked.

"Muriel, hold your tongue," Lord Vegas hissed, turning bright red.

"I will no longer hold anything," Dean's mother shouted, pushing to her feet. She was several inches shorter than her sons, but in that moment, it felt as though she towered over them all. "And I will not stand by and watch my sons behave like their father and besmirch a name that has already been dragged through the mud."

Dean grimaced at that characterization. He hadn't stopped to think that it could be perceived that he and Francis and the others were just as bad as Lord Vegas.

It was at that moment, just as Dean was scrambling for

something he could say that would alleviate the situation—and noticing that Francis and Joseph seemed to be desperate to make things right with a few, choice words as well—that the front door rang. Dean squeezed his eyes shut. Of all the moments for Nan to arrive at the house for supper.

"Are we expecting guests?" Lord Vegas asked, glancing over his shoulder at the parlor door, almost hopeful. He must have thought someone was coming to his rescue.

Instead, Dean's mother said, "I have decided to take matters into my own hands." She turned to Dean. "As you seem so intent on marrying, I have chosen a suitable bride for you—one who has breeding and bearing. One who will increase your standing in society instead of diminishing it."

"Mother, I am already engaged," Dean said, though it came out sounding more like he was muttering. He shouldn't have invited Nan to supper. She was about to walk into a whirlpool.

"This is the first I am hearing of this," Lord Vegas said, standing as the sound of Flynn opening the door was heard. He glared at Dean as he did.

"I am Father."

That was as far as Dean got before Flynn escorted not Nan, but the prim and proper, tight-laced and sallow Lady Heloise Barrington into the room. It took all of Dean's effort not to groan aloud.

"Lady Heloise," his mother said, putting on a smile that was completely at odds with the mood in the room as she swept across to greet the young woman. "How very good of you to join us on such short notice."

"Mama informed me that I was required to attend," Lady Heloise said, glancing over her shoulder to a dour, older woman dressed in black.

"And we are happy to have you here," Dean's mother said. "You remember my sons, Lord Cathraiche and Joseph." She cupped Lady Heloise's elbow and drew her over to stand in front of Dean. "And, of course, Dean."

Dean squirmed as Lady Heloise scanned him from head to toe, then sniffed, as though she were inspecting a racehorse she intended to purchase. Come to think of it, the Barrington family raised horses. Lady Heloise knew how to examine a prize stud, apparently.

"Mmm, yes, Mr. Rathborne-Paxton," Lady Heloise said at last with a nod, as if she approved of the stock.

"I have arranged for the two of you to sit beside each other at supper this evening," Dean's mother went on with a smile. "So that you might become better acquainted."

Without smiling, Lady Heloise glanced from Dean to his mother and back. "Yes, that would be acceptable."

An awkward silence followed. Dean's mother stared hard at him, as if she expected him to carry the conversation. Dean was at an utter loss. He had no idea how to make idle conversation with a woman like Lady Heloise.

Francis came to his rescue. He stepped forward, cleared his throat, and said, "Lady Heloise, how is your father? I saw he has a horse competing at Royal Ascot this year?"

"He does, my lord," Lady Heloise said, nodding gravely, completely expressionless. "We have high hopes."

That was it. Dean could barely comprehend it. The woman had no personality, no facial expressions to speak of, and nothing of any interest to add to the conversation. Francis glanced to Dean with a small shrug, completely at a loss.

"How did your mother enjoy the continent?" Dean's mother asked, evidently not bothered by the blandness of Lady Heloise's personality—or the fact that the elder Lady Barrington was standing right there. It seemed Lady Heloise's mother had as little presence and personality as she did.

"It was lovely," Lady Heloise answered, glancing over her shoulder to her mother.

Lady Barrington nodded.

That was the end of the conversation.

Dean's mother moved back to where Aunt Josephine still sat on the sofa, looking as though she was disappointed that the confrontational mood of the parlor had been replaced by utter banality.

Before anyone could try a new topic, the front door rang again.

Again, Dean winced as Flynn went to answer it. Surely, this time it had to be Nan arriving. Her timing was even worse, now that Lady Heloise and her mother were here. All Dean could do was brace himself for the inevitable.

The inevitable came, but it was not at all what he had supposed it might be. The moment Flynn showed Nan into the parlor, Lady Heloise let out a loud, high-pitched squeal.

"Good heavens, it is you!" Lady Heloise cried out. Her expression blasted into pure joy and excitement, going from sallow to pink in an instant. Her eyes shone with sudden, hysterical tears, and she began to bob up and down as though propelled by some unseen set of pistons and steam. "Nanette D'Argent. It is you, right here in front of me. Nanette D'Argent. *Nanette D'Argent!*" She glanced around as though it made no sense that everyone else in the room was not equally as excited as she was.

Dean started to laugh, then forced himself to cover with a feigned cough. Francis turned away and raised a hand to his mouth. Both of Dean's parents looked utterly confused. Joseph merely gaped.

Nan sent a brief, teasing look to Dean before falling expertly into character. "You are too kind, *mademoiselle,*" she said, throwing her shoulders back and advancing toward Lady Heloise. "I take it you are a follower of zee theater?"

"I am, oh, I am!" Lady Heloise rushed toward Nan, a rapt expression on her face. When Nan took both of her hands in greeting and kissed her on each cheek in the French style, Lady Heloise swooned. Actually swooned. Dean thought he was going to have to leap out and catch her, but she recovered quickly enough to blurt, "I have attended every one of your shows, Mlle. D'Argent. You are the most magnificent thing to grace the London stage in many a year. Your voice is that of an angel, and your dancing is so light that it makes me think you could walk across water."

Dean exchanged a glance with Francis—who had marched to the side of the room to have his laugh, but had turned back to watch the comedy unfold. Dean had to look away almost as soon as their eyes met to keep himself from laughing as well.

"I saw you play Lady Macbeth three years ago," Lady Heloise went on, her color turning brighter and brighter as stars shone in her eyes.

Dean noted Lady Barrington roll her eyes and press her fingertips to her temples. It did nothing to quell his urge to roar with laughter.

"You were wonderful," Lady Heloise continued. "I could feel every bit of your anguish and emotion in every word. It was one of the most transformative experiences of my life. And the way you commanded the stage in *Love's Last Lesson*—"

Lady Heloise was prevented from gushing further as Lord Vegas cleared his throat loudly. "I have not been introduced to this woman," he said.

Dean took a half step toward Nan. "Father, this is Mlle. Nan—"

"How could you not know who this is, Lord Vegas?" Lady Heloise gasped, her eyes wide with offense. Her mother groaned and covered her face with her gloved hands. "This is Mlle. Nanette D'Argent. She is the most famous woman in all of London. She is the leading lady of productions staged by the Concord Theater. Her likeness can be seen all up and down Oxford Street." She turned back to Nan, still clutching one of her hands tightly, and said, "I have every soap and every biscuit you have ever endorsed. I have three of your trading cards. I gave my silver and garnet bracelet to Millicent Spode for the most recent one. It is a rare treasure, but I simply had to have it. I keep it on my pillow so that I might dream of you at night."

Dean's whole body flashed hot—not just with the effort it took him not to laugh uproariously at the admission, but because he'd kept Nan's card on his bedside table as well.

"Are you so very important?" Dean's mother asked Nan, her jaw tight and her expression still shining with disapproval as she did.

Nan pulled her hand out of Lady Heloise's grip with some difficulty, smiling indulgently at the woman, then took a step toward Dean's mother. "My lady, I am but a humble actress. 'Owever, I have secured several engagements to endorse products that have made me quite well known here in London. Surely, you have encountered zees products at your shops, *non*?"

Dean's mother narrowed her eyes as though grudgingly admitting that Nan was more than she'd supposed she was. "I do not care for common, commercial things," she said in a flat voice.

"Oh, but you should, Lady Vegas," Lady Heloise said, still breathless with wonder as she stared at Nan. "Mlle. Nanette D'Argent only lends her image to the finest soaps and the most delicious confections. Why, I believe her visage makes everything taste and smell better than it would otherwise." She paused and pulled her adoring glance away from Nan long enough to ask, "May I be seated next to Mlle. Nanette D'Argent instead of Mr. Dean Rathborne-Paxton at supper?"

A snort sounded from Francis's corner of the room. Dean frowned at his brother—who was bright pink and hiding his mouth behind his hand. Even Joseph was having a devil of a time keeping a straight face. There was nothing Dean could do but go along with it all.

"My lady, I would gladly give up my place so that you could be seated next to this shining star," he said with a bow. He then glanced at his mother as though he had won a point in a tennis match.

His mother frowned back, put out, but also curious. That was enough to give Dean hope.

"Dinner is served, my lord," Flynn announced from the doorway.

"Thank God," Francis muttered, stepping forward.

"You will all follow me," Lord Vegas said, rushing to lead the procession out of the parlor. It should have been Francis's right, since Lord Vegas had transferred ownership of the house to Francis six months before, but Lord Vegas still fancied himself lord of the manor.

"Can I walk in with you?" Lady Heloise asked Nan, breathless enough that Dean feared she might pass out before they reached the dining room.

"But of course," Nan answered, her smile dazzling.

Lady Vegas sighed and offered her hand to Aunt Josephine —who looked as though she were enjoying the whole display immensely—to help her to rise. She leaned close and murmured something in Aunt Josephine's ear. Aunt Josephine whispered back. The two sisters shared a look as though they were plotting something further.

Dean felt the sudden urge to nip whatever that was in the bud.

"May I just have a quick word with Mlle. D'Argent?" he asked, stepping over to touch Nan's arm and draw her away from Lady Heloise—who was practically drooling as she gazed at Nan.

"Of course, you may, *monsieur*," Nan answered.

Her assent prevented anyone else from denying the two of them a moment alone. Dean shooed the rest of them out of the parlor. Lady Heloise loitered by the doorway, gazing at Nan in ecstasy. Even when Francis took her arm and tugged, she craned her neck and continued to look for as long as she could before being pulled away.

Nan snorted into a laugh as soon as the two of them were alone. "Who is that woman and what is she doing here?" she whispered.

Dean took the risk of stepping into Nan and sweeping her into his arms. "She is a silly girl with good breeding whom my mother believes is a more suitable bride for me than you are," he said.

Nan's smile grew sharp. "Ah, yes. I remember. You and your brothers and your unsuitable bride plot."

"It is terribly unsuitable and unfashionable for a man to marry a woman he actually likes and desires," Dean said with feigned imperiousness.

Nan laughed and let him embrace her further. Dean shot a glance to the doorway, and when he was certain they weren't being watched, he kissed Nan quickly.

"I have an idea," he said when he leaned back. There wasn't time for them to be leisurely about it, so he rushed on. "I saw a chink in Mother's armor just now. She is intrigued by the way Lady Heloise reacted to you."

"Oh?" Nan asked. "Do you think so?"

"I am almost certain of it," Dean said. "Which means that the key to gaining Mother's approval for this match is simply to let her see how loved and adored you are."

"And how do you propose to do that?" Nan grinned wickedly. "Are you planning to trade jewels for my latest trading card to give it to her?"

Dean laughed loudly. "No, and I would not give up my card for any jewels."

Nan's brow shot up, but rather than ask about the card, she went on with, "What do you propose we do, then?"

"Mother merely needs to get to know you better. I believe throwing the two of you together, perhaps for lunch in a day or two, once she's recovered from the initial blow of Lady Heloise being more interested in you than me."

Nan giggled. "She would not be the first woman to be so enamored."

"Whatever the case," Dean rushed on, too terrified to think of the possibilities, "lunch with Mother will be precisely the thing to win her over. Once Mother sees you as I see you, as the most beautiful and perfect creature on the earth, she will not be able to help but to give her full consent to our union."

"Do you truly believe that?" Nan asked, more than a hint of doubt in her tone and expression.

"I do," Dean insisted, still the optimist. "You will see it as well. But first, we've another meal to conquer." He shifted to take her arm, escorting her out of the parlor. "Just don't expect this meal to be soothing and peaceful. Not with Father presiding."

"No," Nan said in agreement. She laughed, then drew in a breath and resumed her theatrical persona. "Monsieur, I do believe zat your family is as mad as an entire basket of March hares."

"My darling," he answered, "I do believe you are right."

Chapter Sixteen

For the past two days, Nan had begun to feel as though Dean's tendency toward optimism was catching. Supper at the Rathborne-Paxton house had been a hilarious fiasco in so many ways. Lord Vegas had been a pill through the entire meal. But Lady Heloise Barrington counteracted his venom with adoration—and more than a few randomly blurted bouts of praise that had nothing to do with the conversation at the table. Lady Vegas had remained silent through most of the meal, only speaking to her sister, Lady Dorrington, now and then, and only in whispers.

Nan was certain she could sway Lady Vegas through the luncheon Dean had arranged at the Savoy Hotel three days later. She'd spent the entire, awkward meal at Rathborne House studying Lady Vegas, and she'd come to the conclusion that Dean's mother was ripe for winning over. She simply needed to put aside her prejudices against the mingling of classes and forget that Nan was the daughter of a crofter.

She left morning rehearsal at the Concord Theater with a smile on her face, shifting her parasol and tipping her face up to the sunlight that managed to filter down through the smoke and soot of the London sky, even though sunlight would spoil her complexion. Perhaps not, though. She was trying out a new face cream that Mr. Brown wanted her to endorse, so perhaps she didn't need to worry about dark spots and blemishes after all.

That cheer put a bounce into her step as she made her way down The Strand. It was likely criminal for her to be in such a spritely mood when the specter of Montrose continued to hang over her and the entire production of *The Marshall*, but no one had heard a peep from Montrose since his dramatic appearance several days before. It was enough to give her hope that he'd seen what he was up against when the entire cast and crew stood against him, and that he'd given up. She would cling to that hope for as long as she could.

Which turned out to be no time at all.

"Mlle. D'Argent, Mlle. D'Argent!"

Nan stopped when she heard her name called out and twisted this way and that, looking for whoever had called to her. She burst into a smile when she spotted a young man in working-class clothes rushing up to her.

"*Bonjour, monsieur*," she greeted him. "Is zere something I could 'elp you with?"

"Yeah, there is." A short burst of fear hit Nan as the young man stepped right up against her faster than she could get away. "You could give us a kiss, for one."

Nan took a large step back, closing her parasol and holding it tightly, prepared to use it to defend herself. She kept her smile in place and feigned amusement. "I am terribly sorry, *monsieur*, but I do not give out kisses to strange men."

"That's not what I hear," the man said with a snort. "All you actresses are the same, right?"

Nan lost her smile. "I beg your pardon, *monsieur*, but get out of my way."

She was surprised when the man actually moved away

from her, letting her proceed. She turned down Adam Street, even though she hadn't intended to make the turn so soon, to leave the man's sight as quickly as possible. It wasn't entirely unheard of for her to be pursued by followers. She should have asked Patrick or one of the stagehands to accompany her to the Savoy, but it was so close to both the theater and her flat that she hadn't bothered.

The encounter unsettled her, though, and when she opened her parasol again, she used it to conceal her face as much as she could. Keeping her eyes down had a secondary effect as well. When she stepped out from Adam Street onto Savoy Place, her eyes were drawn straight to the headlines of the newspapers a young man was hawking on the street corner.

"Mismanagement at the Concord Theater," the lad called to her when she stopped to snatch up one of the papers. "Public funds used to pay for scandalous parties."

"Zat is absurd," Nan hissed, not looking at the lad.

She noticed the young man shrug all the same. "That's what it says, Mlle. D'Argent. I'm just repeating it."

Nan sighed and lowered the paper, sending the lad a sympathetic smile. "It is not true," she told him, then fumbled the newspaper and her parasol so that she could fetch a coin from her purse for the lad. "Mr. Cristofori and his partners manage zee theater quite well."

Again, the lad shrugged. "That's not what the papers say." He pointed across to another young man on the opposite street corner who was selling a rival publication.

Nan made an impatient sound, then strode across the street to purchase a paper from that lad. She tried to read both of them while still managing her parasol as she walked on to the hotel. The articles in both publications were similar. They claimed that an unknown source had revealed misappropriation of public funds given to the Concord Theater, salacious parties that flowed with alcohol, opium, and women and men of loose character. Everything was vague. Nothing was stated outright. But it took very little imagination to paint a vivid picture.

"Did you see this?"

Nan was startled out of her thoughts and dropped one of the newspapers as she neared the Savoy Hotel, only to come face to face with Martin Piper. Her initial fright relaxed as Martin bent over to pick up the newspaper she'd dropped. She noticed that he held one of his own.

"It is all lies, of course," she said, maintaining her accent, even though Martin knew the truth. The street where they stood was too well-traveled for her to be herself.

"Of course," Martin agreed with a deep frown. "The Concord Theater has never been given public funds, for one. The money Niall spends comes from the box office and from investors."

"And we both know zat Mr. Cristofori would never finance any sort of scandalous revels." She said as much aloud when she noticed more than a few of the people who walked past them were slowing to take a look, and to listen.

"Niall and Blake are dull in comparison to most other people I know," Martin added with a grin, moving closer to her. "Not as dull as Edward, but I have been working on loosening him up. In more ways than one."

Nan wanted to laugh at his ribald joke. Few, if any, of the people passing them and listening in would have the slightest idea what he was referring to, but under their current circumstances, loose tongues were dangerous.

"Do you know if Cristofori and zee others have seen zees?" she asked, holding up her newspapers. "Zey did not seem to be aware of it at rehearsal zees morning."

Martin frowned. "I don't know if they've seen the papers, but Niall has his hands full at the moment." When Nan raised her brow in question, Martin inched closer and said, "We lost two more stagehands this morning. They said they'd received threatening letters indicating that if they didn't quit the show, they'd lose their lodging."

Nan let out a heavy breath. "And Cristofori is having a devil of a time hiring replacement chorus members."

"Who would have thought?" Martin rubbed a hand over his face. "I would have given my right arm for a part in a West End show when I was just starting out."

"Montrose," Nan muttered. There was no other explanation. The villain hadn't been quiet for the last few days after all. He'd merely been positioning his pieces so that he could make a move toward checkmate.

"I need to go speak to Edward about this," Martin said, holding up his newspaper. He started to walk on. "Keep your eyes open, love. We might be in the soup, but at least we're all swimming together."

Nan smiled and did her best to wave as Martin walked away. It was a small comfort that she had friends to help her deal with whatever storm Montrose was about to rain down on them.

She continued on to the hotel, but it was beginning to seem more and more as though it was not her day for smooth sailing and calm seas. No sooner had she closed her parasol and stepped into the lobby than she bumped straight into a tall, handsome gentleman, spilling her newspapers all over again.

"I am terribly sorry, madam," the gentleman said, bending to scoop up her papers. He spoke with a foreign accent that Nan couldn't quite place—Scandinavian, perhaps—and held himself with a regal bearing. When he stood and organized her papers, then handed them back to her with a smile, she could have sworn there was something familiar about him.

"Thank you, *monsieur*," she said, smiling as she accepted the papers.

The man's expression lit up. "Mlle. D'Argent," he said in recognition.

"*Oui*, zat is who I am." Nan continued to smile, but after her encounter with the man on the street, she was not as eager to meet her followers as usual.

"It is a great honor to meet you, *mademoiselle*," the man said, offering his hand. Nan managed to shuffle her parasol and newspapers so that she could place her hand in his. As the man lifted it for a kiss, he said, "Allow me to introduce myself. I am Prince Petrus of Aegiria."

Nan's eyes went wide. "A prince?"

Prince Petrus's smile turned bashful. "Princes are as common as weeds in Aegiria, I am afraid," he said. "That is what comes with having a large and productive royal family. Though I am, perhaps the least important member of that family, seeing as...."

His words faded, and he glanced around the lobby anxiously. Nan followed his gaze, but she couldn't determine what he was searching for.

Prince Petrus seemed to realize his lack of attention and returned his focus to Nan. "I do not wish to keep you from your business, Mlle. D'Argent. I merely wished to express how much I enjoyed your performance in *Love's Last Lesson*. We do not have theatrical performances as fine as yours in Aegiria."

"Thank you, your highness," Nan said with a smile. "Do not worry yourself on my account. I am a bit early for my engagement."

As soon as she said as much, she spotted Dean rising from a table at the very edge of the restaurant. He looked as though he would rush to her rescue if it turned out Prince Petrus was accosting her in some way. Nan smiled at him in reassurance. As she did, she noticed Lady Vegas and Lady Dorrington at the table as well, both of them frowning at her.

"As it turns out, my engagement is already here," she said, taking a small step away from the prince.

"Then by all means," Prince Petrus said. "Do not let me detain you. It was a pleasure speaking with you, Mlle. D'Argent."

"Likewise, *monsieur*." Nan sent the prince one last smile before heading across the lobby toward the restaurant.

Dean had stepped away from the table and met her halfway there. "Who is he?" he asked as he took her hand and raised it to his lips for a kiss.

Nan tried to hide her smile. If she wasn't mistaken, Dean was a little jealous.

"He said his name is Prince Petrus of Aegiria," she said. She and Dean both glanced back at him. The prince had taken up a position near a cluster of chairs at the other side of the lobby, and the way he watched the door made it clear he was waiting for someone. "He wanted to congratulate me on my performance in *Love's Last Lesson*."

Dean hummed and narrowed his eyes slightly. "Why does he look so familiar?"

"I thought zee same thing," Nan said as they headed toward the restaurant. "But I do not know why I feel zat."

"Aegiria." Dean frowned, walking slowly so that they had as much time as possible to reach the restaurant. "That's that tiny, island kingdom in the Baltic Sea, between Sweden and Poland, is it not?"

"I think so," Nan said, racking her brain to remember the geography of inconsequential European kingdoms.

That was the last chance Nan had to think about other kingdoms or Prince Petrus, or even the troubles at the theater and with the production.

"She looks as garish as she did the other night, when she interrupted supper," Dean's mother said as soon as Dean escorted Nan over to the table.

"Garish," Lady Dorrington agreed with a shake of her head.

Nan fought to keep a kind smile in place and not to be hurt by the barb. "Good afternoon, Lady Vegas, Lady Dorrington. It is so nice to see zee two of you again."

To her horror, Lady Vegas sighed and shook her head. "There's no need to put on that French act with me, girl. I know the truth."

Nan's smile died on her lips, and every muscle in her body tensed. She didn't know what to do. If she dropped her persona for Lady Vegas, anyone within earshot of the table would know the truth. If the wrong person caught wind of it, her secret could be all over London by the evening edition, Montrose or no Montrose. But if she kept up her act, Lady Vegas would likely be offended, which would defeat the purpose of the lunch entirely.

Dean jumped in to resolve the problem. "Nanette has important reasons to maintain her aura of elegance, Mother," he said, taking the newspaper, her parasol, and the weight off Nan's shoulders. "Humor me for now and indulge in a little playacting."

Lady Vegas sighed and rolled her eyes, settling back in her chair. "The entire thing is ridiculous."

"As ridiculous as the daughter of one of our tenants marrying the son of a marquess," Lady Dorrington said with a sniff. She reached for the teacup at her place and sipped it, then made a face as though it were sour.

Nan had conquered the London stage, had faced critical audiences as well as adoring ones. She'd been ridiculed for lending her image to products when she'd appeared on her first soap, and had her love life speculated about in gossip columns. But nothing had felt more daunting than maintaining her smile as she sat across the table from the woman she desperately wanted to be her mother-in-law.

"Are you enjoying your return to London so far, Lady Vegas?" she asked, pretending as though Dean's mother already loved her and they were about to enjoy a lovely meal together.

"Absolutely not," Lady Vegas said, then sniffed and reached for her tea. "My sons have behaved appallingly in my absence. Samuel rushed into marriage with a woman I do not know without waiting for me to return and assess the situation. And my wretched blackguard of a husband has spent the last three days attempting to press me under his thumb once more. I spent thirty years as that man's prisoner, and I will not return to that position. Not when I know the truth."

Nan was grateful the waiter had only just come over to pour her tea. If she'd been drinking it, she likely would have choked at the vehemence of Dean's mother's statements. Although it was a sign of hope that the woman was willing to be so open with her.

"Mother, Francis has that lovely flat arranged for you," Dean said. "I do not know why you torment yourself by staying at Rathborne House when you could be free of Father."

Lady Vegas gaped incredulously at Dean. "Rathborne House is as much mine as it is that vile man's. I raised my children there. I decorated the blasted place. If anyone should move out, it should be him."

Nan inched back into her seat. She'd stumbled into a family matter, and no good ever came from inserting oneself in someone else's family matters.

Of course, as soon as she had that thought, Lady Vegas turned to her and snapped, "I suppose that you wish to take over Rathborne House now, seeing as you are a wicked social climber who has somehow managed to sink her claws into my vulnerable and weak-minded son."

Nan's mouth dropped open, but Dean beat her to replying.

"Mother, I am not weak-minded, and Nanette has not sunk her claws into me. We are in love, and we wish to build a life together." He reached for her hand.

Nan wasn't convinced a display of public affection was the right course of action when Dean's mother was still so dead-set against her. "It is not my wish to impose on zee Rathborne-Paxton family, my lady," she said.

"A likely story," Lady Vegas huffed. "I know your type, girl. You reach beyond your grasp. What do you hope to gain by throwing yourself at my son? His fortune? You realize he has none, thanks to my reprehensible husband. A wolf in sheep's clothing if ever there were one."

The only thing keeping Nan from getting her back up and giving Dean's mother a piece of her mind was the painfully obvious fact that Lady Vegas continued to be deeply hurt by her husband's betrayal. She was furious, and it seemed as though that fury was lashing out at whatever presented itself.

Knowing as much could only help Nan's cause.

"Lady Vegas," she said, making her voice as soft as possible and staring at the woman frankly, "I do not know 'ow much you follow zee theater, but you must know zat I am not only well-known and well-regarded, I am independently wealthy as well. I am not after your son's fortune, and I know he has none."

Her words did nothing to soothe Lady Vegas—who glanced between Nan and Dean as though she wasn't certain which of them she was more angry with.

"I wish to marry your son because he is wonderful and heroic," Nan went on. She paused as she considered the blatantly manipulative idea that suggested itself to her, then decided to risk using it. "Dean would not be such a lovely man nor such a fabulous hero were he not raised by a good and loving mother. Clearly, his father had nothing at all to do with zee man he has turned out to be."

Lady Vegas's eyes narrowed. Nan was certain the woman knew precisely what she was doing, and that she didn't think much of it. "I have never heard Dean described as heroic before," she said.

Nan didn't have the slightest idea what Lady Vegas intended with those words. The woman let nothing show in her expression. It occurred to Nan that the poor woman might have learned through thirty years of a miserable marriage not to let her emotions show. She either approved of Nan calling her son a hero, or she disagreed and felt Nan was being deceptive. The only way to gauge what Lady Vegas felt was to go on.

"Dean has been a treasure to me," she said. "He has protected me from overzealous followers. Of late, he has been my champion against zee threats Montrose has made toward me."

"Montrose?" Lady Vegas's brow rose in alarm.

"Lord Vegas," Lady Dorrington gasped, sitting straighter.

Nan had no idea what the woman meant until she heard Dean mutter, "Good God, what is he doing here?"

She turned to see Lord Vegas stride into the hotel lobby. Curiously, Prince Petrus straightened from where he'd taken to leaning against a counter and started toward Lord Vegas. Lord Vegas only saw the prince at first, though he looked as though he'd seen a ghost as he spotted the man.

Then he turned just enough to see Dean, Nan, Lady Vegas, and Lady Dorrington watching him. The mood in the hotel lobby instantly turned as brittle as an icicle about to shatter.

Chapter Seventeen

Everything had been going so well when.... No, actually, everything had been going horribly. Dean was both frustrated and embarrassed by his mother's continued stubbornness where Nan was concerned. It hurt him to see Nan so much on the back foot that her temper appeared to be on the verge of getting the better of her. And while there was a certain appeal in the idea of watching Nan well and truly lose her temper, Dean did not want that sort of fireworks display directed at his mother.

He was just about to intervene and put a stop to his mother's attacks when everything at their table—and, it seemed, the entire hotel lobby—came to an abrupt halt. Lord Vegas had entered the building.

"What in blazes is he doing here?" Dean muttered to himself.

He stood, resting a hand carefully on Nan's shoulder in a protective gesture. Lord Vegas seemed as though he were there to meet Prince Petrus of Aegiria. Dean could only imagine what that meant. His father couldn't limit his debts and his shame to just England. He'd probably caused a mess in Aegiria as well.

Whatever the case, the moment Lord Vegas spotted Dean staring back at him, the moment he saw that Nan, his wife, and Aunt Josephine were there with Dean, he clenched his hands into fists at his sides, sent Prince Petrus one last look, then turned and marched straight toward the restaurant.

"Good heavens," Aunt Josephine said, leaning back in her chair, as though that would put more distance between her and Lord Vegas. "Why can that man not simply go away and leave good people in peace?"

"Because, like too many others I know, he thinks so highly of himself that he feels he is above reproach," Dean's mother answered.

Dean twisted to gape at her. His mother was right, all things considered. If Dean had been exposed for committing the same sins his father had, he would have withered with shame and retired to the country by now. Lord Vegas seemed determined to plow ahead, no matter what came to light about him.

"What are you doing here, Muriel?" Lord Vegas hissed at his wife as he came to stand near the table. He was livid to the point of shaking as he glared at Dean's mother, but Dean was at a loss to understand the ferocity of his emotion.

"I invited Mother and Aunt Josephine here for lunch with my fiancée, Mlle. D'Argent, Father," Dean answered, inching closer to the man.

Lord Vegas narrowed his eyes and snapped around to face Dean. It didn't matter that Dean was a grown man and a few inches taller than his father, that look and the venom directed at him dredged up far too many memories of Lord Vegas's wrath and the punishments he would mete out on his sons when they stepped so much as a toe out of line. It didn't matter that Lord Vegas had been disgraced and proven to be a hypocrite for the piety he thrust on his sons either. The memories of nights spent on his knees on the hard floor, reciting prayers until the words all blended together, the feel of the cane across his backside and his knuckles when he was so exhausted that he got the words wrong, and the phantom gnawing in his stomach as he was forced to stand in the corner and watch the rest of his family eat their supper while he had none every night for a week had never truly left him.

"We will discuss your wickedness where this trollop is concerned later," Lord Vegas snapped. "You most certainly will not marry her."

"Father, I am already—"

"Quiet, you!" Lord Vegas shouted at him so loudly that the patrons of all the tables around them dropped their meals to watch with terrified fascination. "You will not marry a French actress. I forbid it!"

Dean noted that several of the people who were now watching leaned close to each other and whispered, staring at Nan as much as Lord Vegas. He could only imagine what gossip would come out of this lunch.

That thought was precisely why he battled through all his cold and miserable childhood scars to stand taller and face his father. "I will marry whomever I please," he said.

Lord Vegas sneered at him and shook his head. "Then your name will be stricken from the family Bible." He swept Dean up and down, his lip curled in a sneer, then went on with, "I always did like you the least of all my wastrel sons."

Dean sat down hard, glad his chair was positioned in such a way that it prevented him from falling to the floor. It should not hurt. Cruel words from a man he had never really liked should not hurt like a bayonet in the gut. But right or wrong, Lord Vegas was his father, and it was only natural for every man to want his father's love and approval.

"How dare you show your face in public at a delicate time

like this?" Lord Vegas continued his vitriol, this time addressing it to Dean's mother. He took a step toward his wife, his face splotching red with anger. "My name has been besmirched unjustly, and you tarnish it further by dining out at an establishment such as this?"

Dean wanted to point out that Lord Vegas was clearly there for some sort of rendezvous of his own. Prince Petrus watched the entire scene from the opposite side of the lobby. Dean also wanted to tell his father that Lady Vegas had done nothing wrong, not in the course of her entire life, and that it was his disgrace that threatened to damage her reputation. But his tongue was tied and the wounds of his father's dismissal had left him numb.

Dean's mother cowered away from Lord Vegas, leaning into her sister. "I...I did not think—"

"You never do and you never have," Lord Vegas cut her off. "You always were a silly, weak-minded girl who needed discipline to keep you from wickedness."

"I...I could not say...." Dean's mother seemed to shrink before his eyes, falling back into the form of the thin, cowering woman that she'd been through the torturous years of her marriage.

"You will all gather your things and leave at once," Lord Vegas ordered Dean, his mother, and even Aunt Josephine—who leaned even farther back in her chair, eyes wide, as though the Devil himself were haranguing her. "And if you know what's good for you," he went on, "you will take yourselves straight to church and spend a good few hours praying that God forgives—"

Lord Vegas was cut off by the small, calm sound of Nan clearing her throat. She did more than that. Nan stood, her back straight and her bearing strong, and simply stared at Lord Vegas.

Lord Vegas turned his vicious sneer on her, looking as

though he would raise his verbal sword once more to slay her, now that everyone else lay at his feet. "How dare you stand up against me?" he demanded. "I suppose you have something to say?"

Nan kept her expression completely implacable, though Dean thought he noticed her hands trembling as she placed her fingertips on the table in front of her. "I do have something to say, *monsieur*," she said, tilting her chin up another inch.

Lord Vegas snorted and sneered. "And who cares to listen to a harlot who struts across a stage and prostitutes herself for soap and chocolate?"

A few of the patrons at the nearby tables gasped.

"I daresay quite a few people would prostitute zemselves for chocolate," Nan said, grinning for a moment.

Quiet chuckles sounded from close by. They only infuriated Lord Vegas. "Who are you to show such cheek to a man like me?" he demanded.

"I am zee woman who loves your son," Nan replied without hesitation. "I am zee woman who cares about his mother." She gestured to Dean's mother. "A woman whom you have greatly wronged, *monsieur*. A woman who has not deserved zee 'orrible treatment you have given her."

Lord Vegas turned a darker shade of puce and practically vibrated with fury. Dean pushed away the phantom feeling of the cane across his backside as he wobbled to his feet. He needed to defend Nan against whatever Lord Vegas was about to hurl at her.

But before he could summon up the courage to open his mouth, Nan went on with, "It was not Dean, nor was it his mother, who sank himself so deeply into debt through gambling and whoring zat a man like Montrose decided to come after him. Zees fine lady has never done anything to deserve zee sort of torture you have inflicted on her, *monsieur*."

"What would you know about any of that?" Lord Vegas growled, lowering his voice and glancing around, as if noticing for the first time that they had an audience.

Dean's breath caught in his throat. Nan always excelled when she was in front of an audience.

"I know zat men such as you have hurt women such as Lady Vegas in ways zat are cruel and undeserved for ages," Nan answered. She shifted slightly to stand more firmly by Dean's mother's side and went so far as to rest a hand lightly on Lady Vegas's arm. "I know zat zees woman cares for her sons above all else, and zat you have stood between them, dampening zee love zey have for each other for far too long."

"That is right," Dean's mother said, her voice tremulous, but her body tensing, as though she were gathering strength. "All I've wanted to do for my whole life is be a good mother to my boys. You have prevented me from doing that and from being the mother I've known that they need for too long."

"You are too soft," Lord Vegas spat, his shoulders hunching slightly. "You would have spoiled them. Discipline and education, that is what they needed."

"Young boys need love and understanding, *monsieur*," Nan said. "Zey need encouragement to grow into fine young men. Your son, zee man I have come to love, is kind and heroic, but you had nothing at all to do with zat. He is who he is because of zis woman alone."

"All of our boys are the men they are because of me," Lady Vegas said. She shocked Dean to his core by standing and facing Lord Vegas with the sort of vitality and strength she'd been using against him since he went to her in Shropshire. "I raised four fine young men despite your cruelty, your rules, and your false piety."

"You have done an admirable job despite great odds

against you, *madame*," Nan agreed. "I can only 'ope zat I will be able to raise sons of my own as marvelous as zee ones you have raised."

"Thank you, dear," Dean's mother said, a bit breathless and still struggling, but with feeling. She went on to do something that shocked Dean to the point where he nearly sank into his chair again. She reached for Nan's hand and held it tightly before saying, "I think you should leave, Christopher. I think you should leave Rathborne House as well. You are not wanted there. You are no longer wanted as a part of this family."

"How dare you?" Lord Vegas hissed. He formed his hands into fists again, and this time, his trembling was on display for all to see. Dean had the feeling it wasn't anger, though. At least, not on the scale that it had been before. The man had never stared into the eyes of defeat that way before. He was at a loss, and the only thing he knew how to do was glower.

"Montrose," Aunt Josephine gasped all of a sudden. She was the only one still seated, and Dean could only blink at her at first.

Until he followed the line of her sight across the lobby to the hotel door. Montrose had just entered the scene.

Lord Vegas made a tight, choking sound at the sight of the villain, all color leaving his face. For a moment, Dean thought his father might shatter like cold glass brought into the heat too quickly.

More curious than that, Prince Petrus jerked straight from where he had been leaning against a counter at the other end of the lobby. His eyes went wide at the sight of Montrose. He turned that startled, wide-eyed look on Lord Vegas for a moment before marching hastily toward the hotel door. With a brief glance back over his shoulder, he darted out of the hotel, as though Hell itself were on his tail.

"Oh!" Dean's mother gasped, pressing a hand to her stomach. She had the light of recognition in her eyes, as if she knew who Prince Petrus was. Her initial shock turned into a look of tight fury that she directed at Lord Vegas.

Dean wanted to scream. He couldn't read the emotion in his mother's eyes. She was furious, but he couldn't for the life of him figure out why she would be so upset that Lord Vegas clearly knew an Aegirian prince.

"I will not be cast out of my own house," Lord Vegas blurted. The comment seemed so incongruous that it snapped Dean out of his curiosity over Prince Petrus entirely. "You cannot throw me onto the street when I am the lord and master of Rathborne House."

"Francis is the sole owner of Rathborne House now," Dean reminded him. "You'd best ask him whether you've a right to stay."

Lord Vegas turned to him, looking as though he could murder Dean with his own hands. Instead of doing so, he glanced across the lobby to Montrose.

Montrose did nothing. He simply stood in the center of the lobby, hands clasped placidly behind his back, smiling at Lord Vegas as though they were two friends who had arranged to have lunch together. Something about the smile Montrose wore chilled Dean's blood.

It did more than that for Lord Vegas.

"This is not the end of this," he hissed, then marched away from the table, leaving Dean and the ladies alone at last.

It was somehow fitting that Lord Vegas tripped over the carpet and knocked a bit of cutlery off a table as he made his exit. Once clear of the restaurant, he tugged at his jacket and attempted to hold his head high as he passed Montrose, heading for the door. Montrose sneered at him as he left. As he reached the door, Lord Vegas darted out to the street at a run.

Dean would have felt a thousand times smugger about the way the encounter ended if Montrose hadn't then turned his piercing stare on him and the ladies. The bastard narrowed his eyes in a way that was as much a threat as any words he could have shouted. Dean interpreted that look as exactly what it was —Montrose reminding both him and Nan that he still had their balls in a vise. Well, his balls. He shuddered to think what sort of things about a lady he might put in a vise.

Just as the tension of the moment grew to be too much, Montrose nodded to their table, doffing his hat as he did, then turned to walk out of the hotel as though nothing at all were amiss.

"Good heavens," Dean's mother said breathlessly, still clasping one hand to her stomach while holding Nan's hand with her other. "My heart is racing. I believe I need to sit down."

"You did magnificently, Lady Vegas," Nan said, switching from fierce warrioress to caring potential daughter-in-law as she helped Dean's mother to sit. "I can see where your son gets his lion heart from."

"Thank you, dear," Dean's mother said hesitantly. She glanced sheepishly up at Nan, watching as Nan resumed her seat.

Dean sat again as well. "Are you quite well, Mama?" he asked, reaching across the table to her.

"I am," his mother answered hesitantly. "It is...it is nothing a spot of brandy won't resolve."

Dean burst into a broad smile and sat straighter, catching the eye of one of the waiters. It wasn't difficult to do, as all of the restaurant's waiters and most of the patrons were watching them with rapt attention. As soon as Dean glanced around at them, the fellow diners turned back to their meals. The noise level in the restaurant instantly increased.

"A brandy for my mother," he told the waiter once the man had reached the table. "You'd better make that four," he said as the young man turned away. "I think we could all use one after that." He grinned at Nan as the young man nodded, then walked off.

"I do not normally drink so early in zee day," Nan said, glancing to Dean's mother, "but I think a tipple is in order, *non*?"

Dean's mother laughed anxiously, then burst out with, "I am terribly sorry, my dear. I have judged you unfairly. You have proven yourself to be of a strong and noble spirit and...and I am sorry."

"Zere is no need to apologize, my lady," Nan said, smiling as she squeezed Dean's mother's hand. "Believe me, I understand your way of thinking entirely." She sent Dean's mother a conspiratorial look.

Dean's mother smiled back at her, and Dean's heart shouted in triumph as his body sagged in relief. "I take it we have your blessing now?" he asked, raising an eyebrow.

His mother leaned back in her chair a bit and eyed Nan suspiciously. "I do not know if I can approve of my son marrying a...an actress."

Dean held his breath, panicking for a moment that all had been for naught. Nan didn't seem to be fussed about his mother's reaction, and when he took a second glance at his mother, he recognized the glint of humor in her eyes.

She went on with, "But I suppose there is an exception to everything." His mother burst into a smile and grasped Nan's hand. "Could you forgive me for my initial reticence?" she asked.

"It is perfectly understandable," Nan said, making a gesture with her free hand as if to brush the whole thing away. "We still share a common enemy," she went on, growing more serious.

"Montrose," Aunt Josephine said, nodding.

"He will not get the better of us," Dean said, taking his cue to launch into action. "We defeated him once, and we will defeat him again. He is after Nan...nette," he remembered to use her public name at the last minute, "but he will give up his pursuit of her money as soon as he discovers that she has more friends than he does."

"I hope you are right," Dean's mother said.

A pause followed. Dean couldn't resist asking, "Mother, do you know Prince Petrus of Aegiria?"

"I do not," his mother answered, withdrawing her hand from Nan's and lowering her eyes, though she kept her back straight.

Dean wondered if she was lying. "Does Father know him?" he asked, more confused than ever.

"I cannot say," his mother answered, her voice hoarse.

It was maddening to know that his mother knew more about what was going on than he did. "Mother, could you not—"

"I think zat is enough questions for now," Nan interrupted him, smiling kindly at his mother. "Let us enjoy zee rest of our luncheon together. Your mother and I have quite a bit of getting to know each other to do, *non*?"

"You do," Dean sighed, loath to give things up so soon.

Nan was right, though. They needed to focus on thwarting Montrose's plot against Nan first. The ground Montrose stood on to blackmail Nan was far shakier than the position Lord Vegas had put himself and his family into. It would be easier to accomplish the small defeat, especially since the cast and crew of the Concord Theater were on their side. But once Nan was freed from Montrose's threat, Dean was determined to figure out what connection Prince Petrus of Aegiria had to his father, and to defeat Montrose once and for all.

Chapter Eighteen

The joy of winning Lady Vegas over to her side carried Nan through a challenging week of rehearsals and all the way to opening night of *The Marshall*. There were still so many things to be resolved between Lord and Lady Vegas, she knew. Particularly since Lord Vegas had refused to move out of the family home. Lady Vegas had also refused to take up residence in the flat Lord Cathraiche had arranged for her, which meant that every day at Rathborne House was a bitter battle of wills.

Which explained why Dean not only discouraged Nan from returning to the place for another supper, or perhaps more, but also why he spent more time at the theater and Nan's own flat than he did at home.

"Perhaps I should simply pack up all of my worldly goods and have all of my correspondence forwarded to your address," Dean suggested as they arrived at the Concord Theater in advance of the opening night performance.

Nan laughed and rested a hand on Dean's cheek before turning into her dressing room. "There have been more than enough suggestive stories about me and this production and those associated with it in the last fortnight already, dearest," she said, smiling fondly at him all the same. "The last thing we need is for the press to learn that we are living together in sin."

"It isn't as though we are the only ones in London," Dean complained. He leaned against the wall just inside her dressing room as Nan crossed the room to deposit her purse on her dressing table, then moved to check her costumes for the night.

"I'm certain that's true," she said, glancing back at Dean with a grin. "But how many of those people have Montrose breathing down their necks?"

Dean could only shrug and make a noncommittal sound.

The truth was that even though Montrose hadn't made any more direct threats to her, even though she hadn't seen so much as a glimpse of the man since the afternoon at the Savoy, Montrose's presence had been felt every day and by every member of the production since then.

She wasn't being flippant when she'd told Dean there were enough stories in the gossip columns about her and the other cast members of late. Every day brought some new, sordid speculation or overheard rumor. First, she'd been accused of beating her maid, which had offended Olivia to the point of tears. Then came the articles linking her to half a dozen men throughout London, including Prince Arthur again. Those sorts of articles were easy to laugh off, since rumors of those sort abounded during the best of times. Nan found it laughable that a few articles even purported that she was engaged to Dean. She was endlessly amused that Montrose's storm of false information managed to bury the truth.

It wasn't just her, though. Articles had abounded about Everett, Cristofori, and Martin and their paramours. Everett and Cristofori laughed theirs off, but Martin had grown exceedingly nervous and withdrawn when gossip was directed at his Edward. For a few days, Nan had been worried that Martin would withdraw from the show.

He wouldn't have been the first or only one. Every day, someone else tearfully told Cristofori that they couldn't withstand the pressure any longer. They'd lost half of the original chorus, and Lydia had wept as she'd confessed Montrose's villainy had frightened her to the point where she needed to return home to Lincolnshire for the rest of the summer. Cristofori had hired Lydia's understudy, Justine Peters, to replace her, which meant that Lily Logan had to scramble to learn the lines and blocking so that she could understudy Justine.

"We have managed to hold this production together by a string," Nan told Dean over her shoulder as she searched through the rack for her Act One costume. "I'm not certain how much more we can take, though."

She reached the end of the rack, frowned, then sorted back through her costumes. More than one of them was missing.

"We've made it to opening night," Dean said, his voice far cheerier than hers. "Cristofori tells me that the box office is fantastic so far. Montrose's efforts to turn people away from the show with rumor and inuendo have only increased interest in it."

"Or perhaps people are merely interested in the spectacle of us failing," Nan said. She stepped away from the rack and searched the rest of the room. Perhaps one of the costume department's seamstresses had taken the missing costumes for last-minute alterations.

"Darling, is something wrong?" Dean asked.

"I'm missing two of my costumes," Nan said.

Still frowning, she marched past Dean and into the hall, then out toward the stage. She intended to search out the costume mistress, but instead, she found Cristofori, Everett, Mr. Abrams, and Mr. Delaney, the stage manager who had been brought in to replace the usual stage manager when he had an unfortunate fall two days ago, standing on the stage, gaping up at the fly space.

Dread pooled in Nan's stomach as she changed direction and marched over to join them, Dean following her.

"What seems to be the problem now?" she asked, looking up along with the others.

"The fly space," Mr. Abrams said, pushing a hand frantically through his hair. "Someone's damaged the pulleys. None of the backdrops can be raised or lowered." He dragged his gaze down to stare frantically at Nan. "We can't change the scenes."

Nan pressed a hand to her stomach. That was entirely inconvenient when part of the play took place by the seaside and part took place in a ballroom.

"We can use some of the old flats," Everett said, taking charge. He marched off to the stage left wings. "Where is Martin? We can use some of those large set pieces that he constructed for *Much Ado About Nothing* three seasons ago."

"Dean," Cristofori said, gesturing for Dean to follow. "You helped paint the sets. Can you put together a series of flats that we can slide on and off the stage?"

"I'll do my best," Dean said with a shrug. He moved to follow the others, but paused to kiss Nan's cheek. "Will you be able to manage without me?" he asked.

Nan sighed and shrugged. "I'll do my best."

She kissed him back, then turned to hurry off toward the costume room while Dean headed for the rooms where scenery was stored. Montrose had been busy. She didn't know how he'd managed to get into the theater to tamper with the pulley system in the fly space. Whatever he'd done, he would not get away with it. There was more than one way to ensure that the scenery could be changed.

That determination was trying to form into steel resolve as she threw open the door of the costume room.

"Mrs. Evans, do you know—"

Nan stopped cold at the sight that met her. It looked as though a whirlwind had been through the room. Costumes were scattered everywhere, and the racks that had held them were tipped over and splintered. On top of that, someone had splattered paint all through the room, destroying everything that had been pulled from the racks.

If that wasn't enough, Mrs. Evans, the costume mistress sat weeping on a pile of ruined costumes in the center of the room, a nearly empty bottle of gin in one hand.

"'S ruined," she slurred, throwing her arms wide and gesturing to the carnage with her bottle. "Iss all ruined."

Nan gaped at the mess, despair creeping up on her for a moment. The significance of Mrs. Evans's gin wasn't lost on her. The woman had once suffered from the need of spirits, but she had joined a temperance society several years ago and sworn off the bottle. That resolve appeared to be ruined now.

Mrs. Evans was far more important than the costumes, as far as Nan was concerned. She gathered her resolve, then marched into the center of the room to scoop the woman up under her arms.

"There, there, Mrs. Evans," she said, taking the bottle from her hand and shuffling her out of the room. "They're only costumes."

They were only costumes that were desperately needed for the show. Nan spotted her two missing costumes in one corner of the room before she bundled Mrs. Evans out to the hallway. Both were ruined with paint.

She spent the next half hour sorting Mrs. Evans by taking her outside so that she could expel some of the gin she'd imbibed and so that the woman could have fresh air. She would have handed the task off to one of the stagehands, but they were all furiously busy trying to construct a new set and gather upset chorus girls who had had their costumes ruined.

Time was ticking swiftly away by the time she made it back into the theater.

"Can we do anything to make the chorus look uniform?" she asked Lily as the two of them crossed paths halfway across the stage.

Dean, Everett, Everett's Patrick, and Cristofori were all rushing frantically about, positioning props and set pieces from previous shows and doing whatever they could to build the scene.

"We can give them all garlands or parasols," Lily said in a frantic flash, "but we've a far, far bigger problem."

Nan's stomach turned at that. "Oh, God, what problem now?"

Lily swallowed sickly and said, "Miss Peters is missing."

Nan gaped at her. "I beg your pardon?"

"She isn't here." Lily took a huge, gulping breath. "Her call was an hour ago, but she isn't here. We've only an hour and a half before the curtain rises, and *she isn't here.*"

It took Nan a moment to realize that Lily's distress was because if Miss Peters didn't show up, she would have to go on as the comedic secondary female lead. Lily had been at the theater for more than a year, learning everything she could, but she'd never appeared on the stage before.

"It will be all right," Nan told her, grasping both of the woman's arms, perhaps a little too tightly. "Everything will be all right. You've learned the lines?"

"A bit?" Lily squeaked. "But Nan...I can't dance for shit."

Nan would laugh about Lily's panic and her profanity later, but at the moment it made her want to panic and scream obscenities herself.

"Find Martin," she told Lily. "Tell him to rehearse your

scenes with you. Between the two of us, we will get you through this."

Lily whimpered, but dashed off in search of Martin. The last thing Nan heard from her was her wailed cry of, "I'll have to wear a dress!"

They would laugh about it later. Nan was certain they would all clutch their sides and roll with laughter when they recalled the night...later. At the moment, however, it was all she could do to keep herself from crying. It was all she could do to—

Without warning, as she passed her dressing room door on her way to find Dean, a burly man wearing a scarf over his face leapt out at her. He carried a pipe of some sort that he swung at her legs. Nan shrieked in shock and leapt away from the man. His pipe caught in her skirts, and she felt the weight of it brush against her shin, but it was barely a graze.

The man swore under his breath, then broke into a run, dashing for the stage door. Since it was already open—and the sound of Mrs. Evans could still be heard weeping and retching outside—the man was able to escape into the alley and probably run away before anyone could stop him.

"Nan!" Dean's shout echoed from the stage. The sound of his running footsteps followed, and he appeared in the hall. "Nan, what is wrong?"

Everett and Patrick hurried into the hallway behind him, both skidding to a stop as Dean reached Nan and pulled her into his arms.

"There was a man," she panted, desperate to catch her breath and keep her head about her. "He flew at me with a pipe and tried to smash my shin."

"Probably so you wouldn't be able to dance tonight," Everett said, striding up to join them.

"Not be able to dance?" Dean gaped at Everett, incredulous. "She wouldn't have been able to perform at all."

Lily, Martin, and Cristofori had joined them in the hall, and Lily wailed, "I can't play the leading lady *and* the comedic leading lady in the same performance!"

She burst into tears, then turned and ran off.

"I'll calm her down," Martin said, following after her. Nan thought she heard him add, "Then someone needs to calm me down as well."

"We are not going to let him get the better of us," Dean said, clutching Nan tightly and rubbing her arms. "We are not going to let Montrose intimidate us into folding."

"Now or ever," Cristofori agreed.

As soon as he said that, one of the newer stagehands stumbled through the stage door, his arms full of newspapers.

"Have you seen these?" he said, stumbling toward them and handing everyone a newspaper. "They're accusing practically everyone involved in the production of being a sodomite, even the ones that aren't."

Nan's stomach twisted, but for some mad reason, Everett burst into laughter. "Even the ones that aren't!" he laughed, slumping against Patrick.

Nan gaped at him for a moment. Her initial instinct toward rage over the fact that he wasn't taking things seriously enough turned quickly to wild laughter of her own. It probably wasn't that funny, and she most certainly wouldn't be laughing later if any of her friends were arrested, but in that moment, she needed the laugh.

"Right," Cristofori said, clapping his hands together. "Everyone into their costumes, whatever costumes those are. Design is not important at this juncture, getting that curtain up is. Vocal warm-ups in fifteen minutes."

His burst of authority was just the jolt they all needed. Nan peeled away from Dean's arms, kissing him as she went.

"I have no earthly idea what we will end up presenting to our audience tonight," she said, heading back to her dressing room as Everett walked into his, Patrick following, "but whatever it is, it will be unforgettable."

The truth of those words felt as though it would haunt Nan for the rest of her life, and certainly the rest of the evening. She dressed in one of her other costumes and started applying her greasepaint for the performance, only to discover a horrible smell when she opened the jar of paint. It smelled as though a fish had crawled into the pot and died. She went in search of another one, but it seemed as though Montrose had infiltrated the make-up room as well. Every bit of face paint in the theater smelled of rotting fish.

Time was wasting, so there was nothing anyone in the cast could do but apply paint that made the entire stage area smell like the docks on a bad day. The smell was so bad that it had two of the chorus girls in tears.

"Chin up," Nan told them as she came out of her dressing room with less than five minutes to go before the curtain rose. "At least it hasn't turned your face blue."

"Is it going to turn my face blue?" one of the chorus girls asked, then burst into sobbing.

That set the entire female chorus off. Nan cursed herself for saying anything as she bolted across the stage to where Everett stood, peeking out through a sliver in the curtains.

"It's a full house," he told her as she wedged against him, peeking out through the curtain as well.

Of all the nights for the house to sell out. She glanced up to the Rathborne-Paxton box and was cheered somewhat to see Lady Vegas and Lady Dorrington there. At least she had a friend in the audience.

"I only wish it were a full pit," Everett went on.

Nan was confused for a moment before he pointed downward, indicating the orchestra pit. Nan looked, then groaned as she saw half the seats in the pit were empty.

"He's gotten to the orchestra," she sighed.

"At least the diminished orchestra won't drown out the diminished chorus," Everett said with a half-mad laugh.

"We can tell that to the press," Cristofori said. He was marching past them and had happened to overhear the comment. "If they ask why the pit is so sparse," he said as he turned and walked backwards.

"It's all about improvisation," Everett said, spreading his arms wide.

Nan frowned at him as they walked back to the wings as the orchestra tuned in preparation for the overture. "If I didn't know better, I'd say you are enjoying this more than you should."

"I love this," Everett said, a mad light in his eyes. "I love a day that I know I will never forget."

Nan made a face at him, then rushed to take her place in the wings. The combined chorus—and Lily Logan wearing a dress—was gathered, waiting for their first number, which came directly after Nan's opening aria. The show began with a solo song and dance from her that set the tone for the action that was to follow. She took a few deep breaths, pressing her hand to her stomach and humming the first notes of her song to get ready. When she glanced up, Everett smiled at her from the wings on the other side of the stage.

A flurry of gasps and squeals sounded behind Nan, and she rolled her eyes, wondering what new terror awaited her, as the orchestra began the overture. But for a change, she was met with good news. Miss Peters scrambled through the chorus girls, a long, rectangular flower box in her arms.

"Thank the Goddess," Lily shouted. She immediately tore at the dress she'd put on, frantic to take it off.

"I thought I wasn't going to make it," Miss Peters said. "First, the door in my building was jammed. I had to climb out a window to leave my flat. Then I was accosted on the street, not once, but three times!"

"It was Montrose," Nan said as the orchestra neared the end of the overture.

"Ready?" Mr. Delaney called out to her.

Nan nodded and waved to the man.

Dean stepped into the backstage area from the hallway, smiling and signaling to her that all was well. At last, Nan was certain she could breathe easy.

"Oh, these were waiting at the stage door for you," Miss Peters said, handing Nan the flower box. "I need to take my place."

The curtain was still closed, so Miss Peters was able to dash across the empty stage to the wings on the other side. Nan watched to make certain she was safe as she opened the lid of the box.

When she glanced down, she screamed louder than she ever had in her life. The box did not contain flowers. It was filled with spiders of every description. Hundreds of them. Only after the fact did she realize the box had been sealed with a light layer of paste to keep them in until the last moment. The spiders rushed to freedom as soon as the box was open, covering the front of her dress and her arms, even when she threw the box away.

She threw it right into the anxious chorus girls—who also started to scream and flail and dash about. It took everything and everyone with presence of mind backstage to keep the chorus girls from screaming the house down and running.

Nan sucked in a few, desperate breaths as she batted at her arms and her skirts, trying to rid herself of spiders. She felt her mind crack, felt herself slipping into hysterics. She couldn't do it. She couldn't go on when Montrose kept tormenting her. She could handle rumors in the papers, destroyed costumes, and half an orchestra, but she absolutely could not countenance spiders. She couldn't breathe, she could barely think. She couldn't—

"You're all right," Dean said, rushing up to her and closing his arms around her in a hug. "You are all right. They're just insects. You are far more powerful than them. And I am right here, Dean Rathborne-Paxton, vanquisher of arachnids."

Nan laughed through the tears that threatened her as Dean shook and slapped at her skirts and brushed her arms, ridding her of spiders. There were too many of them to do away with them all, but he did a fair job of cleaning them off, and an even better job of calming her down.

At that moment, the orchestra played the final notes of the overture, the audience applauded, and the curtain whooshed up. After only the slightest of pauses, the orchestra pushed on into the opening strains of her first aria. Nan could barely hear them over the thudding of her heart in her ears.

"You can do this, my darling," Dean said, grabbing her shoulders and pointing her toward the stage. "You are Nanette D'Argent, darling of the London stage. You can do this." He paused, then added, "You cannot let Lady Heloise down."

With a final, mad laugh, Nan surged forward. It took everything she had to smile and hold her arms wide as she took the stage. The audience roared with applause. The spiders dropped off the hem of her dress. Well, some of them did. Another tickled her as it crawled across her face. She refused to let it win, though. She refused to let Montrose win.

With that determination rising within her, she took her place for the opening steps of her song and dance...just as there was a horrible commotion and a crash in the wings behind her.

Chapter Nineteen

Despite his father's militant insistence, Dean had never been much of a praying man. Not truly. But as he turned Nan and nudged her out onto the stage to conquer what could arguably be the most important performance in the life of the Concord Theater, he said a prayer to whatever God was listening that things would proceed smoothly.

He was immediately thwarted by something that sounded like rain, only on the floor in the wings. It was like hundreds of tiny, staccato raindrops falling in and around where the chorus girls stood, waiting for their queue to join Nan on the stage for the first dance number.

The sound was drowned momentarily as Nan was greeted by the audience, but as the applause died down, Dean heard one of the chorus girls murmur, "What the devil?"

A moment later, there was a large thumping crash as one of the girls seemed to fall over her feet as she took a step forward. She grabbed hold of one of the emergency set pieces waiting backstage as if she would use it for balance, but the entire thing tumbled over with a crash, taking the chorus girl with it.

A few of the other girls murmured in confusion as Nan began the first, beautiful notes of her song, and a heartbeat after that, another girl tumbled over for no apparent reason. The others broke into a panic—one already fueled by spiders —and two of the stagehands had to rush in to calm them and see what was going on.

"Marbles," one of them whispered.

Dean blinked at the sheer ludicrousness of it, but sure enough, in the light filtering in from the stage, he could see that hundreds of small, shiny marbles had been scattered in the wings where the chorus girls waited for their entrance. Not only that, as Dean shoved a hand through his hair and gaped at the stage incredulously, he could see dozens of the glittering orbs rolling slowly across the back of the stage.

"They can't dance on marbles," Dean hissed to himself.

That was, of course, the point. If the chorus girls attempted their first dance number on a stage strewn with marbles, it would be a disaster.

"Pick them up," he whispered to the others, bending over to begin gathering them and shoving them into his pockets. "Pick all the marbles up as fast as you can."

He was immediately able to see which of the chorus girls had mettle and which were hopeless ninnies who fell apart in the face of adversity. Some of the girls rushed to do as he'd asked with looks of fearless determination. Some of them burst into tears and had to be prevented from leaving by the stagehands.

"We can do this," a ginger-haired young woman with particularly bright green eyes and an Irish accent said. "We can bloody well do this."

Dean silently gave three cheers for Irish stubbornness as

more and more of the chorus girls bent to search for marbles on the dark floor of the wings.

"We don't have pockets to put them in," another girl whispered, holding up two handfuls of marbles.

"Here." Lily rushed forward with a large bucket, offering it to the girls, who emptied handfuls of marbles into it. She met Dean's eyes and said, "I found it over in the corner. It's probably where they all came from to begin with."

Dean nodded, but before he had time to say anything, the Irish girl gasped, "That's our cue, that's our cue!"

The chorus girls pulled themselves together with amazing speed. Led by the Irish girl, they poured out onto the stage, launching right into the opening stanzas of their song.

The stage was, of course, covered in marbles at that point. Dean shifted to stand by Lily's side, holding his breath as the girls moved to their position, then began their dance. Nan moved upstage from where she'd begun the show, joining the chorus in song. As she did, she stepped on one of the marbles. She jerked—and Dean sucked in a breath—but managed to maintain her composure, although she sent Dean a wide-eyed look as she did.

Dean shrugged, his heart racing for Nan. He nearly burst into a laugh a moment later as the Irish girl adjusted the song's choreography to bend over and gather a few marbles. In short order, the other chorus girls did the same, and by the time they reached the second verse, the chorus was spinning and twirling, bending, and clearing the stage of marbles.

"Right," Dean hissed to Lily. "Hold the bucket out so they can dump their marbles when they come near the wings."

"Yessir," Lily said, a bit too much excitement in her voice.

"We can only assume that whoever tossed the marbles is still here, and that he's plotting more. I'm going to find him." Dean nodded, then moved away from Lily.

"I would say 'break a leg'," she whispered, "but with a stage full of marbles, that is too real of a possibility."

Dean laughed, even though he shouldn't have, and dashed to the very back of the stage so that he could walk behind the backdrop to see what was happening on the other side of the stage. The male chorus was poised and ready for their entrance, and Everett and Martin waited just behind them for their cue to enter at the end of the song.

"Were those marbles I saw on the stage?" Martin gasped when Dean clustered close to the two men.

Dean nodded. "Montrose is here, or else he has a saboteur here helping him."

"I would have thought that much was obvious already from the mess," Everett said, still a little too energized for anyone's good. "He isn't going to stop us from giving our audience the most memorable show of their lives."

"That's what I'm afraid of," Dean muttered. "I'll see what I can do about—"

He stopped as he looked up and caught sight of a shadowy figure dressed all in black picking his way across the fly space toward the center of the rigging where all the trapped backdrops hung.

"Oh, no, you don't," he said, glancing around in search of the fastest way he could get up into the fly space himself.

"I'd go with you, but the number is almost over," Everett said, clapping Dean on the arm. "Get up there and catch that bastard. The show must—"

"Go on, Everett, go on!" Martin hissed, pushing Everett toward the stage as the audience applauded the end of the opening chorus number.

Everett laughed loudly and strode out onto the stage, Martin tailing him, to face a roaring round of applause. The entire cast was now on the stage, so Dean was able to scramble toward the nearest ladder up to the fly space unimpeded.

"Bollocks to this," he growled as he pulled himself up as fast as he could. He'd never liked heights, and the fly space was one of his least favorite parts of the theater. But the show was in jeopardy, and Nan's life and career as well. He would risk heights for her.

That didn't stop him from groaning a bit as he made it to the catwalk that stretched across the upstage section of the fly space. The sound alerted the saboteur to Dean's presence. The man jerked and twisted to stare at Dean, seemingly shocked that anyone had spotted him or that they even knew he was there. The man held a long knife that he'd been using to saw through the ropes tying the backdrop to the bar that held it up. He'd severed one bit of rope, which caused a wrinkle in the scene as it hung down to the stage below, but he hadn't sliced through the whole thing yet.

"No, you don't," Dean said quietly, dashing out onto the catwalk as fast as he could without making too much noise.

Everett was in the middle of his first scene with Nan on the stage below. Dean had never been so grateful for the man's loud voice or his captivating presence. Nan delivered her lines loudly as well. The full chorus was on stage, and at least half of them were sneaking peeks to the space above them.

The saboteur gave up his efforts to ruin the scenery and raced across to the other side of the stage. Dean followed, but he lost sight of the man as his black clothing blended with the darkness all around. He wasn't about to give up his pursuit though. When he made it to the other side, he raced up to the front of the fly space to look around, and when he didn't see the man, he dashed to the back.

That was when he spotted the man lunging for one of the ladders and climbing down. Not to be outdone, Dean leapt for the ladder that was only a few feet from him and scrambled down, hoping to catch the man before he reached the floor.

Only, as soon as Dean's feet touched the floor, a clatter

above made him look up. The saboteur had fooled him. The man had climbed back up to the fly space and now made his way across the catwalk, as if heading to the other side of the stage—the side of the stage where the stage door and his likely escape was located.

"Absolutely not," Dean growled.

He took three seconds to assess the situation as the next song and dance number began on the stage, then pushed ahead, acting without thinking.

The fastest way to the other side of the stage and perhaps the only way to catch the saboteur before he got away was through the dance. Dean rushed out onto the brightly lit stage behind one of the chorus girls.

Immediately, a murmur sounded from a section of the audience near the front of the stage. Too many of the chorus members gaped at him. Miss Peters would have fallen over in shock if Martin hadn't scooped his arm around her as part of the dance.

Dean did the same, scooping his arm around the chorus girl nearest to him and spinning her, as though it were all part of the choreography. He then moved farther toward the center of the stage and grabbed another chorus girl to spin, then another. As he made progress across the stage, smiling and twirling each startled chorus girl that he came across, chuckles rose from the audience. By the time he reached the Irish girl near the far end of the stage, those chuckles had spread, and when the Irish lass refused to let him go, grabbing his face and kissing him soundly, the audience burst into full laughter.

Dean nearly choked, particularly when Nan glanced back at him and came within inches of breaking character to laugh as well. At least she wasn't upset. He feigned comedic surprise —although it wasn't as feigned as the audience likely thought it was—and pushed on, fleeing into the wings.

"That was...something," he whispered to himself as he hurried on, looking for the saboteur.

He caught sight of the tail end of the man as he dashed through the stage door and out into the night. Dean followed, nearly falling over Mrs. Evans as he did. He'd come so close to catching the man, but the best he'd been able to manage was to chase him off. At least that held the promise that the rest of the show would go off without a hitch.

He ran back into the theater, searching backstage for the rest of the first act to see if Montrose had planted any other henchmen among them to disrupt things. Blessedly, as far as he could tell, there had only been one saboteur, minus the one who had tried to smash Nan's leg before the show began. The rest of the act finished, and the curtain closed for intermission as the audience applauded heartily.

As soon as the bottom of the curtain touched the stage, the cast let out a collective sigh of relief. Dean ran onto the stage, right to the center, where Nan and Everett, Martin and Miss Peters stood. Unsurprisingly, Cristofori and Mr. Abrams dashed in from the other side.

"What in Hades is going on?" Mr. Abrams asked.

"Montrose had a saboteur in the theater," Dean explained, panting and shoving a hand through his hair. "I chased him off after my debut performance." He nodded to the Irish girl.

The Irish girl winked at him before herding the rest of the traumatized chorus into the wings.

"Keep your winks to yourself, Molly, he's mine," Nan called to the lass, making everyone laugh.

It was just the sort of levity they all needed.

"We made it through the first act," Cristofori said, as though rallying his troops—or perhaps rallying his troupe would be more accurate, "but we've still another act to come. Just because we chased off one man doesn't mean Montrose has given up."

"I highly doubt he has," Dean said.

"If I were to wager a guess," Nan said, inching closer and taking Dean's hand, "I would say it is about more than money now. The man is motivated by pride and grudges."

"That is a very astute and entirely correct observation, love," Dean said, smiling at Nan.

"It means we need to be ready for more mayhem in the second act," Everett went on, rubbing his hands together.

"I've already set guards on all the doors leading backstage from the house to prevent anyone from coming back and asking questions," Cristofori said. "I'll station Patrick by the stage door to make certain no one else comes or goes."

"If we can just get through the performance, we can figure out how to deal with Montrose later," Martin said with a determined nod.

"I need to change my costume," Nan said, lifting to her toes to kiss Dean's cheek, then starting off. "If I still have costumes yet to wear."

"You cannot do the second act in the buff, love," Everett called after her. "We are not that sort of a theater."

His comment earned a bit of laughter as the rest of them set off to do what they needed to make certain the second act continued without a hitch. Dean made another sweep of the backstage area while the lights were up, but he didn't find anything.

The second act began as smoothly as they could hope for. The chorus seemed more confident after making it through the first few numbers without incident. Dean peeked through the wings at one point to assess what the audience thought of the show. No one had left. That was something. He stood where he could see up into his family's box. His mother was there, but she held a lorgnette to her eyes, so he couldn't read what she thought of what she saw.

That was when he spotted Montrose, just as the second act

hit its midpoint. Montrose stood near the back of a box, a furious grimace on his pale face. He was probably upset that nothing had happened. Dean was just about to smirk in victory when Montrose pushed his way out of the box and disappeared into the hallway.

He was coming backstage, Dean knew it. Despite Cristofori's guards, he would find a way to get backstage to cause more trouble. The problem was, the box Montrose had left from was directly in the center of the house. There was no telling whether he would go to the right or the left to force his way through Cristofori's guards.

Dean clenched his fists as he tried to guess where Montrose would appear. It seemed most likely the man would want to be as close to the stage door as possible, so he headed over to that side.

Nan and Everett were in the middle of their declaration of love scene out on the stage. That meant both that the audience was quiet as they watched in rapt fascination, and that the finale was coming very soon. Dean tried to keep quiet as he traveled behind the backdrop, regrettably making it ripple as he moved. He headed toward the door he thought Montrose was most likely to come through, but all his guesses were proven wrong when there was a scuffle behind him, near the door he'd been standing close to earlier.

He cursed under his breath just as the orchestra started in on the opening strains of the finale—which started off as a tender love song between Nan and Everett, but that would soon turn into a rousing song and dance. He couldn't force himself to be quiet when Montrose was backstage, though.

He caught sight of the man on the other side of the stage as Montrose shoved his way past one of the younger stagehands. He reached into his jacket as he strode right up to the edge of the stage, though he was careful to keep out of the view of the audience. Lily tried to grab him and pull him back, but Montrose pulled a pistol from his jacket and smacked her head with the butt.

Dean saw red. Interfering with a theatrical production was one thing, but if Montrose was out for blood, then Dean would make certain his was the first that was spilled.

Without a care for what it would look like, Dean sprinted out onto the stage, running behind the lines of the chorus as they all burst into song, and racing to reach Montrose. Montrose raised his pistol above his head. The fleeting thought occurred to Dean that the man had no intention of actually shooting anyone, but a gunshot would be enough to cause a panic in the theater.

Of course, when Montrose saw Dean charging at him, he lowered his gun and pointed it at Dean in a panic. A gasp sounded from the chorus members who were positioned near that section of the wings, but the sound was drown by the loud singing and playing of the orchestra.

Dean reached Montrose before he could fire and seized the man's wrist. Montrose was startled enough to drop the pistol, which, thankfully, he had apparently forgotten to cock in his own surprise. Lily was already on the floor after the blow she'd received, and she scrambled for the gun as Dean jerked Montrose forward onto the stage.

The audience. The audience had to see and identify Montrose. If they saw, they would know who was behind the mischief of the night, know who it was threatening the cast and crew and spreading rumors intended to hurt them. If just a few people recognized Montrose, it might put an end to the villain's pursuit of Nan.

"Unhand me," Montrose demanded, trying to jerk out of Dean's grip.

"Not until you agree to leave Nan and the theater and my family alone," Dean growled, tugging Montrose farther onto the stage.

The finale reached its zenith, and even though the noise and movement of the dance pulled focus, murmurs could be heard from the audience. It was exactly what Dean needed.

He turned to assess how many people had seen Montrose, but as he did, Montrose shocked him with a surprisingly potent left hook to his jaw. The blow sent Dean reeling, but it wasn't enough for Dean to let go of Montrose's other wrist. He used the momentum to pull Montrose toward him, then tipped the man over, shoving him to the floor, then leapt on him to pummel the arse as hard as he could.

As soon as Dean threw the first punch, the audience exploded with applause. It was so surreal that Dean laughed, even thought the applause was for the end of the show. His moment of humor cost him, though. As the curtain closed, Montrose shoved him to the side, climbing over him to reverse the beatings. Dean tried to dodge the man's hand and struggle against him, but Montrose was heavier than his thin frame looked.

It was Montrose's turn to be startled into letting his guard down as the curtain opened again and the roar of the audience increased. The chorus formed lines and moved to the front of the stage to take their bow. Dean wrestled with Montrose, throwing him to one side, then attempting to crawl over him again. Montrose anticipated the move, and their battle devolved into wrestling and scrapping with each other at the back of the stage as the chorus moved back, allowing several of the featured players to take their bows.

Only when the applause swelled again as Everett and Nan hurried onto the stage to bow did Dean attempt to pull his focus away from Montrose. Nan glanced back at him with terror in her eyes, but something else besides that. There was a thread of resignation in her expression as well, as if she believed everything was all her fault.

"Get off of me," Montrose growled, pulling Dean's attention back to him. "I will have you sued for this."

"You are the one who broke into the theater and attempted to end this production," Dean shouted back at him. "Well, look at that." He forcibly turned Montrose's face to look out through the feet and legs of the chorus to the audience. "They loved it. They loved every ridiculous moment of it. If it was your intention to ruin the theater or to ruin Nan by sabotaging the production, all of your efforts and whatever money you've spent on this is for naught."

"You forget," Montrose said, grinning viciously up at him. "I still hold the trump card. I could ruin Nan Silvers in an instant just by speaking her name. I could—"

Montrose stopped short as the audience suddenly went quiet. Both Dean and Montrose turned to find Nan standing at the front of the stage, her arms held up.

"Ladies and gentlemen," she said, her voice bright but trembling. "May I have your attention please. I have a very important announcement to make."

Dean held his breath as the bottom tried to fall out of his stomach.

Chapter Twenty

an had never had such a hard time concentrating on performing in her life. If it had been her first show or her first lead, she was certain she would have failed spectacularly. Experience and training enabled her to focus as much as anyone else on the stage for the duration of the second act. That and the fact that Everett seemed to be having the time of his life. She was grateful that the two of them spent most of the second act on stage.

And then the backstage drama made its way out into the footlights, or close to it. As she walked out on stage, a forced smile in place, to meet Everett so that they could take their bows, she caught sight of Dean and Montrose wrestling behind the chorus. It was ridiculous. No, it was completely mad. Her fiancé and the man who was blackmailing her had descended into an actual fistfight—on stage, in front of God only knew who.

It had to end. As Nan grasped Everett's hand so that the two of them could walk all the way to the apron to take their bows, she knew it had to end. Worse still, as most of the audience craned their necks and looked past her and Everett to watch the fight taking place at the back of the stage, she knew there was only one way that it could all be well and truly over.

"Ladies and gentlemen," she said, panic welling within her as she quieted the audience with a gesture. "May I have your attention please. I have a very important announcement to make."

This was it. This was the moment everything she had worked so hard for vanished into thin air. But she had to do it. She could not let Dean put himself in danger on her behalf for a second more. As he'd said so long ago when he explained his and his brothers' reasons for marrying scandalous women, the only way to quench a destructive fire was to rob it of fuel.

She clasped her hands to her stomach as the audience grew quiet, giving all of their attention to her instead of Dean and Montrose as they grappled at the back of the stage. Even Dean and Montrose themselves grew quiet and watched her. Nan could feel Dean's love and encouragement, even though she didn't dare to turn and look at him. That was the only thing that allowed her to go on.

"I have something very important to tell you all," she said, maintaining her French accent and persona for the time being. "You know zat I love you all and zat it is you, my public, who has encouraged me to reach for zee greatest heights of performance."

She paused, gazing out at everyone and taking a deep breath. Her eyes caught on Lady Vegas watching her from the Rathborne-Paxton box. Oddly enough, Lady Vegas wore a smile, as though she were proud of Nan for what she was about to do.

"Zerefore," Nan went on, "it is exceptionally difficult for me to announce to you all today zat *Zee Marshall* shall be my last performance."

The audience seemed to take in a collective gasp. Even Everett looked anxious beside her.

"I love zee theater more zan anything," Nan continued, "but zee time has come for me to retire."

"No!" someone shouted in the house. "Say it isn't so."

"We love you!" a woman shouted. "We love you so much. I love you!" Nan searched for the source of the voice and found Lady Heloise leaning over the edge of one of the boxes, already in tears.

Nan smiled. "And I love you all as well," she said. She paused, gripped her costume over her stomach, and went on with, "But I have not been honest with you." She paused, cleared her throat, then repeated the same words in her actual voice. "I have not been honest with you."

The audience shifted in confusion, glancing up at her as if waiting for further explanation.

Nan cleared her throat and swallowed hard. "I have not let you all see who I truly am," she continued in her own voice. "When I first began my career as an actress, I was given to understand that I needed something special to set me apart. Something like an exciting story of where I'd come from. Something like the persona of someone who I am not."

The murmurs from the audience took on a fevered pitch as more and more people caught on to what she was confessing. Eyes went wide, and a few people seemed livid.

"My name is not Nanette D'Argent," she went on. "It's Nan Silvers, and I am the daughter of a crofter from Shropshire."

The audience gasped. Behind her, Montrose called out, "No! No, you mustn't!"

Nan pivoted to glance behind her. Montrose had struggled free of Dean's grasp. Both men knelt at the back of the stage, panting and sweaty from their struggle. They watched her as intently as everyone else in the audience, Dean smiling at her with pride, Montrose gaping in horror. The chorus split and backed away so that the audience could see both men fully.

That was when Nan knew everything would be all right. Montrose knew he was defeated. The one thing he'd been certain he would be able to hold over Nan's head to extort money from her was gone. His shoulders slumped, and his face lost its color.

Nan had never been happier. She turned back to the audience, beaming instead of cowering.

"I suppose you would like to know the reason I have come clean now," she said, smiling and, dare she admit it, flirting with the audience to the full extent of her abilities.

"Yes," someone called out. "Tell us why you've made fools of us all and why you've spent these many years laughing in our faces."

A few people made sounds of agreement, but others scoffed and huffed in offense at the censure.

"I have never laughed at anyone," Nan said. "I was perfectly content to be who you all needed me to be for the rest of my life. It was a sacrifice I was willing to make to bring sunshine into your life. But then a ray of sunshine came into my life."

It was perhaps a bigger gamble than revealing her true self, but Nan twisted again and extended her arm to Dean. She begged him with her eyes to stand and come forward, and blessedly, he did.

When Dean inched his way up to the front of the stage to join her, she took his hand.

"I would like you all to meet Mr. Dean Rathborne-Paxton —who, as you remember from Act One, made his debut on the stage this evening."

Several people laughed at the memory of Dean's antics with the chorus girls. It encouraged her to go on.

"Mr. Rathborne-Paxton is the love of my life," she went on, smiling at Dean with her whole heart and taking both his hands. "He is the man whom I am willing to give everything up for, the man for whom I have risked it all. He is my fiancé."

She turned back to the audience, grinning at them as though they were in on the conspiracy.

A wave of gasps and—thankfully—sentimental sighs passed through the theater. Nan inched closer to Dean, grasping his hand in both of hers and looking up at him adoringly. Several of the ladies in the audience—and a few gentlemen—let out sounds of sentiment. One young woman even said, "How romantic."

Nan's heart beat hard against her ribs. That was precisely the reaction she had intended with her confession.

Dean perfected the moment by raising her hand to his mouth and kissing her knuckles. "I could not be happier," he said, looking at Nan, but speaking loud enough for the audience to hear.

A glint of mischief filled his eyes. Nan had just begun to wonder what impishness his entertaining mind was cooking up when he turned to face the audience.

"I have only one regret in my recent engagement to Miss Silvers," he said. Nan grinned, impressed by how easily he commanded the stage. He gestured to his family's box. "That regret is that my dearest Mother does not approve of our match. But I implore of you," he said, turning back to the audience before Lady Vegas could do anything other than look startled at being called out. "I implore you, our friends. Can you convince my wonderful mama to give her blessing for Nan and I to wed? Will you do me the honor of speaking on our behalf?"

It was a stroke of utter genius. If Nan hadn't already been in love with Dean, she would have fallen for him completely in that moment.

"Allow them to marry!" someone shouted from the audience.

"Yes," someone else added. "Say you will let them."

"They belong together," another audience member called out. "Can you not see they are in love?"

The audience descended into a riot of cheers and shouts of encouragement, everyone pleading with Lady Vegas to give her consent to the match. The few people who had initially been offended at Nan's duplicity came to her defense now.

The crowd kept up their cheering until Nan and Dean tried to stop them, although it took a shrill whistle and a shout of, "Oy! Let the woman speak!" from Everett to get them to be quiet.

At last, shaking a bit, but with enough understanding in her eyes that Nan was certain she knew precisely what was going on, Lady Vegas rose and said, "But, of course, if you all approve of this match, how could I possibly deny true love?"

Nan could have flown up to the box and kissed her soon-to-be mother-in-law right then and there. The audience burst into applause that was even louder than that at the end of the show. They thundered their approval, all thoughts of duplicity and deceit banished from their minds. Nan could only guess at what tomorrow's headlines would read, but she was willing to wager they wouldn't be about how wicked she was.

As if to cap the entire thing off, Dean swept her into his arms and kissed her with a passion that left half of the audience gasping and the other half cheering even louder. Thankfully, Mr. Delaney brought the curtain down at just that moment.

As soon as the stage was sealed off from the house, Nan pulled herself away from Dean. She laughed, grasping his arms tightly, then threw herself at him in a powerful hug. The cast and crew erupted into applause around them.

"You will pay for this," Montrose shouted, standing and shaking his fist. He only dampened the enthusiasm of the cast and crew for a moment. "You are not worth the mud under my feet," he growled, pointing at Nan. "I don't want your sordid money anyhow. But you!" He switched to pointing at Dean. "I am not finished destroying you or your family. The entire lot of you had better continue to watch your backs."

"And you would do well to watch yours," Patrick said as he stepped up behind Montrose. He grabbed the back of the man's jacket, then wheeled him around and marched him off the stage, saying, "Right this way, sir."

Everyone waited with baited breath until Montrose was gone, then they burst into shouts and applause. Nan jumped into Dean's arms, hugging him tightly once more.

"We did it," she breathed against Dean's neck. "We defeated Montrose."

"For now," Dean said. "I doubt the man will give up entirely, though."

"I don't care," Nan said, pulling back so she could kiss Dean several times in rapid succession. "He will leave the theater alone now. He will leave us alone."

"I could drink to that!" Everett shouted, interrupting the private moment. "This calls for a party!"

The cast and crew burst into more cheering and applause. The temporary set pieces were pushed aside, and seemingly out of nowhere, tables were brought onto the stage, along with crates of bottles of spirits of every kind.

Nan supposed she shouldn't be shocked that there was so much to drink casually lying around the theater. She was more surprised that so many people were able to produce food so quickly. Some had to have already been at the theater, but as the minutes turned into hours, more food and drink were brought in from outside, along with a few of the more important patrons of the theater. That included Lady Vegas.

"You put me on the spot, Dean," she said, scowling at her son as the half-inebriated cast and crew stepped aside to allow the woman to stride across the stage to Dean and Nan, Lady

Dorrington following her. Lady Vegas walked all the way up to stand nearly toe-to-toe with her son. She narrowed her eyes at him, and for a moment, Nan was worried she would rescind her blessing. That was, until she burst into a smile that was the spitting image of Dean's most mischievous look and said, "I found it rather thrilling, actually." She turned to address the theater people who had crowded around her. "I do believe I could grow quite fond of the theater."

The cast and crew broke into applause and cheers for her. Someone handed her a bottle of beer. Nan gasped at the bold gesture, then nearly tumbled over with laughter as the wily old woman tipped it up and drank.

The party continued from there. Nan had never been so happy or felt so free and so loved.

It was late into the night by the time everyone wandered, some stumbling, out of the theater to make their way home. Nan and Dean saw to it that Lady Vegas and Lady Dorrington made it safely into a cab before Dean walked Nan home.

"That went better than I'd expected," Dean laughed as Nan unlocked the door to her flat and let them both in.

"Yes, it did," she said. As soon as they were secure inside the flat, she turned to Dean and threw her arms around his shoulders. "Do you know, I am quite glad that I gave Olivia the night off tonight."

"Did you?" Dean asked, smiling lasciviously down at her. "How convenient. It will give us the time we need to discuss a few things."

Nan's certainty faltered, and she froze for a moment as she gazed up at him. "Such as?" she asked.

Dean grinned. "Such as whether we wish to invite all of London to our wedding next month."

"Next month?" Her brow shot up.

"Well, I've already begun the process of obtaining a license," he said, walking her slowly backwards toward the bedroom. "And it occurs to me that it would be wise to strike while the iron of public approval is hot."

"Yes, that would be best," Nan said, letting him carry her away in more ways than one.

"Aside from the wedding," Dean went on as they crossed through to her bedroom, "it also occurs to me that we should discuss living arrangements."

"A very important topic of conversation," Nan agreed, beginning to work open the buttons of his jacket.

Dean removed his hat and tossed it aside, then peeled Nan's coat from her shoulders. "Do you think that, perhaps, we would do better to live in a luxurious flat near The Strand rather than taking up residence in Rathborne House?"

"I think that would be advisable," Nan said with pretend seriousness, pushing his jacket from his shoulders. "It is far less crowded in this flat, for one."

"And far less contentious for another," Dean finished her thought for her.

"Agreed." She made quick work of the buttons of his waistcoat, tugged his shirt from his trousers, and pulled loose his tie, all while saying, "I think we should begin this particular arrangement immediately."

"Do you think so?" His voice was rough with desire as he fumbled with the buttons of her blouse.

"I think the public will demand it," she said with pretend seriousness, disposing of his waistcoat and pushing his suspenders down. "They want a love story, after all, and since we are theater people, they will want it with a bit of spice to it."

"I have your bit of spice right here," Dean growled.

Nan laughed as they tore at the rest of each other's clothes. As far as she was concerned, they couldn't fall into bed fast enough. Even though the day had been long and mad, she still had enough energy to tumble between the sheets with Dean and to open herself fully to him so that he could kiss his way down her neck to her shoulders.

"You really are the most beautiful and magnificent creature I've ever known," Dean said, nuzzling against the side of her neck.

"And you are one of the funniest and most passionate men I have ever had the pleasure to know," she answered.

"Pleasure? Is it pleasure you want?" he asked, lifting himself above her for a moment.

"Oh, yes," Nan said in deep, sultry tones. "Loads of it."

He surged down, giving her just that. There wasn't an inch of her skin from her neck to her knees that he didn't kiss or lick or suckle. Nan hummed and sighed with pleasure, whimpering when he teased kisses along her inner thighs without quite giving her what she wanted.

"I should return all of these favors," she gasped as Dean tugged her knees farther apart. "I am not averse to those sorts of wicked activities that actresses are notorious for."

"I should hope not," Dean said with mock seriousness as he glanced down at her. "But not now, darling. Right now, I want to make you squeal and cry out my name in ecstasy."

"I shall await your direction, then," she said with a laugh.

That laugh turned into a sigh of pleasure as he dropped a kiss to her belly, then drew his tongue down to the very heart of her. He brought his hand up to slide two fingers into her, crooking them just so, as he teased and sucked his way around her clitoris. It was blissful on so many levels, not least of which because Nan knew that this sort of amazing pleasure would be hers for always now. Dean could be hers, and while they were not free of Montrose entirely yet, she was confident that they would be someday.

All thoughts of Montrose, or anything else but the pleasure Dean gave her, flew straight out of Nan's mind as Dean increased the intensity of his ministrations. Just as she was on the verge of exploding, he moved away from her sex, kissing his way up her belly to her breasts, then on to capture her mouth in a searing kiss. It was beautiful and heady, and when he adjusted his hand to continue the work that his tongue had started, she found herself hurling toward the edge and bursting into a million points of throbbing light.

"I love you, Nan," Dean gasped before positioning himself so that he could sink into her.

Nan groaned with the sweet pleasure of him inside of her as her inner muscles continued to convulse. "I love you, my darling," she panted in return, moving with him.

His movements drew her orgasm out, and just when she thought she couldn't experience more bliss, Dean let out a cry and spilled himself within her. It was magical in every way, and she clasped him tightly with everything she had. The world might not always approve of their wild antics, but Nan had no doubt that she and Dean would lead a colorful and exciting life together. She was thrilled that that life had already started.

Epilogue

I t came as no surprise at all to Francis that his brother Dean's wedding to the famous actress, Nan Silvers—the former Mlle. Nanette D'Argent—was the social event of the summer. After the nail-biting spectacle that Dean and Nan made of themselves during the opening night performance of Niall Cristofori's new play, *The Marshall*, they had made themselves the talk of the town. Every newspaper in London—probably every newspaper in England—had printed the story of how the intrepid Mr. Rathborne-Paxton had won the heart and revealed the secret of one of London's most sought-after damsels.

Francis smirked as he watched Dean and Nan enjoy the attention lavished on them at the massive reception hosted by the Savoy Hotel after the wedding. Friends and strangers alike fawned over the newlyweds. Nan's followers seemed to love her even more because of her daring revelation and the love story that had caused it. They had flocked around Nan and Dean at the church, and they gathered close to the pair now, even with several stout bodyguards from the Concord Theater there to protect them.

"It's a bloody miracle," Sam said, walking up to stand beside Francis near the door to the hotel ballroom. Sam and his own new bride, Alice, had returned from their sanctuary at Francis's estate near Winchester to attend the wedding. "I am absolutely astounded that she pulled it off."

"The public loves a good story," Francis said with a shrug. "Our new sister-in-law has always been popular, but I am pleased to say she is also quite intelligent. I don't think many women could have swayed public opinion in their favor quite as easily." He paused, smiling, and added, "I think Dean has done very well for himself and that he'll be happy."

"I agree," Sam said, laughing. That laughter doubled as the enigmatic Everett Jewel rushed to the corner where the orchestra was playing to lead the guests in a rousing chorus of the popular new song *Ta-ra-ra Boom-de-ay*. "But I was not speaking about the latest Mrs. Rathborne-Paxton."

Francis dragged his eyes away from the entertainment and stared at Sam. "You weren't?"

"No," Sam laughed. "I was talking about Mother." He nodded to the opposite side of the ballroom, where their mother was dancing along to the ribald song in the arms of Martin Piper. "I've never seen her so lively, or so happy," Sam finished.

Francis smiled. "Yes, Mother has been happy since returning to London," he said, feeling a deep sense of satisfaction.

Sam held up a finger to correct him. "Mother has been happy since Father decided to move into the flat you'd originally arranged for her."

Francis snorted. "True."

It had come as a surprise to all of them when Lord Vegas had capitulated so easily and moved out of Rathborne House. Though perhaps the fact that Mother was now feeling her oats, and that she had Aunt Josephine there on her side, had something to do with it. For Lord Vegas, the atmosphere of his house had become intolerable. For everyone else, it had become the jolly home that it always should have been.

"Is that Edward Archibald the MP dancing with Aunt Josephine?" Sam asked, his expression alight with humor at the sight.

"It is," Francis laughed. "Apparently, there is some sort of connection between him and the Concord Theater."

"I heard there was a connection between him and Mr. Piper," Sam added in a mumble.

"Shh," Francis silenced him. "We aren't supposed to know about such things, let alone speak of them." He would feel terrible if any harm came to Mr. Piper or Mr. Archibald, or any of Nan and Dean's theater friends.

Francis smiled, glad that his brothers were happy. Even Joseph seemed to be enjoying himself as he lectured to a group of chorus girls, all of whom seemed more interested in his boyish good looks than whatever he was saying. It was a grand party, if he did say so himself. The only thing that would have made it more—

Before he could finish his thought, his attention was snagged by a young woman he'd met several weeks before marching swiftly through the hotel lobby. Francis excused himself from the party and strode out into the lobby, intercepting the woman.

"Miss Narayan," he said by way of introduction, smiling at her. "I was hoping we would meet again."

Miss Narayan blinked up at him. "I am sorry, I do not know you."

She attempted to move on, but Francis stepped into her path again. This time, when she looked up at him, she had fire in her dark eyes.

"We met in Hyde Park," Francis said. "My wayward brother had thrown a ball at you?"

Miss Narayan's lips formed a thin, firm line. "Do you think you have the right to remind me of such an embarrassing moment on a night like this?" she demanded. "Do you think that because you are some Englishman with an earldom that you have the right to converse with me when we have not been properly introduced?"

The way she spoke was clear and precise with just enough accent to spice her words. It was the force of her words that nearly bowled Francis over, firing his blood and making him breathe faster. No woman had ever dared to snap at him in such a way.

He liked it.

"I merely wished to make your acquaintance again, Rani Narayan," he said with a respectful bow. "As you are one of the loveliest women I have ever laid eyes on. And I note that you remembered I am an earl." He grinned wickedly at her.

A hint of color splashed across Miss Narayan's cheeks. "It was a guess," she said, attempting once again to step around Francis.

For a third time, Francis stepped into her path. This time, the enigmatic rani jumped down his throat before he could so much as open his mouth.

"Do you think that because I am some pitiful colonial and you are a titled Englishman that it gives you the right to be rude to me? Do you think that I will cower at the way you accost me, or that I will fall at your feet in adoration?"

Francis started to speak, but again, she rolled over him.

"I will not stand for such rudeness, my lord," she said. "If we were in my father's kingdom, I would have him lop your head off. Now, if you will excuse me, I am on my way to a meeting of the Women's Franchise League, and I have no wish to renew any acquaintance with you."

She tilted her chin up and marched on. Francis let her go, but he turned to smile at her as she charged toward the door.

He hadn't been lying when he'd said he'd never seen a woman so beautiful in his life. Or one so headstrong and determined. He'd done his research after meeting her that afternoon in Hyde Park. Priya Narayan was, indeed, a princess. One with a sizable dowery to her name. Even without the dowry, the woman was worth more than her weight in gold.

The fact that she apparently thought him no better than a bug on the street was of little consequence to Francis. Once he made his mind up about something, nothing could stop him from following through. And Francis had most definitely made up his mind that Priya Narayan was the next Countess of Cathraiche. All he had to do now was win her.

I hope you have enjoyed Dean and Nan's story! In case you didn't already know, I have a master's degree in Theater, so any chance I get to set a book onstage or off, I'm going to take it! I studied a lot of Theater History while earning that degree, and I wish everyone knew just how exciting and modern the world of the theater was in the 1890s. The concept of celebrity might seem new to us, but it actually dates back for hundreds of years. And like with so many other things at the end of the 19th century, a lot of the concepts that we think are 20th century inventions were actually already in full swing.

Celebrity endorsements of products was a very big deal by the 1890s. I wasn't exaggerating at all when I said that women with the same star-power as Nan—and yes, by the 1890s, famous celebrities were referred to as "stars"—loaned their image to everything from chocolates to cosmetics to chewing gum. Celebrity trading cards were wildly popular in the 1890s. Similarly to how we think of baseball cards as being found in packs with chewing gum, celebrity trading cards in London were often found in packets of biscuits.

Selling one's image to a biscuit or perfume company required a different kind of assistant for an established or up-and-coming celebrity. Like Nan's Mr. Brown, more and more celebrities were hiring agents to manage their careers by the end of the 19th century. The concept of having an agent in the entertainment business originated with literary agents in the early 19th century and before, but starting around the 1890s, many of these literary agents expanded their client lists to include actors and musicians. Nan would have been among the first to have an agent working on her behalf, but she was far from the last. By the 1910s, some of the biggest talent agencies that we still have today, such as the Curtis Brown agency, which opened its doors in 1899, were well-established. As we all know, these talent agencies pretty much run the entertainment industry as we know it today on both sides of the pond.

The story of the fight against Montrose continues soon! Francis, Lord Cathraiche, has his eye on Bengali rani, Priya Narayan, but will he be able to coax her away from her fight for the rights of women around the world in order to woo and win her? Find out next in *Some Enchanted Evening*!

If you enjoyed this book and would like to hear more from me, please sign up for my newsletter! When you sign up, you'll get a free, full-length novella, *A Passionate Deception*. Victorian identity theft has never been so exciting in this story of hope, tricks, and starting over. Part of my West Meets East series, *A Passionate Deception* can be read as a stand-alone. Pick up your free copy today by signing up to receive my newsletter (which I only send out when I have a new release)!

Sign up here: http://eepurl.com/cbaVMH

· · ·

Are you on social media? I am! Come and join the fun on Facebook: http://www.facebook.com/merryfarmerreaders

I'm also a huge fan of Instagram and post lots of original content there: https://www.instagram.com/merryfarmer/

ONE LAST THING! Do you crave historical romance filled with passion and red-hot chemistry? Come join me and my author friends in the Facebook group, Historical Harlots, for exclusive giveaways, chat with amazing HistRom authors, raunchy shenanigans, and more!

https://www.facebook.com/groups/2102138599813601

About the Author

I hope you have enjoyed *Let's Face the Music and Dance*. If you'd like to be the first to learn about when new books in the series come out and more, please sign up for my newsletter here: http://eepurl.com/cbaVMH And remember, Read it, Review it, Share it! For a complete list of works by Merry Farmer with links, please visit http://wp.me/P5ttjb-14F.

Merry Farmer is an award-winning novelist who lives in suburban Philadelphia with her cats, Torpedo, her grumpy old man, and Justine, her hyperactive new baby. She has been writing since she was ten years old and realized one day that she didn't have to wait for the teacher to assign a creative writing project to write something. It was the best day of her life. She then went on to earn not one but two degrees in History so that she would always have something to write about. Her books have reached the Top 100 at Amazon, iBooks, and Barnes & Noble, and have been named finalists in the prestigious RONE and Rom Com Reader's Crown awards.

Acknowledgments

I owe a huge debt of gratitude to my awesome beta-readers, Caroline Lee and Jolene Stewart, for their suggestions and advice. And double thanks to Julie Tague, for being a truly excellent editor and to Cindy Jackson for being an awesome assistant!

Click here for a complete list of other works by Merry Farmer.

Printed in Great Britain
by Amazon

17619517R00142